VAMPIRE UNLEASHED
KEEPERS OF THE CHALICE 1

TAMAR SLOAN

IVY LANE

KEEPER
CHRONICLES

Cover by Sylvia Frost
https://thebookbrander.com/

CONTENTS

CHAPTER 1

MADELEINE

Resolution clings to Maddy in the same stubborn way the unforgiving chill of the breeze tugs at her ponytail and pries at the cuffs of her jacket. Her throat has long since gone raw from the cold, and yet she continues to yell. There's no other choice. Giving in to the hopelessness isn't an option, not when Olivia still hasn't been found.

Not when the late autumn night is fast approaching.

Maddy cups her hands around her mouth. "Olivia!" Her voice carries through the trees, the branches still clinging to orange and brown leaves, but she receives the same answer she has to every other desperate call of the young woman's name.

Nothing.

Over a dozen searchers scattered around the forest holler Olivia's name, some near, others echoing the call in the distance. The college student has been missing for several days now. Olivia was nearly the top of her class, active in the community, and the first friendly face one saw at the local coffee shop where she worked. She isn't the kind of person who would just disappear. There's no boyfriend, no secret drug addiction, or any shocking revelation that would be a reason for her to skip town.

Yet, Olivia just disappeared.

While she isn't a close friend, she and Maddy are more than on amicable terms. Everyone likes the brown-haired, blue-eyed girl. There isn't a soul in the small town of Creed who would wish her harm. There were whispers of foul play, and it's possible that a stranger passing through could have harmed Olivia, but many pray she's merely gotten lost while out for a jog, unlikely as that may be.

It's that hope that still has searchers trekking through the forest, several days after the young woman's mysterious disappearance.

A snapping twig draws Maddy's attention over her shoulder, but it's only Cora. Her best friend disentangles her foot from a fallen branch with a scowl before shoving her hands back in the pocket of her hoodie. Cora has long since stopped calling Olivia's name, letting Maddy yell herself hoarse. Her friend isn't a callous person, yet Maddy knows Cora's thinking about her favorite cozy chair, fuzzy socks, and warm beverage right about now. Hell, so is Maddy, but a person's life is at stake and a horrible, twisting sensation deep in her gut tells her if Olivia isn't found soon, she never will be.

Maddy can feel it like a promise in her bones.

Maddy has long since grown accustomed to what she's always dubbed "the spooks", because like some ethereal specter, the sensation tingling along her bones often brings bad news. She can't explain the odd sensation, or the events that often follow, but she still remembers the first time she felt it. The feeling was akin to dejavu, and when she was only six, she'd grown dizzy with the sensation. The next day, a man down the street had gone missing and was never seen again. "The spooks" had happened over a dozen more times in her life, and while the result hadn't always ended in unexplained disappearances, there had been car accidents and mysterious deaths.

The return of the sensation now doesn't bode well. Maddy rubs her hands up and down her jacket sleeves in an attempt to chase away the feeling.

"Cold?" Cora asks.

Maddy nods, keeping the real explanation for her restlessness to herself. She doesn't want to breathe life into the nagging suspicion sliding up her spine. She peers around the forest which hugs one of the missing student's frequent jogging paths. The search party has been trekking for hours. Over half of the town seems to have shown up. They'd been divided into groups and each one had been instructed to search a certain grid.

But they haven't found a shred of evidence Olivia may have come this way. No ransacked handbag. No lone shoe. No hair tie with a few stray strands twisted through it.

Ahead, a couple of the searchers turn back and head in their direction. An older gentleman who works at the corner gas station is putting a cell back into his pocket.

"They're calling off the search for the night. It isn't safe to be out in the dark."

Maddy scans the trees, almost desperate to find Olivia hunkering in some shadow. "It's going to be cold tonight. What if she's out here?"

"There's nothing we can do. You girls need to get home."

Bristling at the term "girls", Maddy opens her mouth but Cora nudges her in the ribs with an elbow.

"He's right." She watches the man and the woman who must be his wife pick their way back through the forest. "We don't have flashlights."

"I've got my phone." Maddy pulls her cell out of her back

pocket, then realizes she has several missed texts from her mom. "Crap."

Cora raises an eyebrow before turning to follow the couple through the trees. "See? It's your mom, isn't it?"

Maddy flips through the texts. They're nothing out of the ordinary, mostly her mom asking how the search is going, but she can feel the annoyance growing with each text that's gone ignored. Sighing, she types a quick reply then stuffs the phone back into her pocket.

Several of the cars gathered at the head of the jogging trail are already gone by the time Maddy and Cora make it back. Maddy waves to a few more of the searchers, then turns to her friend.

"Meet me at the coffee shop tomorrow morning?" She prefers tea, but Cora is a coffee addict. It's one of the best ways she can convince her friend to study with her. "We have that physics exam tomorrow."

Cora groans as she unlocks her car. "Fine, but it's going to take at least two salted caramel lattes to get me through."

"Deal." Maddy makes her way over to her Ford Taurus, then opens the driver's door and waves as Cora drives past. She's the last one in the parking lot, and as the sky starts to turn from amber and gold into russet and copper, she hesitates.

Once she leaves, night will fall. It will be another day Olivia is missing.

Another day closer to never being seen again.

There's a rustle from behind her and Maddy spins around. A shiver trembles through her, and it has nothing to do with the brisk fall air. She's suddenly certain she isn't alone. Stepping away from her car, she squints, trying to pierce the darkness clinging to the trees. Someone's out there.

"Olivia?" Maddy walks closer to the forest. "Is that you?"

Her pulse hiccups. Had she found her?

A figure steps out of the shadows of the trees. Maddy backs up a couple of steps as she looks at the man, trying to tell her brain it's too early to freak out. Physically, he isn't unordinary. He has cropped brown hair, jeans, and a jacket. His stare, however, unnerves her. It's intense, dark, and strangely familiar, as if she's seen a whisper of his gaze in a dream.

"The search was called off," Maddy says. "The others have gone home." She instantly berates herself. Why did she let the man know she was alone? Her heart rate quickens and her imagination skips into a rampant pace as she wonders if Olivia's been killed, and this is the murderer. Maddy's hand drifts toward her cell in her back pocket. She's never been more conscious of how big the forest is. And how many shadows it harbors.

Will people be searching for her in a few days, just like Olivia?

"I apologize if I've alarmed you." The man opens his hands and turns his palms out, watching her. "My name is Felix, and I've come to introduce myself."

"Um." Maddy continues to inch toward her car. "Maybe we can talk some other time."

Gravel crunches as the man—Felix—takes a single step forward. "The Order of the Knightly Rose needs you, Miss Grimes."

Goosebumps scatter up the back of Maddy's neck. How did this man know her name? For a brief moment, she thinks maybe he's a college club recruiter, but she doesn't recall any collegiate organization called the Order of the Knightly Rose.

"Sorry, I don't know what that is." Maddy puts her hand on the edge of her car door.

Felix's lips curve upward. "I doubt it, and yet you're already a part of it." He looks over his shoulder to peer into the forest. "She isn't in there."

"Who?"

"The young woman you seek." Felix's disconcerting gaze snaps back to her. "She's beyond the reach of the police, now."

Maddy swallows a lump in her throat, chased there by the swirl of nerves in her stomach. "How do you know?"

"Join our Order, Madeleine, and I'll tell you the fate of the girl."

"You're sick," Maddy snaps. "This isn't a game." Her words are sharp, confident, but inside she's reeling. The sensation of dread still clings to her as she lowers into her seat, shuts the door, and locks it.

She starts her car with shaking hands and revs the engine. A quick glance shows Felix hasn't moved, but it doesn't help the edginess tingling along her nerves. She needs to get out of there.

The headlights wash Felix in bright light. He doesn't move. Doesn't raise his arms to shield his eyes. She tries to ignore the peculiar man as she passes, but she can sense his stare piercing her as she pulls away. What the hell was that about? She glances in her rearview mirror, startling to find him gone. It's too dark to see anything, she tells herself. She's overreacting. At least there hadn't been another vehicle nearby, so the weirdo won't be following her.

She thinks about stopping to grab a bite to eat from the burger joint, but after the encounter with Felix, she steers in the direction of her house. Relief washes over her at the sight of the quaint two-story home. Pumpkins and decorative gourds spill down the steps leading to the covered front porch, and the wreath on the front door shivers slightly in the wind. Maddy parks her car behind her mom's Jeep, grabs her bag, then hurries inside.

The scent of chili and banana bread fills Maddy's nose as she shucks off her jacket, then discards her bag on the couch.

"I'm back."

Maddy's mom calls from the other room. "It's about time. I texted you."

"Sorry." Maddy's stomach growls as she walks across the living room and into the kitchen. "I had my phone on silent." She smiles watching her mom dish out a bowl of chili. Her mom loves to cook, though Maddy hasn't inherited any of her culinary talent. She slides onto a barstool, thankful she hadn't stopped for a burger.

"Well, how did the search go?" Her mom sets the steaming bowl in front of Maddy, the dark hair she inherited pulled up in a high ponytail. "Any news?"

"No." Maddy reaches for the package of shredded cheese on the counter, grabs a handful, and drops it into the chili. "I don't think anyone's seen even a sign of her." She picks up a spoon and starts to stir in the melting cheese. "The most exciting thing that happened is some weirdo who talked to me after the search was called off." Maddy shakes off the lingering unease at the encounter. She was just creeped out because Olivia's missing. She shrugs. "He said he was with something called Order of the Knightly Rose."

Her mom grows still, the ladle in her hand poised over the pot. "What did you say?"

Maddy scoffs, trying to make light of the freaky experience. "Yeah, crazy right?" She blows on the steam rising from her spoonful of chili. "The guy said his name was Felix. He wanted me to join, and said he'd tell me what had happened to Olivia if I did. Some sick joke, right?"

But her mom doesn't answer.

Maddy glances up, realizing her mom's staring at her with wide eyes. The unease slinks back, slithering up her spine as if it never left. "Uh, should we call the police? I figured he was just some weirdo or something."

Her mom sighs and puts the ladle back in the pot. "I knew this day would come. I just..." Her voice drifts, then she shakes her head. "Come on. I have to show you something."

"Show me what?" Maddy doesn't get an answer and she puts her spoon down, frowning. Her mom is acting as mysteriously as that Felix guy was.

The house is quiet as they head down the hall, the only sound being the wind whistling against the dark windows. They step into her mom's bedroom, and Maddy hesitates in the doorway when her mom crouches down beside the blue and green oriental rug in front of her bed. To her surprise, her mom tugs one of the corners back. Then, she watches with widening eyes as her mom pries at the floorboards. There's a *click*, and her mom raises a trap door, the hinges groaning.

"Mom, what the hell?" Maddy steps over to the hole in the floor. A cool draft drifts up from the opening. "When did this get here?"

"It's always been here." Her mom's voice is tinged with amusement. She grabs a flashlight from her dresser and heads down.

Maddy, confusion wrinkling her forehead, follows her mom carefully down the creaking steps. Below, her mom flicks a light switch and Maddy finds herself in a small basement. Settled against one wall is a large desk. The other three walls are covered in photos, newspaper articles, and maps of their small town.

"What is this?" Maddy whispers. Her gaze zeroes in on a photo of a smiling Olivia with her friends at a volleyball game.

Maddy's mom leans against the desk. A few tendrils of hair frame her face having escaped the ponytail, and weary lines pull at the corner of her eyes. "I've been investigating disappearances in this town for the last decade."

"But...but why?" Maddy can't piece together why her mom

has a secret room under their house, and photos of all these people...why is her mother involved?

"Madeleine, I'm a hunter, and just like Felix, and I know what's happened to all of these people." She waves a hand to the photographs depicting mostly women, but also a few men, who've disappeared over the past several years.

Maddy glances at them, then at her mom. She can feel the foundation of everything she's ever known slowly unraveling.

Olivia.

Felix.

Now, her own mom.

"What happened?" she asks, crossing her arms as if that will help hold everything together.

"Vampires, Maddy. Vampires."

CHAPTER 2

MADELEINE

A deep and incessant headache throbs behind Maddy's eyes as she works on trying to sweep the revelations that kept her up all night back under the rug in her mother's bedroom.

Vampires.

The word echoes through her with disbelief. No matter how much effort she puts into trying to fit their impossible existence into the mold of a lie, she knows her mother spoke the truth. Maddy saw that secret room beneath their floor for herself, she had no choice but to hear about the mysterious disappearances that have been increasing.

But more than that, something in her very bones tells her what her mother said rang true.

With a sharp exhale through her nose, Maddy drops her pencil and picks up her steaming coffee mug. Today is definitely a day that needs something stronger than tea. The college café she favors is packed. It's not so much the coffee that has students returning day after day, but the quirky, eclectic atmosphere. The Bean Buzz is full of mismatched chairs and tables, along with a few couches in the corner that are hard to snag, and instead of Styrofoam cups, the café uses real mugs. None of them are part of a set and Maddy always enjoys seeing which cup she'll end up with every time she visits. Today hers has a cat with purple pajamas, a trail of Zs following in its wake.

What's more, this is the cafe that Olivia worked in.

The black coffee warms Maddy's throat and she tightens her lips a bit at the bitterness of the beverage. Usually, she opts for a caramel latte, but this morning she's gone with the strong stuff to keep her awake enough to study. Especially seeing as she didn't get much studying done with the offer of joining a secret vampire hunting league hanging over her head.

Maddy glances over at Cora. Her best friend hasn't looked up from her book on nuclear physics for nearly an hour now. Maddy admires her focus. Her ignorance that science has all the answers. She sets her cat mug down and turns her attention to the pages of notes in front of her and bunches her eyebrows, reading over the words as if she can use the concept of ion implantation to chase away the offer the strange man, Felix, has extended.

Cora mumbles something to herself, then scribbles a note down on a piece of paper beside her thick book. Maddy chews on the inside of her cheek. The petite redhead has been her best friend for as long as she can remember. They do almost everything together, and confide in each other with all matters of life. Maddy desperately wants to tell Cora about what she's learned, and yet she's hesitant. She can scarcely believe it herself, and she was *there*. She can't imagine what Cora will think.

No, she knows exactly what her friend would say. She'd tell Maddy she'd been hit with a crazy stick, was obviously studying too hard and she needs a break.

The voice of Maddy's mom echoes in her mind from last night. *You cannot tell anyone what I've told you, Madeleine. It is far too dangerous for you, and anyone you divulge this secret to, understand?*

Maddy flips the page she'd been staring at and tucks it behind her notebook with a grimace. How is she supposed to keep something like this to herself? She needs to talk to someone about the insanity trying to creep into her life.

The chair scrapes across the floor opposite Maddy as Cora stands, mug in hand. "I'm heading to the bathroom and getting another cup. Need anything?"

Maddy shakes her head mutely, still staring down at her messy scribble of notes. Cora's just disappeared behind the door sporting a bean in a skirt when someone taps Maddy's shoulder. She cranes her neck to find her friend, Gabby, smiling down at her.

"Hey," Maddy says.

Gabby slides into a chair beside her. "Hey to you." Her hands are wrapped around a tall, slender mug covered in various emojis. Her gorgeous blonde curls spill down her back and her blue eyes are bright for so early in the day. She crosses her leg over her knee, drawing attention to the pink miniskirt she wears despite the cool weather. Gabby is gorgeous, and looks like she should be one of those mean girl types, but she has a heart of gold and a mouth full of snark for anyone who tries to belittle her friends. Maddy's not sure why the second year took a shine to her when she first arrived, but she's grateful Gabby did.

"Not studying today?" Maddy asks, noting Gabby's lack of books.

"I think I have a handle on things." Gabby's smile fades as she stares at Maddy. "Girl, you look like you spent the night in a cement mixer. Are you okay?"

Maddy stretches her legs out under the table, suddenly feeling restless at Gabby's question. "No, not really."

A line of concern furrows between Gabby's delicate eyebrows. "Do you want help studying?"

"It isn't that. It's..." Maddy taps her finger on the edge of her notebook and purses her lips, hesitant to say what's really on her mind. Oddly enough, she almost senses it would be easier to bare her soul to Gabby than it would be to Cora. Maybe it's because there's that one degree of separation. Maybe it's because Gabby's a year older. Maybe it's because there's a glint in Gabby's blue eyes that seems to already know this is far deeper than the usual things an eighteen-year old faces.

Maddy gives herself a mental shake. She's trying to justify herself. But she can't tell Gabby about this. She can't tell anyone.

Her shoulders sag a little and she decides to talk about her problems in general terms. "I guess I just have a big decision to make and I'm not really sure what to do about it."

A trio of male college students stroll by and one of them hesitates, eyeing Gabby from her head down to her long, slender legs. He starts to smile at her but she quickly gives him a deadpan "not on your life" sort of look and he continues on his way. Maddy wonders what it would be like to stop a man dead in his tracks without having to lift a finger. Judging by the expression pinching Gabby's face, it's more than annoying.

"Anyway, a decision?" she says. "About school?"

"No." Maddy glances around, but there's no one nearby. Cora's made it out of the bathroom and is standing in line for more coffee, her foot tapping impatiently. "I guess it's more of a family thing."

Gabby nods slowly and takes a sip of her coffee. "I see."

Maddy tilts her head to the side, wondering if she's given away too much. Having not had her father in her life due to her parents' divorce, she clearly just insinuated her mother's involved. "Do you?"

"I just meant, I know what it means to make decisions revolving around family." Gabby uncrosses her leg, shifts, and sets her knee across her other leg. She leans back in the chair and folds her arms. "Been there, done that."

Maddy wonders what she means, but doesn't pry. "I guess I'm just stuck. It's like, I know what I should do, but it isn't necessarily what I think I should want to do, if that makes any sort of sense." She takes a sip of her coffee, then grimaces. It's gone cold. Perhaps she should have taken up Cora's offer to grab her another one. "It was just kind of sprung on me and all of a sudden I feel this obligation to take part in something I knew nothing about."

Gabby squints her eyes in thought. Across the room, Cora finally makes it to the counter to place her order. "You know what I think?"

"What?"

"I think you should do what your heart thinks you should do. Too often people try to work things out in their head and then their thoughts get so scrambled by all the shoulds and should-nots, they end up making decisions they regret."

Maddy lets out a hollow laugh and closes her notebook. There will be no concentrating on studying now. "Don't most people think the opposite? That following your heart leads to rash decisions?"

Gabby shrugs and one side of her cream wide-collared sweater slips over her shoulder. "I still say follow your heart. There are times in life when certain people are presented with... family matters...and they need to take up the mantle and do what's right. It may be scary and new and dangerous, but destiny is often funny that way."

A long moment of silence stretches between them, only broken by someone laughing about something in the background. A nervous swirl unfurls in Maddy's stomach as she stares at her friend and mulls over what she just said to her. If Maddy didn't know any better, she'd think Gabby knew exactly what she was talking about. It's in the way Gabby said "family matters", then spoke of a new and dangerous destiny. Maddy never said anything of the sort.

"Gabby, do you—"

A buzzing sound comes from Gabby's purse and she holds her finger up. She glances at the screen, swipes her thumb across it, then answers.

"Hey, you."

Maddy turns her attention away to give Gabby privacy. It's obvious who she's talking to from the husky note in her voice—her boyfriend, Colt. Those two are practically inseparable, and judging from the way they look at each other, that's the way they prefer it. A quick tap on her own cell tells Maddy it's eight-forty-seven. She has class at nine, and the physics labs are clear on the other side of campus. She sighs and starts to shove her books into her messenger bag.

Beside her, Gabby stands. "Sorry, Maddy, but I need to go." She gives Maddy's shoulder a squeeze. "Call me later and we can talk some more, okay?"

"Sure." Maddy watches Gabby flounce from the café, not feeling one bit better about getting even a little bit of her worries off her chest. If anything, she's even more conflicted.

Cora is leaning against the counter, talking with another girl from their class while she waits for their order. Maddy stands and flings the strap of her bag over her shoulder. Still mulling over Gabby's advice, she taps out a text to Cora telling her she'll see her later as she rushes through the café door.

Before she has a chance to press send, Maddy runs into something. Hard.

Her feet shuffle as she tries to maintain her balance and her strap slips from her shoulder. The sudden weight of her bag dropping into the crook of her elbow makes her cell clatter to the sidewalk. She hitches the strap back up and then notices a chest in front of her.

"Crap, I'm sorry." Maddy lifts her chin.

Any further apology is promptly lodged in her throat.

Eyes widening, she drinks in the sight of the guy before her. Tall, sandy-haired, and sexy as hell, he wears a T-shirt that fits his athletic shoulders like a second skin. She's never seen him around campus before. If she had, she'd certainly remember. The noise of the café and fellow students fade away as she continues to stare at him, lips parting.

His eyes are green. Mint green. Cool and mossy, yet somehow bright and full of vitality. They widen slightly as he stares back.

But the next second, he lifts a questioning eyebrow and Maddy's teeth click as she snaps her mouth shut. He crouches, snags her phone from the concrete, and shoves it at her.

"Watch where you're going." His tone is sharp as he sweeps past her without another word.

Maddy turns, clutching her phone and scowling, wishing she thought to snip an insult back at him as he disappears into the crowd.

He may be hot, but he's also a douche.

CHAPTER 3

CALEB

Maddy.

Caleb's been watching her for some time and her name finally fell from the lips of her friend. And now she's right in front of him.

He's seen her around town and campus several times. Something about her intrigued him, caught his attention and wouldn't let go. Though he can't quite put his finger on it, he has to admit she's certainly pleasant to look at. The way her raven hair spills over her shoulders just begs to have fingers run through it and her dark mocha eyes drink him in like she's never laid eyes on a man. It's not lost on him the way her pupils dilate, the dark centers eating up her earthy brown irises. He nearly groans, impossibly wanting to lose himself in it. Getting that reaction from women has always sent a wash of pleasure swirling through his body, but this is sharper. Deeper.

He hadn't expected that.

She stares at him, pulse quickening and pink lips parting. He can smell the lingering smell of coffee on her breath, but it's nearly overpowered by the subtle change in her scent, heavy with attraction. The same attraction which is starting to roll her heartbeats faster. For a moment, he thinks about smiling at her and asking if he can walk her to class. He wants to hear her voice. Speaking just to him.

He wants to keep losing himself in the earthy magic of her gaze.

But reality swoops in and punches him hard in the gut when another scent makes his throat burn.

He can't take an interest in any woman. Not anymore.

So, he lifts an eyebrow, the gesture heavy with question. Maddy closes her mouth so hard Caleb can hear her teeth click together. A blush warms her cheeks, increasing the irritating need scorching through him.

Caleb crouches down and retrieves her phone. The girl blinks, a slight raising of her eyebrows telling him she's going to speak. Before she can utter a word, he shoves the cell phone at her and chisels his voice into sharp stone.

"Watch where you're going." He moves past Maddy and hears her breath catch. As he starts winding through the other students, he swears he picks up the stabbing sensation of irritation. A grim smile presses against his lips. It's better—safer—to be unlikeable than to get involved, even with someone as beautiful and intriguing as Maddy. God, her skin had looked soft, and her *smell*...

Caleb shoves his hands in his pockets with a growl in his chest. A few girls part in front of him, clearly alarmed by his surly attitude. Deep down, he knows he shouldn't blame Maddy for his growing anger, but it's easier to place blame on her than it is to admit she isn't at fault. If she hadn't collided into him, he would never have realized just how gorgeous those eyes were up close, or her scent, like rosewater and bad decisions.

He stalks past the science building, making an effort not to look over his shoulder to try and catch a glimpse of the girl latching onto his mind. The air outside is crisp and clean, and the breeze cutting between the buildings of campus work to wash away Maddy's clinging scent. It's only a matter of time before some semblance of balance returns to his mind.

The sound of tennis shoes scuffing the sidewalk, incessant chatter, and the tap-tap-tap of fingers on phones grates on his nerves. He angles toward the administration offices, knowing the collection of buildings are less crowded during this time of day. Caleb kicks a loose rock with the toe of his black boot, then pauses and cants his head, catching hushed voices nearby.

"...don't want to do that." It's a female voice, quiet and laced with uncertainty. A familiar one.

"You have to or I'll tell everyone you were the one who vomited all over Brandon Foster's two-thousand-dollar couch last Friday." Another woman, but her tone is sharp and sneering.

"But I didn't. I wasn't even there."

"It doesn't matter, Stacy. No one will believe you over me."

Caleb's teeth grind together. He thought he recognized the softer girl's voice, and coupled with the name Stacy, he realizes it's his neighbor, and some other chick is bullying her into doing something she doesn't want to do. He's heard enough and stalks toward the direction of the voices. Rounding the corner of a brick building he finds someone, the apparent bully, walking away with a retreating Stacy at her back. Caleb lets Stacy go for the moment and keeps his concentration locked on the student suddenly watching him with hopeful eyes.

The bully tucks a curl of hair behind her ear and gives Caleb a coy smile. "Uh, hi."

"You shouldn't pick on people who don't have the confidence to stand up for themselves."

The student's smile falters under Caleb's steel words. "I...I wasn't," she squeaks.

Caleb barks a humorless laugh. "Right. Mind telling me what you're trying to get Stacy to do?" He keeps his hands stuffed in his pockets to ensure his posture isn't threatening.

The girl wrings her hands together and glances over Caleb's shoulder, as if searching for a way to leave, or maybe even someone to rescue her. There's no one there. "It's nothing." She lifts her chin, momentarily defiant. "It isn't your business."

"Not my business? I know Stacy. She's a sweet person who doesn't need any trouble." His muscles tighten, trying to keep the simmering anger under control. "Do I have to ask you again?"

The bully's gaze drops to the ground. "Stacy gets extra credit for working in the administration offices, and she's a big computer geek. I told her to go in and make some changes to the attendance record. I've messed up in a lot of classes and the university might not allow me to attend exams."

Fear drenches her voice and as Caleb pulls the sharp scent in, wondering what's going on for her. Is she worrying about disappointing her parents, or is it something more sinister, like punishment, that has her so on edge and desperate?

He wants to be the bad guy. He wants to tell this girl off for her manipulating, but he senses so much more than he used to. People have undercurrents. The emotions they don't want others to see. In fact, he's living proof people aren't what they seem.

If this girl isn't all bad, then maybe he isn't either...

He shakes his head with a sigh. "Look. College is hard, but that doesn't mean just because you mess up, you take others down with you, okay? Don't do it." The girl nods mutely and he jerks his chin. "Now go on. Get out of here."

The student hurries past Caleb and he peers around for Stacy but she'd already been hurrying away when he arrived. He takes off after her. If she follows through, she could be expelled. Colleges don't take lightly to that sort of manipulation. Her parents are decent people, and more than once they've mentioned their daughter's dream to go into law.

Caleb rounds the building but Stacy is nowhere in sight. He clicks his tongue as he searches for her. He should have asked the other girl which building Stacy was heading to. Committing his neighbor's scent to memory wasn't something he's ever considered, so he can't pick out her trail amongst the myriad of other smells lingering in the air. Then, he catches the sound of voices. He twists and turns, finally settling his eyes on an open window on the building to his left. Even though it's three floors up, Caleb squints, tips his head to the side, and listens. It's subtle but he's certain he can hear Stacy's voice.

He hurries up the steps and into the building. A hallway stretches before him, lined with doors leading to different offices. A sign a little way down indicates the elevator is around the corner, but Caleb opts for the stairs on his immediate right. By the time the door closes, he's nearly two floors up. He reaches the third floor and leaves the stairwell. Glancing up the empty hallway, he can pick out Stacy's voice.

His footfalls are silent as he creeps toward it, quickly registering a second voice—a punishing tone that cuts her off.

"This is completely inexcusable. I thought better of you, Stacy. I have no choice but to write you up. You'll be receiving a letter concerning this matter."

Caleb peeks into the room. A man frowns down at a pale-faced Stacy, who stares at her feet. A screen on a computer behind them shows the attendance record for a sociology class. Stacy must have been caught mid-act, probably because she's never done anything like this before. Down the hall, Caleb hears the elevator ding so he quickly slips inside the office.

"Caleb?" Stacy's eyes round at the sight of him. He's barely ever spoken to the junior, so it's no wonder she's surprised to see him.

The man narrows his gaze at Caleb. "You'll have to wait outside. I'm having a chat with Miss Anderson."

Stacy's in deep trouble, and there's only one way out of this mess. Caleb steps closer to the man. "Sir?"

The man's nostrils flare as he turns toward Caleb, but then his body sags so slightly no one would notice. Caleb's stare holds the man's gaze.

"You know Stacy isn't the sort of person to break the rules. She gets good grades and always tries her best. She's clearly being manipulated, wouldn't you agree?"

The man glances at her, then back to Caleb. "Yes, maybe so."

"I think that we can let this one infraction slip, don't you?"

"Well, yes, I suppose."

Caleb smiles. "Excellent. If you're comfortable with it, I'm sure Stacy and I could right whatever wrong she was threatened into doing. Would that be okay, sir?"

"Yes," the office administrator says, his voice almost a monotone. "That will be fine." Without uttering another word, he heads through a door at the back of the room.

After waiting a beat, Caleb crosses over to the computer. A few quick taps and he rights the wrong Stacy committed. He even left the bully able to take her examinations. Then, he turns and faces Stacy.

"You need to learn to stand up for yourself, you know."

"Thank you," she gushes. Stacy takes a step forward, arms raised, and Caleb quickly grabs her shoulders, a little faster and a bit rougher than he intended. Her arms cross her chest and she takes a half-step back, her cheeks once again pink.

Caleb clears his throat. Stacy had clearly just been trying to hug him. He's not a hugger. "Just, you know, don't do this kind of thing again." He pats her shoulder then puts a bit of distance between them. The attraction Stacy feels for him tickles his nose and he scratches the side of it. "You're better than that."

"Well, thanks for the help." Stacy hesitates a moment longer, then rushes out of the office.

Caleb rubs the back of his neck. He hates awkward encounters. As he turns to leave, a breeze comes in through the window, making papers flutter on the desk.

Goosebumps scatter up the back of his scalp and his stomach rumbles as a coppery scent fills his nostrils.

Blood.

Caleb hurries out of the door without a passing glance at the few people in the hallway. His throat is on fire. His mouth floods with moisture.

Striding away, he does everything in his power to keep a leash on the monster lurking beneath his skin.

The monster he hates.

CHAPTER 4

MADELEINE

S tudents jostle past Maddy but she stands rooted to the spot, scowling at the guy as he disappears through the crowd. He didn't have to be so rude. It wasn't as if she'd run into him on purpose. With a shake of her head, she hitches the strap of her bag farther onto her shoulder, determined to go to class and put the unpleasant incident behind her.

If only it hadn't started so...pleasant.

Shaking her head, she steps forward, only to stop. Lifting her foot, Maddy discovers a wallet. It must have slipped out of the guy's pocket when he retrieved her phone from the sidewalk.

For a moment, she contemplates leaving the wallet there. It would serve him right if someone came along and stole whatever cash or cards he has inside. She isn't a vindictive sort, however, and she stoops down and grabs the wallet. She stares down at the brown leather and runs her fingers over the worn edges, tempted to take a peek inside. Despite the fact the man had been rude, she'd still found him incredibly attractive. She can't help but wonder what she'd find inside. Does he use mostly cash, or strictly debit cards? Is there a photo of his girlfriend?

What's his name?

Curiosity eats at Maddy, but she shoves down the temptation. It takes several steps to realize she's trying to follow the guy instead of just hurrying to class and turning the wallet into lost and found later. She falters. Ditching class isn't the best idea, but they aren't doing much apart from reviewing for exams. She can miss one day and besides, she wouldn't mind seeing the guy again and giving him a piece of her mind on the rules of social etiquette.

Her decision made, Maddy jumps up on her toes, trying to see which way he was heading, but there are so many people milling about, she's afraid she's lost him. Just before she's ready to turn around and try to make it to class in time, she spots the guy's sandy hair heading toward the administration buildings.

"Hey!" Several students eye Maddy as she shoves through the crowd but the guy she's pursuing doesn't pause when she hollers for him. Pursuing him only fuels her irritation and she's more determined to catch up to him with each step. The crowd of students thins when she nears the administration offices. Maddy catches sight of him as he turns a corner between the old, brick buildings.

She approaches but when she catches the sound of his harsh voice, she slows. She edges up to the building and pressed her back against the rough brick. A sharp breeze blows toward her and she brushes hair out of her face with a huff of irritation. The guy's speaking to someone, but she can't make out what he's saying. His tone implies anger and impatience, which is obviously his baseline. At least it doesn't seem to be personal.

A moment later, a female student hurries by, her face pale and eyes wide. She doesn't notice Maddy against the wall as she clutches her purse tightly.

For a moment, Maddy watches the student quickly retreating. Her nostrils flare with indignation. Apparently, the guy is more of a douche than she assumed. Does he get off going around and harassing female students? Maddy doesn't make a habit of getting into confrontations, but this guy has her rankled. She rounds the corner, ready to give him a piece of her mind, only to find he's already gone.

There's only one direction the guy could have taken. Determined to catch him before he disappears for good, Maddy rushes down the alley between the two buildings. She reaches the end in time to see a door shut in a nearby building. Hoping it's him and out of options, she hurries to the door. Inside, she's met with a long stretch of hallway but no sign of the guy. She does, however, catch the echoing footsteps of someone hurrying up the stairwell.

Maddy spots a sign for the elevators and quickly makes her way to them. There's no telling which floor the man would have gone to, if that was even him in the stairwell. She chews on her lip, stares at the buttons, and makes a guess. After jabbing her finger on the button for the third floor, she clenches the wallet in her hand and hopes she's right. A moment later, the elevator dings and the doors slide open. Maddy's heart leaps as she catches sight of him slipping into a room.

Damn, he's fast. She slows her steps as she approaches and listens.

To her surprise, the guy's convincing what must be a teacher or administrator to let some girl off the hook for trouble she seems to have caused. Maddy leans closer to the door, trying to piece the story together. Apparently, the student had been bullied into doing something and the apparent douche is trying to set things right.

Had the girl in the alley been the bully? Maddy wants to be angry at this guy, but if he told off a bully and was willing to stretch his neck out for the girl inside the room, maybe he isn't so bad, after all. He also seemed to be quite persuasive. The man he was speaking to agrees to take it no further.

A door closes within the office, likely leading to an adjoining room. Maddy slides closer and risks a peak through the narrow window in the door. The girl tries to give the guy a hug, but he holds his arms up a bit and quickly steps back. Maddy lifts a hand to cover a smile. She'd been ready to berate him for his bad attitude but seeing him so socially awkward is a bit...endearing.

The girl thanks him, looking a little awkward herself, and approaches the door. Maddy quickly moves out of the way and leans against the wall, trying her best to appear as if she were waiting for a friend. The student pays her no mind as she passes. Down the hall, a woman curses as she drops a stack of papers, then sticks her finger in her mouth. Maddy can sympathize. Papercuts were the worst. She's about to quickly help the woman gather the papers when the guy she'd been following steps out of the office.

Maddy freezes as the guy's eyes snap immediately to her. Perhaps it's because her first encounter with him had been in a crowd outside of the café, but here in the quiet, near-empty hallway, she notices something about him.

He's different from any guy she's met before. Really different. She can't quite put her finger on the reason, but something about him seems to set him apart from other men. Perhaps it is the way he studies her, as if he recognizes her and she isn't someone he's merely seen for twenty seconds of his life. No, it's deeper than that. Maddy could have sworn there's an aura about him that sets him apart from everyone else, a sort of strength or even danger that makes him different.

Whatever it is she's sensing from him, Maddy doesn't shy

away, even when his eyebrows lower and a muscle ticks along his jaw.

"What do you want?" He growls the words so low, the woman who dropped the papers shuffles by without a pause, still sucking on her paper cut.

Maddy's pulse quickens at the way the man's nostrils flare and he grinds his teeth. *Is he really that annoyed with me?* She clears her throat and tilts her chin up. "I just thought you might like this back." She holds up the wallet. "Though with your serious lack of manners, maybe I should have left it on the sidewalk to give you a good dose of karma."

The guy's gaze bounces back and forth between the wallet and Maddy. He reaches a hand to the back pocket of his dark wash jeans, jeans that fit him in a way that should be criminal, and realizes his wallet is, indeed, missing.

"Uh, thanks." He reaches out and takes the wallet. Without another word, he brushes past Maddy.

"Hang on just a second." Maddy quickly steps in front of him. "I heard what you did."

He raises an eyebrow. "And?"

Maddy blinks. The guy doesn't even bother hiding the fact he persuaded an administrator to let the girl go, or that he very likely threatened the bully. "Why did you do it?"

"I don't know what you mean." He stuffs his wallet in his back pocket. "I have places to be." He sidesteps, but Maddy shadows the movement.

Admittedly, she's enjoying seeing him getting frustrated.

"Get out of my way," he snaps.

Maddy props her hands on her hips. "You know, you really need to learn how to talk to people, especially to someone who missed class and went out of their way to return your wallet."

"I already thanked you." He speaks through clenched teeth, as if determined to keep more words trapped in his mouth.

A small smile quirks at the corner of Maddy's lips. "Are you always this cranky?"

For a moment, he does nothing but stare down at her. Despite the line pinched between his eyebrows, there's a certain sort of curiosity playing in his light green eyes. It fascinates her far more than it should.

He spins around her in a blur, rushing off before Maddy can get another word in.

Watching him disappear through the door to the stairwell, Maddy's smile deepens. Perhaps the guy isn't so bad, after all. Maybe he's just socially inept. As she heads towards the elevator, she can't help but wish she'd peeked in his wallet after all and gotten his name.

Her phone buzzes in her pocket as the elevator doors close behind her and she answers the call from her mom.

"Hey, Mom."

"Maddy, I know you have class, but could you come home?"

Maddy's heartbeat skips. "Is everything okay?"

"Yes...just...I need you to come home for a little bit."

"Okay, sure. I'll head that way."

The elevator doors slide open and Maddy steps into the hall. The mystery man exits the building and Maddy shakes her head, determined to work him out of her mind as she steps outside and heads to the parking lot on the other side of campus.

He was a nice diversion, but now reality has set in.

Her mother needs to talk to her. And after what Maddy learned last night, she doubts it's to discuss what they're having for dinner.

CHAPTER 5
CALEB

The interaction with Maddy repeats through Caleb's mind like a movie scene on an unbroken loop. He lingers on every word, and every detail about the girl. He certainly hadn't been prepared to see her outside that office. After watching her casually for weeks, the sudden surprise had tilted him back on his typical behavior when put off his game...irritation. It's the best way to get people to back off.

Only, Maddy hadn't seemed the least bit fazed by his gruff attitude. If anything, she'd seemed amused.

Caleb slams his car door shut and stuffs his hands in his pockets, thinking about the little smile playing on her pink lips and the steel set of her stance as she'd faced off with him. He has to admit, he likes the fact that she's strong-willed enough to push his buttons and not stand down when any other student on that campus would have retreated. She surprises him, and that isn't easy to do. Not to mention she's pretty. No, not pretty. Maddy's downright beautiful. There's just something intriguing about her flashing brown eyes, the delicious sound of her quickened heartbeats, and the way her hands had settled stubbornly on her squeezable hips...

30

Groaning, Caleb roughly runs his fingers through his hair and crosses the pavement on quick steps. Now isn't the time to be thinking about Maddy and truth be told, he shouldn't even be thinking about her at all. Nothing could ever happen between the two of them, not with what he is now. It's best to put a stop to his fascination with the girl and put his focus on what lies ahead.

The large brick building in front of him seems abandoned at first glance. Many of the dingy windows are cracked or missing panes entirely, scraggly, dead weeds hug the edges of the walls, and a plastic grocery bag dances by on a cool breeze, as if the trash couldn't even be bothered to linger outside the building. According to the faded lettering painted on the brownish-red brick, the warehouse used to once house a bakery. The Creed Baking Co. had long since faded into history in favor of the wholesale market, but a faint light shining behind one of the cracked windows shows an ounce of life left in the old place.

It's a strange sort of place for one to reside. Caleb figures those inside wanted something unassuming and forgettable. Indeed, an abandoned bakery was the last place one would think to find a group of people dedicated to hunting and slaying vampires.

The Master called Caleb shortly after he'd left the administration building, telling him about a tip pointing to a residence of hunters. According to his Master, this group of hunters are believed to have attacked a vampire stronghold in Mercy City a couple of months ago before arriving in Creed. Caleb had quickly jumped at the chance and agreed to check it out. Not only does he need the distraction and has been craving an adrenaline-induced release lately, but he's also hoping he runs into *him*.

Anger, dark and deadly, seethes through his veins, and he welcomes it. Feeds it. Revenge is only a matter of time.

Caleb steps behind an evergreen tree to observe. The distant sound of traffic fades to a hum inside his head and he tilts his face toward the light breeze. He picks up the sharp tang of a dumpster piled with garbage, and the earthy scent of the pine needles and sweet sap of the tree, but nothing else.

For a long time, Caleb tailed the hunters before they managed to slip through his grasp and disappear. He finally found clues that pointed toward them taking up residence in Creed but until now, he hadn't been able to unearth their whereabouts. Like a thorn in his palm, he'd dug and picked, trying to find them, only to be growing more irritated with each passing day.

He wonders if the Master had been the one to find the hunters, or if it had been one of his other followers. A little annoyed that the discovery had gone unnoticed by him, Caleb's at least relieved to be the one put on the case.

It's the only way to make sure this is done right.

He studies the building and watches the window glowing with faint light, but no shadow passes over the panes to indicate even a single soul within the walls of brick. No one leaves or comes in. Caleb doesn't hear a single breath or heartbeat, though he's still too far away to likely pick up on any. His Master received word on activity here just this morning. If there's anyone inside, it's unlikely they've left in such a short time.

Caleb steps out slowly from behind the tree and approaches the building. He shoves his hands in his pockets and stares down at the ground, doing his best to appear as nothing more than a passerby. He nears the building, but just as he's a few feet from the brick face, a sharp tingle like the biting static of electricity ripples over his skin. A metallic taste fills his mouth and he grimaces, taking a step back.

The building is warded.

"Damn." Caleb tilts his head back and eyes the roof. The entire building is likely protected, so getting inside through a roof access or a window may prove impossible. At least now he knows there are, indeed, hunters within the old bakery, otherwise there would be no protection magic.

He continues his slow stroll, wishing he had the ability to break through the spell. He rolls his tongue around in his mouth, doing his best to sweep away the residual taste touching the ward had brought. The chance is slim, but there may just be a weak spot in the hunters' defenses somewhere. Continuing along the wall, he turns right at the corner, every few steps swaying closer until he can sense the lightest brush of static on his arm. It sends goosebumps across his skin and raises the hairs on the back of his neck.

With sharp eyes, Caleb sweeps the area with his keen gaze, but he still sees no sign of any other life nearby. The breeze shifts and blows at his back, taking any scents that might give him clues away from him. The ward holds steady along the left-hand side of the building. Caleb takes another right and faces the back. There's an alley running the length of the wall, with a metal building across that seems to be used for storage. All of the windows are on the second floor on this side of the wall and Caleb frowns. He doesn't like that someone could be watching him, but he can't see them.

He suddenly catches the sound of rapid heartbeats and he stills, eyes snapping toward the right side of the alley. A pair of cats burst around the corner, one chasing the other and both growling and hissing. They pass by Caleb without a glance. He stares up toward the windows, but the noise of the little beasts hasn't seemed to draw anyone's attention.

He shakes his head after a moment and starts down the alley. The ward is strong all the way around. They've been careful. Perhaps his Master knows of a way to break through them.

Caleb's hands clench in frustration. If only he could get inside and see who exactly was a part of this hunting party...

A faint whooshing reaches Caleb's ears. His heartbeat skips into overdrive as he jumps to the side in a blur of movement. There's a rush of wind. A thud that's far too close. The tearing of metal. Caleb's boots skid through the gravel of the alley and when he comes to a stop, he finds a wooden stake piercing the metal of the building beside the bakery. He narrows his eyes at the polished timber. If he'd been a fraction slower, he'd have been impaled through the chest.

He cranes his neck to find a man peeking out of a window above with a hard, piercing stare. He seems unordinary, and yet Caleb would recognize the man with the short, brown hair even yards away. A familiar sort of cold spreads through him, his veins frosting with hatred as his lips peel back in a snarl.

The man leans out of the window with a glare to match his own. "Foul, wretched animal." He follows his scathing words with a string of curses. "Get out of here. Next time I won't miss."

Caleb leans casually against the metal storage building and crosses his arms. He keeps his eye on the hunter above, if the man's planning on throwing another stake at him, he would have done so already.

"I can't say it's a pleasure to see you again, Felix." Caleb's tone is light, even leaning toward amicable, but there's nothing friendly in the steel stare he holds on the hunter. "Though it has been a while. We haven't seen each other since Mercy City."

When Felix destroyed Caleb's future.

Felix sniffs. "And much too soon for my liking. Leave. You won't be finding your way in here."

"Oh, I will." Caleb smirks. "I can guarantee it. You can hide in there all you want with your little friends and your pointy wooden toys, but I promise you, Felix, I will do everything in my power to make sure you never leave Creed alive." He risks a quick glance up and down the alley, assuring himself Felix hasn't sent any hunters to outflank him.

Felix barks out a laugh, the sound cold and devoid of an ounce of emotion or mercy. "Who do you think you are, making such threats? Has your ego inflated so much? Or do you just take pleasure in being your vile master's dog?"

Caleb's teeth scrape together as he clenches his jaw. If anyone in the vicinity is a dog, it's Felix, hunting down others like a ravenous hound. A strange sort of pain echoes through Caleb at the thought of believing hunters to be equal to dogs. It's a dishonor to his late aunt, Kenna DeVoe. Felix had been her lieutenant in the Order of the Knightly Rose. That had been before she died, however, and Felix had gone on to carry her legacy while Caleb, well, he'd been cast down to live in the sea of quarry the hunters now pursued.

"This isn't over." Caleb pushes away from the wall. "I'll be seeing you again, Felix." He gives the hunter a mocking salute and stalks down the alley, vowing to make sure Felix will suffer for his sins of the past.

No matter what.

CHAPTER 6

MADELEINE

Silverware clinks against plates as Maddy plunges her hands in the hot, soapy water. She pulls out a knife and pinches the sponge over the blade. Her thoughts are a frenzied tangle. So much has happened just in the past day. A young woman has been allegedly killed by a vampire, and now Maddy has a decision to make. After hurrying home from school, her mother had told her that Felix had called. He's requesting a meeting with Maddy.

He's going to extend the invitation, yet again, for her to join the Order of the Knightly Rose.

Maddy, the vampire hunter.

She snorts quietly to herself and puts the knife in the other half of the sink to be rinsed, then grabs a spoon. The last thing she would have thought of becoming in life was any sort of hunter or agent, much less one who hunted beings who live off human blood. The thought makes her want to shudder but she focuses on the steaming water and does her best not to linger on an image of piercing fangs.

A glance at the clock on the wall shows it's nearly two in the afternoon. Maddy hadn't gone back to school after having a talk with her mom about Felix and what he would expect. Instead, her mom told her about her own role as a hunter as they'd made spaghetti and a salad for lunch. It just seemed so unreal to Maddy. She wanted to ask if her father had been involved as a hunter, as well, but he was a sore subject after the divorce, so she didn't voice her curiosity aloud.

Even after hearing her mom's side of things, Maddy still isn't certain she wants to become a hunter. What about her friends and school? Would she even have authority over her own life anymore? True, she hasn't yet decided exactly what she's going to do after school. She's been waffling over the decision, but nothing has settled right with her. Could it be because she was meant to do something else?

Maybe something daring and dangerous?

"Let me get those." Maddy's mom steps up to the sink and gives Maddy a light bump with her hip, a smile playing on her face.

Maddy shakes her head. "It's all right. I'm nearly done." She senses her mom's stare on her as she finishes up the dishes.

"Madeleine, I know this is a lot to take in." Her mom smooths out a wrinkle in her shirt, then picks a white fuzzy off of her black leggings. "But I think you should seriously consider joining the Order. It's in the family, and it's very difficult for us to lead normal lives when we're meant for something so much greater."

Maddy dries her hands on a dishtowel, then folds her arms and leans against the counter. "Aren't moms supposed to convince their daughters to stay out of trouble, not plunge into it head first?"

Her mom's lips curve in a patient smile, but there's a tightness around the edges of her eyes. "I want you to become a hunter so you will stay *out* of trouble. Vampires exist, and now we know there are some right here in Creed. I want you to be able to defend yourself, and to protect others if the occasion calls for it."

If there had been someone like her around, a young hunter, would Olivia, the missing student, have been saved? Maddy isn't certain, but the prospect of preventing something like that from happening again puts a little fire in her belly. She thinks about what Gabby told her. Her friend said to follow her heart and spoke of destiny as if she'd been scooped up by the wings of fate, herself.

Maddy peers over at her mom. "I'll talk with Felix, but I'm not guaranteeing I'm going to agree to join the Order."

Her mom nods and pulls her cell out of her pocket. "That's all he wants is for you to listen to him and at least consider this. I'll give him a call."

Maddy heads to her room and picks up her phone where it's charging on her bedside table. She has a couple of missed calls from Cora, and one text from her complaining that she missed meeting her for lunch. Maddy taps out a quick response to apologize and tells her something came up at home and she'll call her later. Then, she brushes out her long, dark hair before pulling it back into a ponytail. A nervous flutter unfurls in her stomach, feeling as if she were preparing to go into a job interview. Perhaps that's exactly what this is.

Several minutes later, her mom calls for her. Maddy's cheeks puff out and she heads out of her room and down the hall. Felix smiles at her as her mom closes the front door behind him.

"Madeleine, what a pleasure it is to see you again."

Maddy isn't certain "pleasure" is the term she would use. Felix is an imposing man, despite the friendly features of his face. The first time Maddy encountered him, something about him struck her as dangerous and the sensation hasn't lessened. If anything, Maddy almost feels like her mom has invited a wolf into their home. Lurking beneath Felix's façade is a vampire hunter, and given all of the movies and shows Maddy has seen about them, she can only assume vampires and hunters are, in reality, ten times deadlier than in the imagination.

Felix extends his hand toward her. Maddy steps up and shakes it, refraining from glancing at her mom for reassurance. If he was dangerous to her, Maddy's mom wouldn't have let the man step foot into the house. The head of the Order gives her fingers a tight squeeze, then nods with approval.

"You have a nice grip, Maddy. That will suit you well as a hunter."

Maddy withdraws her hand and takes a step back. "I haven't decided anything yet."

Felix's smile deepens. "Then I had best get to the persuading."

The three head to the living room. Maddy settles into her favorite green chair. It's plush and creaks slightly from a loose spring as she crosses a leg over her knee. Felix takes a spot on the couch and Maddy's mom excuses herself so the two can talk.

"I know you must be very curious, so I'll just get right into it. As I said before, I'm the leader of a chapter of the Order of the Knightly Rose, and I'm here to extend you an invitation to join. As much as I would love to have you in our ranks, this isn't something to choose lightly. The life of a hunter is not easy, but it's deeply rewarding." Felix clears his throat and his tone takes on an almost professor-like quality. "The Order of the Knightly Rose is a reinvented form of the Knights Templar. I assume you know about them?"

Maddy nods. "Yes, of course. They were a military sect formed during the Crusades."

"True, for the most part. However, the Crusades themselves were really a war between the supernatural. The religious conflict was actually a front. Since then, the Knights Templar have vowed to end any supernatural threat."

"Hang on." Maddy holds up her hand. "You're saying super-natural as if there are more than just vampires out there." Felix stares at her, unblinking. Maddy lets out a slow breath as the realization sinks in. "Wow." What else exists in the world among humans? Does she even want to know?

Maddy's mom walks from the kitchen with a pair of steaming mugs. "Tea?"

Felix offers a smile. "Ah, yes. Thank you."

Maddy takes her cup wordlessly, but doesn't take a sip as she holds it in her hands. Her mom gives her a brief, reassuring smile as she leaves.

"After Dracula's merciless—"

"*Dracula?*" Maddy leans forward. "Like *the* Dracula?"

Felix's lips press into a hard line and Maddy gets the impression he isn't used to being interrupted. "Yes, *the* Dracula. After his merciless killing of many hunters, the Van Helsing's took the lead and reinvented the dying Knights Templar into the Order of the Knightly Rose, and our war was restricted to vampires, alone." He pauses to take a sip of the tea, then sets the mug down on the end table.

That's going to leave a ring, Maddy thinks. She wants to know more about Dracula and the Van Helsing's, but Felix continues before she can form a single question.

"For many years, we've been working from the shadows to eradicate the vampire scourge on this earth. We even had a hand in killing off the King of the Vampires, and several council leaders. Then, we worked on taking down the Masters."

A bright light blazes behind Felix's gaze, burning with triumph and justice. It makes the strange fire in Maddy's belly flicker with a yearning desire to be a part of this world she's known nothing about. What would it be like to be part of something so…big? Felix is talking about protecting people. Saving lives. Still, she's hesitant.

"If you killed all of their leaders, why are the vampires still such a problem?" Maddy finally takes a sip of her tea as she waits for Felix to answer. Her mother's gone heavy on the honey, and Maddy wonders if it's the way Felix prefers it, and how her mother had known.

"The vampires were cast down for a while, but they returned to their old ways. Eventually, they resurfaced in full public in Mercy City at the same time a girl named Arielle touched something known as the obsidian. As such, the dark influence spread, making the vampire community active. The vampires went under demon employ and were responsible in the murder of Kenna DeVoe."

Maddy doesn't want to interrupt, but she's having a hard enough time trying to untangle everything Felix is telling her without random names being thrown in. "Who is Kenna DeVoe?"

"She was the leader of the vampire hunters," Felix says. "Her family were all descendants of the Van Helsings. Her death caused quite a rift in the Order, but I took up the mantle of the Order of the Knightly Rose." Felix leans forward, his elbows on his knees and a hard stare pinning Maddy to the spot. "Vampires are running amok, even with the number of demons becoming less. Their evil must be reigned in. I've been working hard to rebuild the Order to fight against the vampire menace. Madeleine, I need every hunter I can get my hands on."

Maddy's heartbeats race in her chest. She dwells on Gabby's advice and the words of her mother, tapping her fingers on the arm of her chair. College student or vampire hunter? The decision is huge, and yet, there's that fire burning within her that she hadn't known until today.

She swallows, then tilts her chin up. "All right," she says. "I'll do it. I'll join the Order."

Felix claps his hands together. "Excellent! I knew you'd make the right decision."

She smiles faintly although it's far too early to tell if she's made the right choice. She just hopes those flames burning within her will blaze a trail for her.

And not reduce her to a pile of char and ash.

CHAPTER 7

CALEB

The sky is gray and Caleb's thankful for the heavy blanket of clouds that have taken up most of the sky. He'd clung to the shadows as he raced after Felix. The hunter had left his warded building not long before. Deciding it would be easier to stay hidden, Caleb left his car behind and had followed Felix on foot. He needs to find out what the leader of the Order is up to so he can relay the information to the Master, who doesn't have a tendency to be patient. He'll be waiting on news from Caleb about the tip pointing to a band of hunters.

Felix had turned into a residential neighborhood and now Caleb's staking out a house the hunter disappeared into. It's a quaint, cozy-looking home. The cottage-style seems more suited to a forest near a creek than it does in this suburban neighborhood. The resident has decorated for fall, with pumpkins and gourds trickling down the front steps. A few shadows move inside, and the Jeep and Ford Taurus tell Caleb there's more than one person in there, aside from Felix.

Caleb peers at the mailbox from his spot across the street. The last name *Grimes* is scrawled across the side in looping letters. He frowns. The name seems familiar, but he can't place it. His attention snaps back to the house. The curtains are closed, so he can't make out faces, only the silhouettes of those within. After a moment, even the shadows disappear. He clicks his tongue, watching and waiting.

The family inside must be important to Felix, somehow. He isn't the kind of man who makes house calls. Caleb smiles, already thinking of ways such information can be used as leverage. He pulls out his cell and deliberates as he taps on the recent calls tab. His finger hovers over Morgan's name for a moment. Caleb's closest friend would want to be privy to this kind of information, but he thinks better of it. The Master would want to know first, and Caleb doesn't want to risk discipline for not following the chain of command. He taps the number at the top with his thumb.

Barely half a ring later, the Master answers. "What have you found?" No greeting. No assurance that Caleb is alright. Information, first and foremost.

Caleb keeps his eyes on the house as he speaks. "You were right about that building. It's warded, and when I tried to find a weak spot, I was attacked by Felix."

"Felix." The Master's voice hisses with mockery and hate. "If he's here, then the Order has taken up residence in Creed. I was hoping it was merely a stray group of hunters. The Order always hangs around, like a foul smell."

Caleb squeezes the cell in his hand, and keeps his breathing steady. The Order. The Knights. Once, they had been friends. Once, he had hoped to join their ranks. Now he's an enemy, and all they want is his death.

"Felix left the building not long ago," Caleb continues, pushing away the painful thoughts. "I followed him to a residential neighborhood. He was invited into a home on West Pine

Drive. I can't see who's inside to know what we're dealing with here."

A dark chuckle rumbles through the phone and the sound grates over Caleb's nerves. "That is excellent news. I'll send you some backup. I believe Morgan and a few of the other boys are downstairs. I want you to get as much information about this family as you can. There must be a good reason the head of the Order thinks they are important enough to warrant a house call. Do not attack them. Information only, do you understand?"

"Yes, Master, I understand," Caleb says dutifully, even if it leaves a bitter taste in his mouth.

The vampire Master expects loyalty. To do any different is a death sentence.

"I want as much information on those living in that house as you can give me. After we find out who they are, then we will discover a way to use them against Felix and the rest of his pathetic Order."

A car passes and Caleb continues to lean against the wide trunk of the maple tree, watching the vehicle slow and then park along the curb outside of the Grimes residence.

"Looks like they have company," Caleb says. "I'll let Morgan know where to find me."

"Stay alert." The Master hangs up after his usual parting words.

Caleb eyes the dark tinted windows of the car, but other than the bare shapes of the driver and a single passenger, he can't make out who's inside. They don't exit the vehicle, and instead keep the car idling. Caleb leans slightly around the tree and snaps a quick photo of the license plate to run through their database later. He waits for nearly thirty minutes before the front door of the house finally opens. Felix steps out onto the porch, laughing as he waves to someone.

The sight of him makes Caleb's muscles tense. He could get to the hunter in a matter of seconds and he wouldn't see him coming, even with those in the car likely working for the Order. Caleb wonders what his neck would feel like, snapping in his hands, and how long the light would take to leave his eyes. Felix takes a step away from the door and smiles at a young woman as she joins him. Caleb's breath catches as Felix walks with her down the front steps.

No.

Maddy.

Caleb nearly gives away his position but he holds steady as Felix walks around the front of his sleek black car in the driveway and opens the passenger door. Caleb watches, stunned, as she climbs in. His first instinct is to call out to her, to tell her not to go with such a vile man, but that's ridiculous. He can't let Felix or the other hunters know he's there. Felix gives a nod to the driver of the car beside the curb and then climbs into his vehicle. The engine purrs to life and Felix backs out of the driveway, then heads down the street, the other car following close behind.

Tapping a quick message to Morgan that Felix has left the residence and is in motion, Caleb follows the vehicles. A small grin touches his face as he runs. He loves the speed and the way his feet eat up the sidewalks and lawns. Humans don't notice his passing, as he's little more than a blur. He revels in his strength and speed, yearning to unleash them on Felix. He holds back, however, unwilling to face the Master's wrath if he breaks the vampire leader's orders. Far too much is at stake.

Felix's car stops at a red light and Caleb curses as he studies Maddy's profile. What is she doing with Felix? She certainly doesn't seem like the type to mix with such a foul sort of company. Then again, Caleb's been wrong about things before. The light turns green and he keeps several yards behind. As soon as he realizes where they're going, he sends another text to Morgan, letting him know to head toward the old bakery on the west side of town.

A few minutes later Caleb is back across the street from the brick building wrapped in the hunters' ward. He slides into his car, then watches as Felix parks outside of the bakery. One of the men from the other vehicle opens the door for Maddy. For a brief moment, she glances across the street and Caleb stills. She doesn't seem to notice him, however, and she turns to listen to Felix as he speaks to her.

Caleb watches her and his fingers tighten a fraction on the steering wheel. Irritation flickers through him and he rolls his shoulders in an effort to dispel the sensation. He lets out a sharp sigh through his nose as Maddy is led through a door.

"What on earth are you doing with the hunters?" Caleb mutters.

Could she possibly be a hunter, as well? No. She doesn't seem like the type and besides, she would have confronted him while they were on campus. A hunter wouldn't miss the chance to bring down a vampire. If she isn't a hunter, however, then what could Felix possibly want with her?

A thought occurs to Caleb. Maybe she isn't a hunter *yet*. Felix would be wanting to grow his numbers, and the only way to do so would be to recruit new members of the Order. He thinks about the beautiful girl with the sexy, snarky attitude, and the way she'd confronted him without a care in the world. What if she were getting involved in the Order?

That would suck. He was just beginning to find her interesting.

Caleb glares at the door as it shuts behind Maddy and the hunters. He isn't certain how she's involved, but the only way he's going to know for sure would be to somehow insinuate himself into Maddy's life.

Caleb hadn't been able to decide if he wanted to get to know Maddy better, or keep his distance from her.

Fate, it seems, may have just decided for him.

CHAPTER 8

MADELEINE

The metal door closes behind Maddy with a thud that echoes with a disconcerting amount of finality, as if it's too late to go back out into the regular world again. She stares over her shoulder at the door and glances through one of the windows. She can't see the car parked across the street from inside the building. She was certain she spotted Caleb watching her from the driver's seat.

"Is something wrong?" Felix watches her, his eyes flicking to the window curiously.

For a second, Maddy thinks about telling him she thought she saw a man she knew watching her, but thinks better of it. "No, everything's fine."

She turns away from the window. The guy in the car probably hadn't even been Caleb. Why would he be following her around and watching her, of all people? He doesn't even like her, evident by his attitude around her earlier that day. That fact annoys her. She doesn't deserve to be disliked by someone who doesn't even know her. Indifference, sure, she could understand that, but he didn't have to be so rude.

Maddy turns her focus on her surroundings. "Wow. It didn't seem like it would look like this from the outside."

The entire space, once a massive bakery, has been transformed into a modern, open floor plan. The walls are still reddish brick, but they pair well with the rugs, couches, and chairs placed around the living space. A few lamps glow on mismatched end tables and on the far side of the room, a counter divides the living space and a large kitchen stocked with stainless steel appliances. A stairway runs up the left-hand side of the room.

"The bedrooms are upstairs, along with a few offices. Each hunter gets a room with an attached bathroom." Felix smiles patiently as Maddy opens her mouth. "Before you ask, no, you are not required to stay here. You are more than welcome to, of course, and you may use your room anytime you need a moment to yourself. There will be times we are out late on missions and tasks, and a comfy bed available immediately after will be more appealing, I'm sure. There will also be times when it is safer for you to stay here."

Maddy doesn't like the sound of that. She thinks about her mom, and wonders if there was such a danger, if she could really leave her at home alone while Maddy's tucked away safely with the Order. She hopes she will never be put in such a situation. Although, her mom's also a hunter. She must have a room of her own? Another part of her life Maddy never knew about.

"We have a large training room, as well, but we'll get to that in a moment. May I take your jacket?" Felix has hung his coat on a hook next to the door.

Maddy shrugs it off and hands it to Felix, where he hangs it beside a row of other jackets and coats. Clearly, she isn't the only hunter here beside Felix and the two men who followed them. She hadn't seen where they'd gone once they walked inside.

"Right." Felix claps his hands together. "Time for introductions." Almost as if on cue, a few people emerge from the kitchen and then more pound down the stairs.

Maddy turns her attention to those coming from the kitchen first. One man looks like a UFC fighter, with a shaved head, muscles fit to crush a man's head, and the assurance of an athlete. He's holding a half-eaten banana and studying Maddy with a weighted stare. The other two with him are a young man and woman, both wearing athletic wear and sweating as if they've been running a marathon. They watch her curiously with matching blue eyes beneath their blonde hair.

"This is Oleg," Felix says, pointing to the muscled man. "He is our weaponmaster, and in charge of training all of the hunters. With him are the twins, Laura and Matthew. They've been hunters for several years now."

Maddy blinks in surprise. The siblings don't appear much older than her. How come she's being brought into the game so late?

"And these five are Jess, Antonio, Kai, Oliver, and Daryl."

Smiling and giving a polite nod, Maddy tries to burn all of the names to memory. Jess will be easy. She's the only female in the group of five who came downstairs. She doesn't seem particularly pleased, though whether it's Maddy's inclusion in the Order or another matter, she isn't certain. Jess crosses her arms and the septum piercing in her nose somehow makes her seem more intense. A young man with Asian features smiles at Maddy. She assumes he's Kai, and the man with the tanned complexion and black hair must be Antonio.

The only two left are Oliver and Daryl. One is a tall man with broad shoulders and a face made for breaking hearts. The other is shorter, skinnier, and was sporting a pair of rectangular glasses. This man drops his stare to the floor.

"I'm Daryl." Then, he jabs his thumb at the handsome one. "That's Oliver. People always assume it's the other way around."

Maddy peers around at the group. "Nice to meet you. I'm Maddy." She turns to Felix. "So, you have eight hunters in the Order?"

Felix chuckles. "Oh no, we have more than that. The two who escorted us here have left already, and the others are out of the city on vampire business, hunting elsewhere." He gestures to one of the couches and Maddy sits. Felix and Oleg take up chairs opposite of her, while the rest of the hunters disperse to return to whatever they'd been doing before Maddy arrived.

"Whenever you are in this building you will be trained to fight vampires. Not only will you need to help us get rid of those abominations, but you also need to be able to protect yourself should one happen upon you."

Maddy's leg jumps up and down, a nervous habit she's never been able to break. "Is that expected, to randomly run into vampires?"

"You can never be too sure." Oleg speaks, his voice an even timbre. He leans his elbows on his knees and folds his hands. "They can be anywhere, even in plain sight. You could have walked right by one today and you'd never know it unless you knew what to look for."

Goosebumps prickle at the back of Maddy's neck. She doesn't like the prospect of vampires walking around unnoticed, much less that she could have actually seen one in her lifetime and never realized.

"You will be evaluated via tests." Felix gives Maddy an intense stare, making her shift uncomfortably. "I hope you pass them with flying colors. Once you do, the real work will begin."

Maddy holds up a hand. "Wait. How much time is this training going to take? I can't just drop everything else in my life to do this. I have family and friends, plus school I need to think about."

"Your schooling will not be affected. You will continue to go about your college life as normal, and I assure you that I expect nothing but good grades from you. My hunters are more than just vampire slayers. I expect much out of them, both physically and intellectually. Once you're qualified, you will be asked to join us on certain missions."

The weight of Maddy's decision falls heavily on her shoulders. Perhaps she'd been too rash, enamored by the growing idea of making a difference in the world by taking down monsters. After seeing the other hunters, with their athletic builds and confident natures, she's not so certain she qualifies to be a part of the Order. She picks at a loose thread on the arm of the couch, this decision starting to crowd her chest.

"You know, your mother is a great hunter." Felix nods his head. "Yes, a very fine hunter, and I know you will be one, as well, Madeleine."

The compliment about her mom makes Maddy feel a fraction better, but nerves still coil in her belly.

"I need to get you into condition as soon as possible." Felix stands and begins pacing across the rug, a steely glare settling on his face. "All of our focus needs to turn to eliminating the vampire chapter in this town. Their numbers are growing here and we need to learn the reason. Several people have gone missing now, a large number for a place such as this. I know vampires are behind this, but it's unusual for so many to congregate in a town without a huge population. They need to feed, and it worries me that the girl you've been searching for in those woods will not be the last."

Maddy thinks about Olivia. Could she still be alive, or had

she been...eaten? Would the vampires have turned her into one of them? She shudders at the thought and the sensation reminds her of the unusual, foreboding tremors that have always plagued her. Could "the spooks" have been warning her about the vampires, or could it be about joining the Order? Maybe it was just about Olivia and the other missing residents of Creed.

"Could Olivia still be alive?" Maddy asks quietly.

Felix grunts. "Maybe. It's difficult to tell. Many of the younger vampires cannot control their thirst and will drain a body after their first bite. Others keep humans as blood slaves, to feed on whenever they are hungry. I'm not so sure the latter is better than death, truth be told."

Maddy swallows the disgust at being a vampire's slave, used only for blood. She doesn't want that to be Olivia's fate, but she doesn't want the student to be dead, either. "I'll do what I can to help," she promises.

Oleg suddenly stands, towering over her. "You. Me. Training room." He points toward the direction of the kitchen.

Maddy blinks. "Now? But I don't know anything."

"Exactly." Oleg reaches down, grabs her arm, and yanks her up.

Maddy squeaks at the sudden movement and glances back at Felix. He doesn't give her a nod of reassurance or a wish of good luck, but just stares at her, as if he's hoping he made the right decision.

The training room is through a pair of double doors on the other end of the kitchen. The walls are covered in weapons and mats line the slick floor. A fighting ring takes up space in one corner, dummies are scattered throughout the room for target practice, and there are even climbing ropes. Maddy has the distinct impression she's been suddenly yanked back into high school gym class, and the thought leaves an unpleasant taste in her mouth.

Oleg walks to the wall with the weapons and Maddy notices the rows of stakes for the first time. They're wooden, and polished to gleaming. Her heartbeats tick faster as Oleg plucks one of the sharp stakes from the wall and presses it into her sweaty palm with a wide, wicked grin.

"Let's see what you're made of, Baby Hunter."

CHAPTER 9

CALEB

For a long while, Caleb sits outside of the weathered brick bakery, curiosity eating him alive from the inside. Maddy had to have been invited to join the Order of the Knightly Rose. There's no other reason Felix would bring her here. Caleb just wishes he understood why Maddy had agreed to join. Was she related to Felix, somehow?

Caleb drums his fingers on the steering wheel. No. If Felix had a daughter or niece, he would have known by now. A close family friend, perhaps. He hasn't seen any sign of Maddy since she disappeared into the building and it has been well over an hour. He can't explain why, but the muscles between his shoulders just won't loosen until he sees her safely outside once again.

Maddy may be unsettling, and annoying, but nobody deserves a punishment as severe as working under Felix. Though it's absurd, Caleb wishes he could tell her the truth about who, and what, he is, but he can't. What would he say to her? It's not as if he can walk up to her and say "Hey, remember me? I'm a vampire".

He huffs a short laugh at the thought, and yet, the Order

only recruits those who were aware of the existence of the supernatural. Surely that means Maddy knows about vampires and other supernatural entities? If that's so, then what connection does she have with the Order?

And if so, it's even more important that Caleb keep his true identity a secret.

The phone on the center console buzzes. Caleb picks it up and reads a text from Morgan. He has information to discuss. After casting one last look at the Order's building, Caleb starts his car and heads down the street. Morgan and a couple of the others are waiting for him in a parking lot outside of a row of small businesses. Caleb parks his car and unlocks the door. Morgan slides inside while the others wait in his car.

Caleb nods at his friend. He likes Morgan. The tall vampire with the mop of messy brown hair is easy to get along with and is a great guy to have guarding your back. He's an adept fighter, and loyal to the Master and fellow vampires to a fault. If anyone needs help out of a tight spot, Morgan is the man to call.

"What did you find out?" Caleb told Morgan to find out information about the Grimes instead of following him to the bakery. He needed to know how Maddy and her family are connected to the Order.

Morgan twists in his seat and scratches at the stubble peppered along his jawline. "Right, so the girl, Maddy, well, her mom is the one involved in the Order."

Caleb's head jerks in surprise. "Involved? How so?"

His friend scoffs. "How do you think? She's a hunter. Or was, at least. We aren't certain if she's still active or not. You know how they are, though. Once you're in, you're in."

Caleb's aware of that sentiment all too well. The leather creaks beneath him as he shifts in his seat, the restlessness he'd had while waiting on Maddy to leave the bakery still lacing his muscles. He needs to do something. Move. Run. Feed. Anything to get his mind off the young woman.

"We should capture the woman," Morgan muses quietly.

"Maddy? Why?"

Morgan quirks an eyebrow at him. "No. The mother. It would send a strong message to the Order that we're not to be messed with. Besides, the Master will not want his plans to be interrupted by those self-righteous, nosy pricks." Morgan glances out of the window, staring toward a dollar store. "The death of a hunter may just put a stop to the Order."

Alarm races through Caleb, quickening his pulse. The last thing he wants is more senseless killing, but especially not Maddy's mother. The thought of taking away someone so important to her tightens his chest in an unexpected way. He keeps his face neutral and tilts his head in a show of deep thought.

"I think we need to handle this in a different way," he says.

Morgan swings his stare away from the dollar store, and the young women walking inside. "What do you mean?"

"If we kill a member of the Order, they'll retaliate. We have numbers in this city, but so do they. The Master won't want a war on his hands right now." Caleb leans back in his seat. "We need to take this slow, cautious. We watch them and see what they're trying to do. If something major comes up, then we intercept."

"What about the girl?"

Something about the way Morgan speaks rankles Caleb. Does Morgan suspect his intentions toward Maddy? Caleb shrugs a shoulder. "I'll watch her, maybe even try to get closer to her and learn more about the Order and why they have decided to come to Creed."

Morgan taps a finger on the window sill for a moment, then

speaks. "Sounds like a good plan to me. Just don't let this girl stab you in the heart."

Caleb ignores his friend's jab. As if he would let some inexperienced hunter get to him so easily. "Keep a watch on their house. I want a report on any comings and goings. I'll relay the information to the Master." He pinches his chin. "See if you can get Gideon to trace the family's ancestral line."

"Why do we need to know the family history? They're hunters and that's all there is to it."

Irritation prickles through Caleb but he bites down on a snippy retort. Morgan is always too practical, and never thinks too deeply on anything. He likes being pointed in a direction and following through with never a thought as to why he's doing so. Caleb prefers to see things at all angles.

"The Order only recruits those whose ancestral lines stretch back to the warriors and members who existed when the Order was the Knights Templar," Caleb explains. "It is rare for them to employ those from the outside."

Morgan nods slowly. "So, in other words, you think this girl they've recruited could be something special?"

Caleb had been wondering as much. Maddy faced off with him, when most other humans are naturally put off with his bristly edges. There's no doubt in his mind she has a hunter's soul. He can sense it in his very bones. "Maybe. It's hard to tell. You and the guys just keep an eye out and let me know what you find."

Morgan climbs out of the car with a promise to keep Caleb up to date. Caleb stays in the parking lot for a few minutes after the others leave, trying to think of a way to get into Maddy's life without being too obvious he's trying to be there. He glances over at the dollar store, and then pauses. Through the storefront windows, Caleb can see the girl Maddy usually hangs out with nearly every day. Her best friend, most likely. Perhaps even a relative, maybe a cousin. He glances skyward, thanking the fates for the opportunity unfolding before him.

He's already got Maddy offside, and it's best for both of them if he doesn't get too close. He can't afford to get emotionally invested in any of this. He's a vampire, after all.

Caleb studies himself in the rearview mirror and combs his fingers through his sandy hair. Then, he gets out of the car and strolls over to the store. A mechanical bell sounds when he enters and he nods politely at the cashier who greets him. There's no sign of the girl, so he peruses the aisles close to the front. He doesn't want her slipping by unseen. Then, he catches sight of her. A quick peek into the next aisle finds her surveying the selection of candles. He watches as she picks one up, sniffs it, wrinkles her nose, then sets it back. After a few minutes, she picks out a large jar candle and heads his way.

Caleb ducks back around the corner before she can see him. He listens to her footsteps and the sound of her heartbeats drawing nearer. Just before she reaches the end of the aisle, Caleb turns the corner and runs right into her. The girl gasps and the collision causes the candle to fall from her hands. Caleb quickly catches it before it can shatter on the floor.

"Oops." He curves his lips upward in a charming smile as the girl collects herself and holds up the candle. "Sorry about that. I need to pay more attention. Are you okay?"

The irony that this is how he should've responded to Maddy earlier today isn't lost on him. What would it have looked like? Would they have talked a little longer? Maybe organized catching up for a coffee?

Shaking away the unruly thoughts, Caleb keeps his gaze steady and warm on the girl. He's here for a reason and he needs to remember that.

For a long moment, the young woman stares at him, a sense of confusion and attraction permeating from her pores. She clears her throat as she tucks a strand of red hair behind her ear. "Um, yes. I'm fine. Thank you." She takes the candle, a blush blooming across her cheeks.

Caleb tilts his head. "You look familiar. Do you go to school here?" He puts his hands in his pockets and takes a step back, appearing as non-threatening as possible.

"Yes, I do."

"Ah." Caleb snaps his fingers. "I saw you at the Bean Buzz."

"Yeah, I love that place." She starts tilting the candle back and forth between her hands and her pulse quickens.

Caleb breathes in her nervous excitement. "Maybe we can get a coffee sometime." He pulls out his cell. "If you'd like?"

The young woman seems taken aback but quickly recovers. "Oh. Sure!" She gives Caleb her number. "I'm Cora, by the way."

"Cora with the candle." Caleb winks at her. "I'm Caleb. I'll give you a call soon. Maybe we can do dinner instead of coffee."

Cora's heartbeats tick even faster. "That would be great."

Caleb smiles at her, then continues down the aisle, giving her a nod. "See you soon." He turns away and a crooked smile lifts his right cheek.

Getting into Maddy's life proved easier than he'd thought.

CHAPTER 10

CALEB

Silence is heavy in the air, broken only by the rattle and rustle of a cool breeze through the autumn canopy. Shadows blanket the park and a few stars wink overhead through the building of thick clouds. Caleb walks down the asphalt path alone, his hands in his pockets and his mind deep in thought. He'd spent the whole day yesterday waiting on new reports from the guys but had heard nothing. Instead, he'd turned his attention to getting into contact with a reliable source of his, and preparing for his date with Cora in a couple of hours.

The path winds through a patch of forest, past a field used for soccer games, and then the playground. A light pierces the darkness up ahead, and as Caleb draws closer, the glow of a cell phone makes the face of his friend glow.

Bryn stares down at her phone and doesn't look up as Caleb approaches. There's a fine line between her eyebrows and her finger flashes across the screen, a digital sword cutting through falling fruit.

A chuckle rolls through Caleb's chest. "You're still playing that game?"

The young woman doesn't answer, but a few seconds later, she lets out a heavy sigh. Out of lives, she sets the phone on her lap then pats the bench beside her. "It's my favorite, but I just can't beat my high score."

Caleb slides onto the bench. "You're the determined type. I'm sure you'll get it. How are you?"

Bryn sweeps a bright purple lock out of her face. Her hair had been pink when he'd met her months ago. She shrugs beneath her jacket. "Oh, you know. Same old, same old."

An amused grin lifts Caleb's cheek. "Is it? Because it seems like the "same old" has been changing an awful lot lately."

"God, isn't that the truth." Bryn reaches into a bag sitting beside her, rifles around for a moment, then pulls out a round sucker. "Want one?"

Caleb shakes his head. "Pass."

His friend unwraps the sucker then sticks it in her mouth. Caleb picks up the sickly sweet scent of cotton candy. He wrinkles his nose. "Those will rot your teeth, you know."

"Like I care." Bryn spins the sucker in her mouth for a moment as she eyes Caleb. "What was it you needed to see me about, anyway? There's a karaoke party I'm missing."

Caleb snorts. He's heard Bryn sing, and the girl can't carry a tune no matter how hard she tries. He definitely admires her commitment, though. "Sorry to keep you." He crosses an ankle over his knee and leans back against the bench, shifting to get comfortable. "I want to know what you know about Felix." Caleb's feelings toward the hunter had changed deeply since meeting Bryn. He hadn't hated the man, then. Now, all he can think about is ending him.

Bryn's mouth makes a loud sucking noise as she pulls her candy past her lips. "I do have new information on Felix, but you're not going to like it."

"I highly doubt I'd enjoy any information on that man. What is it?"

"After Kenna's death..." Bryn pauses, flicking her green eyes to Caleb with uncertainty. The death of his aunt is a touchy subject. "Well, you knew about Felix's standing in the Order. He had influence, but after Kenna's death, he separated from the main faction. He started to pursue his own vision of how the Order should be."

An owl passes overhead, silent to human ears, but Caleb picks up the subtle shift of air over the bird's wings. He knows about Felix breaking off from the main Order of the Knightly Rose. Though Caleb can never be a part of the Order he still feels a sense of vengeance over the fact Felix is trying to turn Kenna's vision of the Order into something else entirely.

"You're cracking the wood."

Caleb glances down. His fingers are curled around the edge of the bench seat, and the thin planks are starting to groan under the pressure of his clenching fingers. He blows out a sharp sigh through his nose and works his fingers loose.

Satisfied the bench isn't going to collapse beneath her, Bryn continues. "Felix took a few of the Order members with him, too. At first, I was surprised when I found out. You know how loyal those hunters are to their mission, but then I found out something."

Caleb waits a moment and tries not to lose his patience as Bryn samples her sucker again. He clears his throat after a moment, raising an eyebrow.

Bryn pulls the sucker free and points it at him. "You knew Felix from before. Did he strike you as the kind of man to rebel against the cause?" She continues before Caleb can reply. "He never would have broken away from the main faction if it wasn't for a strange man Felix met some time after Kenna's death."

Caleb tries to recall Felix associating with an unknown man, but during his pursuit of the hunter, he'd never noticed the Order member meeting up with a stranger.

"Who is he?" Caleb asks.

"I can't be certain, exactly." Bryn twirls the sucker in her fingers. "But, I think I may have an idea. You haven't been the only one watching Felix. I've kept my eye on him since he left Mercy City. This guy Felix is tangled up with something...else. I believe he is part of a mysterious organization."

The bench squeaks as Caleb shifts, turning to face her. "What organization?"

"I don't know." Bryn crosses her ankles and pops the candy into her mouth, tucking the sucker into her left cheek. "No one knows. There's darkness in it, though. That much is certain." She rubs her hands up and down her arms, as if the thought gives her goosebumps.

Caleb is silent for a moment, tilting his face skyward and watching the clouds swirl in the sky. "This darkness, what do you know about it?"

"Not much, but I can sense it and so can others I've spoken to about Felix. He was touched by this...darkness and it's spreading like an epidemic and corrupting those who come into contact with it like an infection." The sucker cracks under Bryn's teeth as she bites through the rest. She crunches for a minute, then pulls the stick from her mouth and hops up. She walks a few feet away and tosses the stick in the trash can. "I've never heard of anything like it. This darkness, it makes people do things, Caleb. It gives them chaotic, dangerous thoughts."

Restless, Caleb stands as well and paces. "A darkness from an unknown organization." He scrapes his fingers through his hair. "That's just freaking fantastic."

Bryn folds her arms against the sharp breeze. It blows her vibrant hair around her face. "This organization is far more of a threat to the supernatural world than the Order is itself, Caleb. Something needs to be done."

With all of his encounters with Bryn, she's never one to be negative. Now, he can sense her worry, and even fear, like a sour layer on his tongue. He closes the distance between them and squeezes her shoulder.

"I'm going to get this figured out, okay?" he says. "I'll look into it. The darkness in this organization has to be coming from somewhere."

Bryn nods, but her lips twist to the side doubtfully, not the least bit placated. "Just be careful. I've been tracking them for a while now, and this organization is in full recruiting mode. Felix and his small band of hunters might just be one of the few working for them. They may even be recruiting outside of just the hunters. It's difficult to say. This organization moves frequently and I doubt they'll be coming out into the open anytime soon."

"I'll do what I can, Bryn." Caleb isn't certain if the Master would even take an interest in this new, mysterious organization, especially when his focus is so pinpointed on Felix and his group of hunters. The wind shifts and Caleb's back stiffens as he catches the scent of others in the park. "Come on, let's head back toward town. I don't want the police placing the blame of those missing on me."

For a few minutes, they walk together in silence. Finally, Bryn speaks. "You won't be the only one trying to find out what's going on. Those who believe in Kenna's vision for the Order are doing their best to slow down the progress of this organization, but the darkness has been spreading past their control for some time now. I fear even they will not be enough to hold it back soon."

Caleb fights the urge to rub his temples. This new development is the last thing he needs right now. There's enough on his plate with Felix, and now Maddy. He glances down at Bryn, her slight frame hunched against the wind biting at their backs.

"I hope you're keeping safe in all of this, and not taking unnecessary risks."

Bryn grins up at him. "Me? Take risks?"

Caleb shakes his head. Given what he knows about Bryn, she's more than capable of taking care of herself, but if this darkness is as bad as she's implying, he doesn't know how safe any of them would be soon.

They leave the park and pause beside Caleb's car where he left it outside of a café. "Just keep in touch, okay?" he says. "I need to know if this darkness spreads farther or if you get new information on this secret organization."

"Yes, sir." Bryn salutes him, her spirits starting to lift slightly. "Hey, do you want to come do karaoke with me?"

Caleb barks out a laugh. "Not on your life. I'd like to keep my hearing intact."

His friend's lips stick out in a pout, then she shrugs. "Your loss."

"I have a date, anyway." Caleb pulls his cell out of his pocket. "Which I need to go and get ready for if I want to be there in time."

Bryn eyes him up and down. "You have a date and instead you've been *working*? You need to get your priorities straight."

Caleb thinks about Cora and how he's going to try and use her to get information on Maddy. It makes him feel dirty, especially considering he's looking forward to learning everything he can. "Oh, trust me, Bryn, my priorities are right where they need to be."

CHAPTER 11

MADELEINE

Adeep moan rumbles through Maddy as she sinks into the bathtub. She hisses at the heat and watches the steam curl from the foamy layer of bubbles floating on top. After easing herself in water up to her chin, she lays her head back against the porcelain and closes her eyes. The rose scent of her favorite bubble bath swirls around her and she soaks it in, letting her muscles work loose in the hot water.

She's sore in places she didn't even think were possible. It's a little over twenty-four hours since her training lesson with Oleg and she'd only been able to climb out of bed a few hours ago. Her mother had seemed amused when Felix dropped her off the night before and Maddy had waddled inside. Oleg was a very, *very* unforgiving trainer. She thought her high school gym teacher had been bad, but the hunter had been relentless.

Curling her fingers in and out slowly, Maddy can still nearly feel the press of the wooden stakes in her hand. She'd been shown how to block, defend, and attack in drills that were burned into her mind, even if her body felt like a beaten bag of mush. Oleg was expecting her again tomorrow, so Maddy had to get moving. She couldn't bear the shame of limping into that building, especially if the other hunters were there.

The back of Maddy's neck burns at the thought. It had been bad enough that a few of them had decided to drop by the training room when Oleg was working her so hard, she was nearly to the point of vomiting. Kai had chuckled and told her it only gets worse. That certainly didn't put Maddy in a better mood.

She pops a bubble and turns her thoughts to Caleb. Had that been him watching outside of that building? It didn't make sense, unless he's decided to become a stalker.

God, he's gorgeous. Maddy shakes her head at the thought. He would never go for her, and she isn't sure she wants him to. He'd been rude to her and besides, she has enough going on in her life now without worrying about some guy, no matter how hot. Her eyes drift closed and the steam makes her drowsy. She would like to see him again, and maybe...

A sudden knock on the bathroom has Maddy jumping and water splashes on the floor as she lurches up. "Yeah?"

"Honey, Cora is here," her mom says. "She says it's urgent."

Maddy frowns. *What could be wrong?* "Okay, I'll be out in a second." A tingle of regret passes through her. So much for a long, relaxing bath.

She climbs out and wraps a towel around her, then pulls the drain on the tub. Cora is already waiting in Maddy's room and when she spots her friend emerge from the bathroom, she springs to her feet.

"Oh my God, Maddy. You'll never believe what happened." Cora is practically bouncing.

Maddy eyes her, noticing her cute dress and strappy heels. "What?"

"The cutest guy ever asked me out on a date!"

"That's great, Cora." Maddy crosses over her white faux fur rug and pulls open a dresser drawer. She looks over her shoulder at her friend. "So why are you here?"

Cora bites her lip for a moment and red tints her cheeks. "I was kind of hoping you would go with me."

Maddy's lips part and she blinks. "Go with you? *On your date?* Oh, come on. You can't be serious."

"Please, Maddy." Cora folds her hands together. "I promise I'll make it up to you."

"Cora, I'm beyond exhausted." Still keeping the towel tucked around her, Maddy shuffles into a pair of panties, the movement making her sore muscles throb. "And I'm hurting like you wouldn't believe."

Cora studies Maddy for a moment. "Yeah, you are moving kind of...stiff. What happened?"

Crap. Maddy can't tell Cora about the whole vampire hunting organization. "Uh, yeah, I decided to take some taekwondo lessons. People have gone missing, so you never know when it will come in handy."

Her best friend raises an eyebrow and frowns. "Taekwondo?"

Maddy nods as she searches for a pair of pajama pants and matching shirt. "Yep."

Cora lets out an exasperated breath and snatches the cotton fabric from Maddy's hands. "Will you do this for me? Please?"

"Cora." Maddy rolls her eyes and tries to snatch her pajamas back. "I'm not going to be some third wheel on your date. You can do this. Look at you. You look hot."

Her best friend glances down at her dress. It's a lavender purple that darkens to gray and ends right at the knee. The gray and silver shoes are a perfect match. As if the outfit isn't enough, her red hair is a glossy halo around her face, light makeup making her green eyes pop. "Do I really?"

"Absolutely! You've got this. Go and have fun with this guy. You deserve it."

Cora is silent for a moment, then plops down into Maddy's desk chair. It rolls backward a couple of feet. "I'm just so nervous."

Giving up on retrieving her pajamas from Cora, Maddy pulls out an oversized T-shirt, wiggles it over her head, then lets the towel fall to the floor. "That's normal. Bringing a friend with you on a date is not. You need to be confident."

Cora scoffs. "Confidence is not in my biological make-up and you know it. This is my first date, Maddy." Her voice nearly whines.

Maddy sits on her bed and crosses her legs. "Not true. Didn't you go out with Trevor Lacey in tenth grade?"

"Yeah, and it was a disaster. He took me roller skating, remember? I sprained my ankle and my mom had to pick me up to take me to the emergency room."

Maddy barely suppresses a giggle. "Well, maybe this date won't be so…adventurous. It's just dinner, right?"

Cora fiddles with a pen on Maddy's desk. "As far as I know." She clicks the pen several times, then peers at Maddy with wide eyes. "I'll make a mistake or say something stupid. I know I will."

"You will not." Maddy feels bad for refusing, but Cora needs to learn to be more independent. Her parents had always sheltered her too much and she isn't the most social person as a result.

But Cora doesn't give up easily. "You won't be a third wheel. Please, just come along. Maybe you can leave halfway through or something." She pauses, then switches tactics. "I only met this guy in person once, briefly. What if he turns out to be a psycho?"

"I doubt he's a psycho." Maddy drums her fingers on her

knee. What if the guy is a nut, though? Can she really let Cora go on this date with a guy she didn't know? Worse, can she live with herself if something does happen? Maddy groans. "Why are you guilting me into this?"

Cora squeals and dashes over to Maddy, then throws her arms around her. "Is that a yes?"

Maddy's cheeks puff out with a sigh and she peers toward her bathroom door, wishing she were still in the bathtub. "*Fine. I'll go. I'm not going to stay the whole time, though. You won't be able to get to know the guy with me hanging around.*"

"Maybe you can just happen to be strolling by right before I head into the restaurant. We can chat for a few minutes, then you can go." Cora grabs Maddy's arms and yanks her up. "Come on. You need to get dressed. And no jeans."

Before Maddy can argue, Cora has thrown open the closet door and is rifling through the small collection of dresses. Finally, she pulls one out. "Oh, this is the one."

Maddy smiles. She does love the black dress with the thin straps. It's elegant and hugs her curves in the right places. "As nice as it would be to dress up, Cora, that kind of defeats the purpose of me just happening to see you, doesn't it?"

Much to Cora's dismay, Maddy picks out a pair of skinny jeans and a long sweater. She finishes the ensemble with ankle boots, her jacket, then throws a slouchy beanie over her hastily tied back hair.

"Girl, you are never going to get a guy dressing like that," Cora says as they head out the door.

Maddy laughs and unlocks her car. "I don't have time for guys." She cranks the heat, then backs out of the driveway. "So, where are we heading?"

"*Arlo's.* Can you believe it?"

No, Maddy can't. Arlo's is the most expensive restaurant in

town, and is the only one that doesn't serve something dripping in grease or could be taken home in a paper sack. "Are you sure?"

"Yes, I'm sure." Cora lifts her small purse. "Need to see the text?"

Maddy waves a hand as she turns off her street and toward the main road that cuts through Creed. Cora bobs her head to the music thumping through the speakers, her spirits lifted by her friend's presence. Maddy can't help but smile. "So, he's cute, huh?"

"Beyond cute. Like, the hottest guy I've ever seen. I'm sure he'll be the hottest guy you've ever seen."

Maddy chuckles. "We'll see." She thinks about Caleb. "I've seen some stunners lately."

Arlo's is in the middle of town. It's a classy looking building, with dark awnings that stand out on the white brick and soft light glowing from the wide windows. Maddy parks along the curb and watches a couple enter, both dressed to the nines, and wishes she'd worn that dress after all.

"You ready?" Cora opens the door and steps out.

Maddy grumbles to herself and joins her friend on the sidewalk. "I'm serious, Cora. I'm not staying long. Where is this guy?"

Cora glances at her phone, then opens a message. "He's waiting inside."

The pair of them step inside. The delicious aroma of Italian food and the chatter of voices greet them. Maddy freezes when her gaze suddenly locks with a familiar face a few tables away.

Caleb.

What is he doing here? Maddy thinks frantically. She could kill Cora for dragging her here. Of all the places that man could have gone to eat, he chooses the same place as Cora's date.

Out of the corner of her eye, Maddy sees Cora wave to someone, but Caleb still holds her gaze. Sweet mother god, he looks good. Maddy's heart thrums in her chest as he rises from the table and approaches.

Maddy and Caleb speak simultaneously. "What are you doing here?"

CHAPTER 12

CALEB

The sound of conversation and the clink of silverware fade to the background. Caleb latches his focus on Maddy's heartbeats, which thunder behind her ribcage as she glares at him accusingly. Cora glances uncertainly between them, her unease masking the floral scent of her perfume. He turns his attention to her.

"You look lovely." His words elicit a blush across Cora's cheeks.

Maddy takes a step forward. "I said, what are you doing here?"

A few of the nearby diners pause to watch them. One, a pre-teen who seems to be out at dinner with his parents and grandparents, raises his eyebrows hopefully, eager to witness drama unfold. Caleb straightens his back.

"I'm here for a date with Cora. Obviously."

The young hunter opens then closes her mouth. She huffs and turns her attention to her friend. "This is the guy?"

"Yes." Cora draws out the word slowly, her eyes casting over Caleb as if she perhaps has made a mistake. "Why?"

Caleb speaks before Maddy has a chance to ruin his date,

and his chances at finding out more information. "Cora, I take it you know her."

Cora grabs Maddy's sleeve and tugs her closer, as if she were going to use her as a shield. "Maddy has been my best friend for years. I guess you two know each other?" She gives Maddy a meaningful stare.

Caleb hides a smile. Clearly, Maddy hasn't spoken of her run-in with him. "We've bumped into each other a couple of times. I must not have made a good impression. I'm Caleb."

Maddy sniffs, though Caleb catches her taking in his appearance with an appreciative glance. He'd chosen dark jeans and a gray button-up with thin lines of black. He hates feeling covered up, so he'd rolled the sleeves up to his elbows. Cora is very pretty in her dress, but he wants to snort at Maddy's appearance. Her faded jeans, jacket, and slouchy hat look extremely out of place in the upscale Italian restaurant.

He also has to admit she makes casual look damn good. The figure-hugging jeans actually make his mouth a little dry.

Maddy clears her throat and Caleb raises an eyebrow. "So, what are you doing here?"

"Uh, well, she was passing by when I was walking in and wanted to meet you." Cora's pulse quickens, giving away the lie.

"I needed to make sure you aren't a psycho who is going to hurt my friend." Maddy narrows her eyes. "The jury's still out."

Caleb grinds his teeth together. If Maddy decides she doesn't want Cora here and leaves, he loses his chance to find out information about Felix's new hunter. He offers a genuine smile. "I completely understand." He holds an arm out toward his table. "Ladies, would you like to join me?"

Cora smiles back at him. Maddy stares at him deadpan before following her friend. Caleb signals the waiter as the girls sit.

"What can I bring you to drink?" the man asks.

Cora chooses water, along with Caleb, and Maddy asks for sweet tea. The waiter nods with a promise to be back soon. Maddy flips open the menu and stares at the elegant script. Her eyes bulge at the prices.

"Think I have enough for a side salad." Maddy's words are so quiet, but Caleb catches them.

"You two order whatever you like. My treat."

Cora smiles shyly, but Maddy seems dubious. Then, she shrugs. His date makes a simple choice and decides on a garden salad with chicken. Maddy, however, tells the waiter upon his return that she wants the lobster bisque, cannelloni, and a Caesar salad.

Caleb raises his eyebrows. "Hungry?"

"Just a little," Maddy says lightly.

Cora waves her hand. "She just needs sustenance to make up for her work out." She ignores the sudden glare Maddy cuts her way. "Maddy has taken up taekwondo."

The corner of Caleb's lips quirk up and he pulls in the scent of warm embarrassment prickling beneath her skin. "Taekwondo, huh?"

Maddy responds with a mere shrug and takes a sip of her sweet tea. She hasn't offered Caleb a smile or a kind word since she arrived. Instead, she's peering at him as if he's done something wrong. He'd sensed her attraction for him before. Could it be she is irritated, even envious, he asked Cora out on a date? The thought pleases him. Perhaps he can use her jealousy against her. He leans toward Cora.

"So, Cora, tell me something interesting about yourself."

"Oh, um." Cora's eyes dart at Maddy but her friend offers no help. "Well, I have a cat named Booger."

Maddy groans quietly. "Cora is a great artist." She grins at her friend. "Like, really good. You should see some of her work."

"I'd love to see it sometime," Caleb says. The food for

Maddy and Cora arrives, and while Caleb ordered a pasta dish, he just sips at his water. After a few minutes, Cora excuses herself to the bathroom.

He angles his head, deciding to make the most of the unexpected opportunity. "So, Maddy, have any hobbies?"

Maddy wipes a bit of sauce from the corner of her mouth. "I don't have time for hobbies."

"Taekwondo taking up all of your free hours?"

Maddy pushes her plate of half-eaten food away, then leans forward and points her finger at Caleb. "You're up to something."

"Me?" Caleb widens his eyes. "I'm not up to anything. You're the one date crashing." The corner of Maddy's eye twitches. Caleb's delighted to note the quirk.

"What's your endgame here?" Maddy settles back against her chair. "I know you've been following me. Are you some kind of stalker?"

Caleb barks a laugh. "Me, following you? You're the one who chased me down to the administrative buildings."

"I was giving you back your wallet. You're the one who was watching me from your car the other day. Don't think I didn't notice. Now you're on a date with my best friend? It seems... shady." Maddy takes another drink of her tea and when she speaks again, her voice lowers. "I think you're using my best friend to get to your actual target: me. I'm not going to let you hurt Cora. If you want something from me, then confront me about it. Leave Cora out of your games."

Perceptive. Caleb hasn't given Maddy enough credit. She's more quick-witted than he'd realized. He has to rescue this plan, and fast. If Maddy gets the chance to block him from Cora, and herself, he'll have no choice but to move forward with taking her and her mother out of the equation. Caleb stares as her eyes flash beneath a thick rim of lashes, the burning in her gaze reflecting a fiery soul. No, he doesn't think he wants to extinguish that just yet.

He rubs the back of his neck. "I've obviously gone about all of this the wrong way. I've never been particularly good with people."

Maddy rolls her eyes in disbelief and stabs a piece of meat with her fork, then shovels it into her mouth.

"I just wanted to thank you for returning my wallet. It has some sentimental things inside of it, and it means a lot to me that it wasn't lost forever. So, thank you." Caleb leans over and squeezes Maddy's shoulder.

For a long moment, Maddy goes still. She stares at him, her pulse quickening, and the scent of warm desire filling Caleb's nose. His fingers tighten slightly, and for a second, he's just as surprised as she is that he's touching her. More surprising, he doesn't want to stop. Something inside of him flickers to life, and he suddenly wishes he were on a date with Maddy, making her laugh and learning everything about her. Dangerous, foolish thoughts.

Abruptly, Maddy brushes Caleb's hand away. "I call bull. Who stalks someone just to thank them for returning a wallet?" Her fork clatters to the plate. "There's some other reason you're following me, and I'm going to find out why." She pushes her chair back and stands. "I need to go."

Cora returns at that moment. "Maddy, are you okay?"

"Yep. Fine. Everything's fine." Maddy's words are clipped and she's very purposefully not looking in Caleb's direction. She offers her friend an apologetic smile. "Sorry, Cora, but I'm going to head back home. If you need a ride later or something, let me know."

"I have no problem driving her home," Caleb says.

Maddy still doesn't look at him. "I don't want to impose on your date."

"You're not bothering me." Cora's words are steeped in desperation.

Caleb holds back a sigh. Humans often react to him like this. Something in their nature tells them he's dangerous. Perhaps it's a sense of self-preservation in the face of an apex predator. Either way, Cora's human instincts are telling her being alone with Caleb isn't a good idea.

"It's all right," Maddy says. "I have some homework, anyway."

Cora lowers into her seat, looking ready to bolt. "This close to exams?"

"Yep." Maddy jerks a quick nod. "I'm behind on a couple of things, so I better get to it. You two have fun. Thanks for the free meal, Caleb." She turns to leave, then stops.

A bar stretches across the room not far from their table. Several people seated along the gleaming surface have paused and turned their attention to a TV mounted on the wall. A reporter stands outside of the forest that borders the town. Red and blue lights flash behind her.

"...has gone missing. *This is the second college student in less than a week to have disappeared inside these woods, and she joins the growing list of missing persons in and around Creed.*" A photo of the student flashes in one corner of the screen.

Aubrey Henwood. The name forms on Caleb's lips, and when he glances over, he realizes Maddy is watching him. She plants a hand on her hip.

"You know her?"

Caleb nods, turning away from the TV as the reporter continues speaking about Aubrey. "Yeah, I was in a book club with her a few years ago in Mercy City. I didn't even know she'd moved around here." His finger taps the table. "All of these disappearances...there is something very strange going on around here."

Maddy continues to stare at him, hard. Her eyes narrow slightly and she frowns like she's trying to work out a puzzle. "Yes, I agree."

She spins on her heel and walks away and Caleb's eyes trace her denim-clad curves. He quickly yanks his gaze away. He needs to get himself under control. Especially now that another girl has been taken.

The Master is putting them all in danger.

CHAPTER 13

MADELEINE

T he eraser of Maddy's pencil taps out a rapid beat on the page of her textbook as the words blur together. She reads the same sentence several times, then sighs sharply as she leans back in her chair.

"This is ridiculous," she mutters. Maddy's going to fail her exams because she can't get a certain man out of her head.

Caleb had looked gorgeous at the restaurant. He was sharp, yet still casual enough to not appear too rich for her blood. He'd even done the thing guys did with their sleeves and had them rolled up to reveal his well-sculpted forearms, hinting at what the rest of him looked like underneath that buttoned-up shirt.

"Stop. Stop. Stop." Maddy bangs her head lightly on the headrest of her desk chair. Thinking about his body isn't helping her get him out of her mind. Besides, he's on a date with Cora, though the thought burns her up inside. There was definitely something strange about Caleb and the way he was acting. He'd been more than polite with Cora, yet Maddy couldn't shake the impression he'd been there for her. After confronting him about it, she was even more convinced. His excuse that he merely wanted to thank her for the wallet had been beyond lame.

Maddy's stomach swirls a bit at the thought Caleb had truly wanted to be there with her. If he wants to know more about her, why go through Cora? That's the part she doesn't understand. Caleb doesn't seem like a creep, or a bad guy, but there is something about him that has her back up.

There she is again, thinking about Caleb. Maddy drops her pencil onto her desk and grabs a bottle of water. It's nearly nine in the evening. She'd left the restaurant a mere twenty minutes ago. Hopefully Cora is opening up a bit more. She really needs to get more of a social life beyond piles of books. Maddy chugs half of the water down. Then, she flips open her textbook, determined to work Caleb out of her mind by memorizing equations.

The bedroom door swings open suddenly and Maddy jumps.

"Oops, sorry." Cora walks in and plops down on Maddy's bed.

Maddy swivels her chair around. "What are you doing here?" Her thoughts swing to Caleb. If Cora is here, then Caleb dropped her off. He knows where she lives now. Maddy isn't certain if she liked the fact or not.

Cora's shoulders slump slightly. "After you left, Caleb seemed distracted. I think he was hung up on that Aubrey girl who went missing. Maybe she was an ex or something? Anyway, we cut the date short and he just dropped me off."

"Well, that's lame." Maddy folds her arms across her stomach and stretches out her legs. "He didn't even let you order dessert?"

Cora snorts. "Girl, after what you ordered the poor guy was probably broke."

A grin stretches across Maddy's face. "You know I love my

carbs. Besides, he offered so I just took him up on it. I wasn't about to just order a salad."

Cora shuffles back on the bed, then undoes the straps on her heels and drops them on the floor. "Ugh, my feet are killing me. That restaurant was nice, but I hate wearing these things." She pauses and purses her lips, staring at Maddy.

"What?"

"I have a question," Cora says. "Do you like Caleb?"

Maddy lets out a short laugh and puts a hand on her chest. "Like Caleb? Are you serious? That's insulting."

"Why is it insulting? He's hot, and has nice manners."

Maddy's mouth works for a moment. "He may have had nice manners tonight, but the other times I've seen him he's been nothing but rude to me."

Cora lifts an eyebrow. "Are you sure you don't have feelings for him? You two seemed to hit it off pretty good. He seemed interested in you, too."

"I definitely do not." Maddy stands and grabs a bag of mini candy bars off her bedside table. She slides onto the bed beside her friend and offers her the bag. "Trust me. He's just someone I bumped into a couple of times. And he wasn't interested in me. He was just being polite. You're the one he asked out, after all. He's not my type, anyway. Much too pretty."

Maddy's tone is confident, but a small voice inside of her tells her it's a lie. That she's arguing a little too strenuously. He may have been stalking her, but he also seems like a perfect gentleman. Could he really be so bad? There's no use denying to herself that she finds him incredibly attractive. Caleb looks sculpted by some god, and those eyes... She takes a piece of candy out of the bag Cora is holding, tears the wrapper, then pops the chocolatey goodness into her mouth, chewing a bit more ferociously than is necessary.

"God, I think he's absolutely gorgeous." Cora digs into the

bag for another piece of candy, looking relieved at Maddy's assurances. "How can a guy be too good-looking for you?"

Maddy shrugs, but stays quiet as she chews. Cora doesn't know that Caleb's been watching her from his car, and she begins to wonder if he'd been watching her while she was in that café, too. What are the chances she'd bump into him? Her mind lingers on the chills she keeps getting. They'd always happened before, but now she was experiencing the strange sensation almost every day. It couldn't be a coincidence.

Cora chatters about the date, and the things she likes about Caleb. Maddy half-listens, but her thoughts are still stuck on Caleb. Maddy joins the Order, and then suddenly, Caleb seems to be trying to get into her life.

Maybe he's a spy. Maddy wants to dismiss the idea, but the thought needles into her brain and stays there. Caleb isn't a part of the Order, or he would have mentioned it now that Maddy has accepted her role as a vampire hunter. Still, that doesn't mean he doesn't know about the Order. Has he been sent by other hunters to keep an eye on Felix and his recruits? Maddy thinks about asking her mom or Felix about it, but something makes her hesitate. She barely knows Caleb, and sure the man infuriates her, but she doesn't want him to get into any trouble, or even hurt.

The room is quiet and Maddy realizes Cora is staring at her. "I'm sorry, I was zoning out. What did you say?"

"I said, are you really sure you don't like Caleb? I mean, I think there was a connection between us and I'd like to give us a shot, but I won't move forward if you're interested in him." Cora's smiles, but behind her gaze, there's a fraction of hope.

Maddy throws her arm around Cora's shoulders. "Girl, he's all yours. You definitely need to take him off the market. You two would be so cute together, and he's obviously interested in you or he wouldn't have taken you out to such a swanky place. You have my full support."

Cora hugs Maddy. "Thank you! He's supposed to call me tomorrow, so we'll see but I'm super hopeful about this. I really appreciate you tagging along earlier."

"No prob." Maddy waves a hand. "Did you want to stay the night? I bet you're ready to get out of those clothes."

"No, I better head home. I have some studying to do and all of my books are in my room." Cora hops off the bed and scoops her shoes from the floor. "If I hear from Caleb, I'll let you know. He mentioned he needed to go grocery shopping. Do you think he's a good cook?"

Maddy shrugs a shoulder and stands beside her friend. "Who knows? Maybe for your next date he'll sweep you off your feet with filet mignon, grilled veggies, and tiramisu made from scratch or something."

Cora sighs. "I bet he's an amazing cook." She smiles brightly. "I'll see you tomorrow."

Maddy waves and hears her mom tell Cora to be safe driving home. Her friend's car pulls out of the driveway and Maddy curses under her breath. She'd given Cora her blessing and now regret prickles through her. She may have had a chance with Caleb. She admits, she finds him intriguing, and yet, he's possibly been stalking her. She can't forget that, no matter what lame excuse he gives her.

After a moment of deliberation, Maddy slips on her boots and heads down the hall. Her mom is reading in the living room and she looks up as Maddy grabs her jacket off a hook by the door.

"Where are you off to?"

"Just going to the store to grab some energy drinks," Maddy says. "This studying will be the death of me."

Maddy's mom frowns. "Well, be careful. And don't get too many of those things. They aren't good for you."

"I won't." Maddy heads out of the door and gets in her car. Her destination is the grocery store, but she isn't going for the energy drinks. Cora said Caleb was going grocery shopping and Maddy is determined to find him. She needs to find out what his true motivation is with her, and if he really is interested in Cora. The last thing Maddy wants is for her best friend to be screwed over by some jerk playing games.

Maddy waits outside the most popular grocery store in Creed. Her fingers drum the steering wheel as she watches the glass doors slide open and people walk in and out. A nervous sort of flutter fills her stomach, and she isn't certain if she's eager to see Caleb again, or if she's uncertain about confronting him. After nearly an hour, she curses and leaves, telling herself this was a stupid idea. She stops at a red light and watches a young woman, likely a college student, hurry by in the dark. Maddy frowns, her attention going to the latest missing person. Had it been vampires? The thought makes Maddy shiver.

When Maddy finally makes it home, she finds Felix's car in the driveway. Her heart races and she hurries inside, hoping there isn't bad news.

"Ah, Maddy, there you are," her mom says. She frowns. "Where are your drinks?"

"Oh, they were out of my favorite." Maddy shucks off her jacket. "Hi, Felix. Everything okay?"

The leader of the Order shakes his head. "I've just gotten word the city will be announcing a curfew on people hiking on the forest trails. Other strict rules are being set into place, as well, and for the better. By now, I'm sure you're aware there is another missing girl."

"Named Aubrey? Yeah, I saw." Maddy crosses her arms. "Is it vampires?"

"Yes, we're certain of it. What bothers me is they don't usually take so many people at once. It draws too much attention to not only the authorities, but hunters like us." Felix's dark eyebrows slant together, chiseling a groove in his forehead. "These vampires are up to something, and if we don't find out soon what it is, I fear for the humans in Creed."

CHAPTER 14
CALEB

Cora waves at Caleb from the corner table in the Bean Buzz café. He's met her here a couple of times already over the past few days. He likes Cora. She's sweet and is beginning to come out of her shell as she grows more comfortable around him. He slides into a chair and offers her a smile.

"Morning," he says. "Cold out today, isn't it?" Autumn is quickly drawing to a close and is offering the first sampling of the coming winter by way of gray skies and a biting wind. He pulls off his jacket and drapes it across the back of his chair.

"Yeah, it is." Cora's cheeks are still flushed from the cold and her fingers are wrapped around a porcelain mug. "Need anything to drink? The line is horrendous today."

Caleb glances over his shoulder. The café is packed with students trying to ward off the cold with hot caffeine. "Nah, I'm good." He turns back around and peeks at the schoolwork she's studying. "Abstract expressionism, huh?"

"It's just an elective, and not my favorite, but most of the other art classes were already full." Cora sips her coffee, then frowns at her art book. "I think abstract is ghastly. I'm more into impressionism. You know, like Monet and Renoir. Maddy says I should be doing art or art history instead of working toward a degree in elementary education."

Caleb leans forward, capturing Cora's attention. "So, if you like art so much, why are you doing education instead?" he asks, genuinely curious. Cora is someone he would've been friends with in his past life.

"My parents are teachers, and I do like kids. I know teaching doesn't make much money, but it's more of a guarantee than art would be. Sometimes I wish I could listen to Maddy, though."

Caleb's ears perk up, just as they always do when Maddy is mentioned. "Sounds like she's a good friend. I suppose she knows what she's going to do in life?"

A laugh bubbles from Cora. "Not hardly. She's indecisive about her career. She wants to do something adventurous, but doesn't know what yet. Personally, I think she just wants to get out of this town. I could see her being a travel blogger, living out of some renovated bus or something."

Free-spirited. Adventurous. Independent. Over the past few days, Caleb has been getting to know Maddy without outwardly asking her friend questions about her. It hasn't been the easiest thing to do, but he'd managed to pick up several tidbits of Maddy's personality from Cora. One of them is Maddy's deep sense of love and loyalty for her friends and family. That worries Caleb, because it would mean Maddy would either cling to Felix out of a sense of obligation, or he will have difficulty prying her from his side if the need were to arise.

Not for the first time Caleb wishes he had a more friendly rapport with Maddy. He's crossed paths with her a couple of times on campus, but she always shies away from him. The few times Maddy hasn't been able to avoid him, such as when he's with Cora, she barely talks to him. Even when she does, her words come off clipped and rude.

Caleb knows Maddy's been following him. Several times

he's sensed a presence, and more than once he's caught her scent nearby. He grinds his teeth together, thinking that she may already be becoming the hunter Felix is trying to mold her into being.

"Caleb, are you okay?"

Caleb pulls his gaze from the nearby window where he'd absentmindedly been glaring at the passing students and turns his focus to Cora's worried expression. He gives her a soothing smile. "I'm fine. Just a lot on my mind, I guess."

Cora nods in understanding. "Did you want to talk about it?"

Suddenly, Cora's sweet, compassionate gaze is too much. "I'm good." Caleb scoots his chair back. "Actually, I have some friends I forgot I was supposed to meet up with. Can I call you later?"

Disappointment flashes across Cora's face but she quickly covers it with a smile. "Sure, that's fine. I'll see you later."

He pulls on his jacket and is met with frosty air as the door swings shut at his back. Guilt niggles at the edges of his consciousness. Cora likes him. He can sense it. Smell it. What's more, she's a nice girl. And he's using her. He shrugs his shoulders as if he can shake off the unwanted feeling. He's trying to protect Maddy and her mother.

Pulling his cell out of his pocket, he taps a recent contact. "Morgan, meet me at the corner of the parking lot by the football field. I need those reports." His friend says he's on his way and Caleb ends the call.

There's a tightness in his chest that refuses to ebb. Before he met with Cora at the café, he received a text from Morgan that they had some news for him. He could've stood Cora up, but that felt worse than meeting her and having to cut it short. Although he's not so sure anymore, he doesn't question the need to leave and meet his friend.

Morgan may have information that could mean the difference between life or death for Maddy and her mom.

The parking lot is mostly empty. Many of the students have filled the spaces closer to the central part of campus where they'd have less walking on this cold morning. Morgan's already waiting beside Caleb's car when he arrives. Caleb unlocks it and the two sit inside.

"Alright, what's the news?" Caleb asks. He turns the radio up a bit, just in case there are any prying ears in the vicinity. Not only could other vampires who aren't involved find out something they shouldn't, but the Order has their ways of spying, as well.

Morgan stares out of the window, keeping an eye on their surroundings. "The girl's mother has been seen meeting with Felix and some of the Order members. We've managed to get close enough to hear a couple of times. They are mostly discussing the missing girls and trying to locate them."

Caleb rubs his jawline, the whiskers prickling his skin reminding him he needs to shave. None of that surprises him. He'll have to decide what to do about it...once he knows exactly what he's dealing with. "What could the Master be planning? Why is he abducting young people?" He'd known after the third person went missing that it was vampires, and no vampires would dare take people, much less college students, in Creed without the Master's knowledge. Caleb's tried to look at the situation from all angles, but he just can't understand what the Master is thinking.

In the passenger seat, Morgan shrugs. "Who knows?" He slides his seat back, giving his long legs room to stretch out a bit. "The guys haven't heard anything about it. Whatever the Master is planning, he's keeping all knowledge of it close to his inner circle." Bitterness laces Morgan's words. He's incredibly loyal to the Master and wants to do his part in helping his leader further their cause. Morgan will do anything to prove it, too, and yearns to be more in the fold.

Caleb couldn't care less about being closer to the Master, and more than once Morgan has told him for someone so adept at leadership, Caleb lacks ambition. There are many things Caleb lacks. Ambition isn't one of them. It just isn't where Morgan can see it.

"Whatever he's planning, it can only be good for the vampires," Morgan says.

Caleb isn't so certain. "I don't know." He watches a group of guys on the other side of the parking lot, heading toward the locker rooms at the corner of the football field. "I think his activities are risking too much scrutiny, especially from the Order. If this continues, even the humans will notice."

Morgan bursts out in a laugh, earning a scowl from Caleb. "What? Do you really think we have something to fear from humans? Even with the Order nearby, there's only so much they can do against our numbers. The Master knows what he's doing. The time of the vampires is at hand." Morgan nudges Caleb's arm.

Caleb nods, but can't help but hope that things haven't changed too much. He has plans to help the humans, somehow, but he also has no choice but to obey the Master. Caleb's aunt was not only a hunter, but Kenna was the leader of the Order of the Knightly Rose. He has a love and respect for humanity that no amount of blood will wash away, and yet the fist of vampirism squeezes him more tightly every day. He keeps his thoughts to himself, however. The others would see his feelings as treachery, and word would spread to the Master like wildfire. The head vampire will force his hand and Caleb will be made to do what is instructed of him, even if it's against his wishes. Especially if the Master catches wind that he's getting too attached to a certain young hunter.

Speaking of Maddy... "What about Maddy's ancestral line? Have you found anything there?"

Morgan turns away from the window. His lips twitch and mischief sparks in his eye. "*Maddy?*" He draws out her name in teasing tones. "Are you telling me you're on a first name basis with a target?"

"Don't be stupid," Caleb snaps. "That's her name. What else am I supposed to call her?"

His friend scoffs. "I don't know. Hunter. Girl. The Doomed One. Take your pick."

Caleb tightens his grip on the part of him that wants to lash out. Maddy isn't just a hunter, and he certainly doesn't want to think of her as some doomed being. His thoughts are irrational, but no matter how hard he tries to shift them into their proper place, he can't think of Maddy as a target anymore. The more he's been learning about her, the less he likes the idea of Maddy falling under the Master's wrath, or Felix's for that matter.

"Okay. What have you found out about the hunter?" Caleb asks.

"Nothing, but I think I know how to find out." Morgan returns to staring out of the window, though there's been no sign they're being watched. "One of the guys said he overheard Elias talking about some witch here in Creed." Elias is one of the Master's closest followers. "And not just any witch, but a blood witch. You know they can read a person's blood as if the truth in our veins were written on a page."

Caleb grimaces. He doesn't like the idea of getting involved with a witch.

"So, if we had a vial of the girl's blood..."

"I'll get it." Caleb doesn't like the idea of Morgan or any of the others getting too involved with Maddy. "I've already got a plan in mind."

Morgan shrugs, happy to let Caleb do the dirty work. The

guilt Caleb tried to shrug off earlier crawls back under his skin, and this time he knows it's here to stay. He already hates himself for what he'll need to do to Maddy.

All the dancing around Maddy, trying to save her from being hurt, has been for nothing.

What he has to do next is the exact opposite of that.

CHAPTER 15
MADELEINE

Gravel crunches beneath the tires of Felix's car as they pull into the parking lot outside of a large building. Maddy presses her head against the window and takes in the structure. It appears to have been a church at one point, with its peaked roof and a tower on one end that would have held a bell. The windows are boarded up and she wonders if there's stained glass behind the aged wood. Weeds sprout from the parking lot and along the edge of the building, a clear sign the property has been neglected for some time.

"What is this place?" Maddy takes off her seatbelt as the other members of the Order park beside Felix.

"Another, much safer, location where we can carry on our activities in private."

Maddy frowns and climbs out of the car. She hadn't spotted Caleb, or anyone else, the past several times she'd gone to train with Oleg. She eyes the brick walls of the church and fails to see how this place could possibly be any safer than the other brick building.

"How is this any better?"

One of the other Order members, the guy called Antonio,

walks to her side as they head toward the building. "This location has been severely warded against any unwanted entities. A few of the older Order members have been here all day putting up spells and barriers."

Maddy's been learning about such things alongside her physical training, but she has yet to learn how to do what she could only describe as a sort of magic. She's kind of glad. She's still trying to wrap her head around everything else, let alone the ability to wield magic. Her skin tingles as she goes through one of the large double doors at the front of the church. Dust motes swirl in the light, filtering through the cracks between the boards on the windows and Maddy coughs.

"We'll get this place cleaned up and usable," Felix says. He puts a hand on Maddy's shoulder and guides her further inside. "It used to once belong to a local chapter of an organization known as the Grail Keepers."

Maddy's ears perk up at the mention of another supernatural organization. "Grail Keepers?"

"Their original mission was to protect the Holy Grail, but they also moved toward protecting numerous supernatural artifacts and relics from organizations like The Tenth Legion and Cain."

"Cain?" Maddy folds her arms across her chest. The old church is drafty and the bite of the cool air brushes her cheeks. As in Cain from the bible? As in the dude who killed his brother, Abel?

Felix nods, a tightness at the corner of his eyes. "Yes. Cain lived on, and developed some sort of personal grudge. He killed all of the Grail Keepers, save for one. Now this place, like many others, is abandoned and there are artifacts left behind."

Three of the Order members are kneeling down in front of the dusty altar, using a metal bar to pry at one of the large stone tiles that make up the floor. Maddy watches as they carefully lever it up while another pulls out several metal boxes. They replace the thick stone tile and open one of the boxes, pulling out a variety of objects.

Relics.

Felix watches along with her. "We can use them," he says. "They will give us power against the vampires and their Master."

"The spooks" trace their unwanted fingers along Maddy's skin. The warning sensation puts her on alert. "Do we need them? Haven't hunters done just as well against the vampires without help from relics?"

A few of the other Order members, mainly Jess and Oliver, mutter at Maddy's question.

Felix's nostrils flare slightly, but he keeps a rein on his patience. "Kenna was the greatest hunter to have lived, and while she did kill the vampire King and many of his Masters, she also met an untimely death. We are not going to be so powerless." He walks over to metal boxes and Maddy follows. Settled among the odds and ends of jewelry, cups, and daggers, is a book with a worn, leather cover and strange writing in gold. Felix runs his finger along the spine. "We need these to supernaturally enhance our few numbers if we want any hope of taking down the vampires and their Master."

Maddy studies the assortment of relics dubiously, noting the way Felix reaches in to run his finger over a tarnished goblet sitting beside the book. She touches one of the wooden stakes strapped to her side. She's barely used to using these when training. Being gifted with some sort of magical abilities is not something she's certain about. The spooks are unsettling enough as it is.

Felix's hand moves back to the book. "Let's get this stuff somewhere safe—"

The door at the front of the church creaks and a stranger

strolls inside. He and the other Order members immediately take on defensive positions. Maddy's hands hover beside her hips with uncertainty. The odd, purple-haired girl can't be a vampire or she wouldn't have gotten past the wards.

"Who are you?" Felix barks.

The young woman peers around the church. "You're trespassing. This property belongs to the Grail Keepers."

Felix straightens, and relaxes a fraction. "You know Reign?"

"I do. My name is Bryn and he sent me here to check up on this place. He's looking to install a chapter here soon, given the disturbing rise in vampire population in Creed."

Shoulders tensing, Felix narrows his eyes at the newcomer. "I thought this place was abandoned. The Grail Keepers have gone extinct, save for Reign. How could he possibly open a new chapter?"

Bryn walks past Felix and his Order members without a care. She spots Maddy and a curious light flickers in her eyes. "Reign's found a few more Potentials, and once trained, they may very well come here." She picks up a necklace from among the relics and studies the wedge of quartz nestled in a cage of intricate wire. "We'll be taking the relics with us back to Mercy City, as these are the property of the Grail Keepers."

"We?" Laura, one of the twins, eyes Bryn with distaste.

Bryn ignores the sour look from the Order member and keeps her attention on Felix. "I brought a crew with me." She smiles slightly. "We can't risk these artifacts falling into the wrong hands."

Maddy flicks a glance between Felix and Bryn, half-expecting the leader of the Order to argue. It almost sounds as if Bryn is insinuating the Order members are the wrong hands, but surely that isn't what she means.

Several more people enter the church and the Order members step forward, hands inching towards weapons. Felix holds up a palm and they stand down. Maddy's heart ticks faster in her chest at the tension billowing in the room. The members of the Grail Keepers file over to the boxes, closing them and picking them up, shredding Felix's plan to strengthen his own forces. He says nothing, but when one of Bryn's crew grabs the box with the book, his fingers curl into fists.

Maddy steps up beside her leader and speaks in a low voice. "Should we do something?" A young man walks by with a box full of relics.

Felix grunts. "There is nothing we can do. It would be unwise to make a move against the Grail Keeper's wishes." He turns his back on Bryn and the others, and pulls a piece of paper out of his pocket. The paper is yellow with age, and the ink faded, but the scrawl of Latin words is still visible. His voice is barely above a whisper as he speaks to Maddy. "Those relics were not the only means of empowering ourselves. This is from the book. It can put the vampires to sleep forever. A witch had done the same thing back in 1692. That spell was broken by the obsidian's influence. I've gotten word the obsidian has been contained, which means the spell can now be reenacted, and will never again be broken."

Maddy's eyes widen. A spell that could put all of the vampires to sleep? "If we can do that, couldn't we just go around and stake the vampires once they're asleep?"

"I like the way you think." Felix offers her a smile. "It would take time, but yes, we could. It would be the best way to ensure the vampires stay gone for good this time. First, though, we need to find the right witch to enact the spell."

Maddy opens her mouth to ask about witches, but a throat clears nearby. Both she and Felix turn to find Bryn watching them. The young woman tucks a strand of her violet hair behind her ear. The last of her crew members leave the church, taking the remaining relics and artifacts with him.

"Felix, you have permission to set up training camps for your Order here for the time being. This church is on thirty acres of land and you may use it as you wish. Once Reign and the Grail Keepers return, however, you will need to leave."

The Order leader nods. "That is acceptable, and please extend my gratitude to Reign. It has been a long time since I've seen him. It's good news that he has found Potentials. The fall of the Grail Keepers was a grave loss to the world."

"I'll tell him." Bryn sweeps a glance over the Order members before settling her sharp gaze on Felix once more. "Do take care. There are more monsters out there than you realize." She turns to leave and the heavy church door closes behind her with a resounding thud.

Uncertainty and suspicion thread into Maddy's mind. Something about Bryn hadn't seemed right to her. There was an edge of threat lacing the woman's tone and Maddy has a hunch Bryn was not as friendly to the Order as Felix may perceive.

"All right, everyone. Let's take a look around and see what needs to be done around here."

Felix and the other Order members begin to disperse but Maddy hesitates, staring at the door Bryn had gone through a moment before. "Felix? I'll go outside and check things out."

"Fine. Just be careful." Felix barely pays attention to her. He seems distracted by a pile of old hymnals, filtering through them as if he may find something useful.

Hoping Bryn hasn't already left, Maddy hurries through the door. There's a large van outside in the parking lot and one of Bryn's companions slides the passenger door shut in the back. Bryn is beside the van with her back to Maddy.

Maddy starts to raise her hand to flag the woman down, then pauses. Bryn pulls a knife from her belt and crouches. She sticks the blade in the dirt and draws a straight line on the ground.

What the hell? Maddy doesn't move as Bryn straightens to a stand. A second later, she looks over her shoulder to find Maddy watching her. A smile stretches across Bryn's face before she slaps the side of the van twice.

"All right, let's get going." Bryn hops in the front passenger seat and the van pulls away.

Maddy's pulse quickens and she rubs her arms against the trepidation scattering over her. She promises to keep a watch on everyone's back, because something tells her those Grail Keepers are not their allies.

CHAPTER 16

MADELEINE

A knot forms in Maddy's chest and she stares toward the road, listening to the distant hum of the Grail Keeper's van traveling down the road, and the occasional clatter or voice from inside the church. The hairs rise on the back of her neck. She reaches back and rubs a hand beneath her ponytail, finding goosebumps across her skin. The rest of the Order remain inside, exploring. Nothing seems amiss, and she attempts to brush off the prickly sensation of unease as simple nerves due to the move to the new location.

Gravel crunches underfoot as Maddy walks across the parking lot to where the van had been parked. She pauses and stares down at the straight line Bryn had etched in the dirt with her knife, then crouches down to get a better look. There's nothing unusual or special about the line. Why would Bryn do such a thing? Does it mean something, or is it perhaps just some way to throw Maddy and the Order off? She can see someone doing something like this to make others wonder if it meant something. Perhaps Bryn and the other Grail Keeper crew are having a good laugh, thinking about Maddy pondering over a line in the dirt.

She holds her hand over it, tempted to wipe the ridiculous marking away, but for a split second, she's certain her fingertips tingle.

A whooshing sound reaches Maddy and she straightens, turning her attention to the forest bordering the church. At first, she sees nothing but the trees and the dying sunlight flickering gold and orange through the dead canopy. Then, she catches a flash of movement and a chill runs through her. The logical part of her wants to tell her it was a bird or squirrel, but a deep-rooted instinct is telling her to run.

A mere few seconds later, Maddy makes out a face as a person dashes through the trees and straight toward her. She's never seen anyone move so quickly. Their limbs are barely a blur, and their footfalls hardly make a sound, even over the dead leaves on the forest floor. Fear seizes her throat and she barely sucks in a gasp.

Vampire.

A thrill ripples through her and for a split second, a sense of awe prickles along the edges of her fright. For days she's heard about vampires, read about vampires, and been training to fight against vampires, but this is the first moment she's seen a supernatural entity with her own eyes. Until now, she hasn't quite believed in their existence. The momentary excitement evaporates as the vampire closes in at an alarming rate.

Maddy curses at herself and pulls out the pair of wooden stakes strapped to her thighs. The vampire, a male, leaps the last several feet. Maddy's heart skips into overdrive as the man opens his mouth wide, revealing a pair of sharp fangs. The vampire takes a swing at her, but Maddy quickly sidesteps. She slashes out with the stake, missing the vampire by mere inches. He growls in frustration as the two whirl to face each other. To Maddy's dismay, more vampires emerge from the forest.

The vampire chuckles at her and Maddy scowls. She thinks

of the missing college students and draws on the anger. They could be dead or missing because of monsters like these. Maddy leaps toward the vampire, catching him off guard. The training Oleg has been drilling into her takes over. Her body and mind give way to offensive and defensive tactics. Pride and triumph bring a fierce smile to her face as one of her wooden stakes sinks into the vampire's chest.

A billow of ash peppers Maddy's face and sticks in her hair. She has no time to give a thought to the disgusting layer of grime. A hand reaches toward her and she strikes out. The sharp tip of the wooden stake draws a burning line down a female vampire's arm. Hairs raise on the back of Maddy's neck and she spins, stake slicing through the air. She manages to take down another vampire, but a few more still remain.

"Felix!" Maddy screams. She tries to stake the female vampire, but the woman is fast and dashes aside. Several more vampires run through the forest and join the ranks of their brethren. Maddy pulls in sharp breaths through flaring nostrils, her wide eyes picking up each movement. Inevitability stares her in the face.

She's going to be overrun.

The front doors of the church crash open and the Order of the Knightly Rose rush to Maddy's aid. The two groups clash in yells and kicks, slashing stakes and flashing fangs. Felix joins Maddy's side and the two face off against a trio of vampires. One of them makes a dash for Maddy and she plants her feet, raising her stakes. The vampire crashes into her and carries her to the ground. A grunt rumbles through Maddy's chest as the air squeezes from her lungs. The man smiles fiercely down at her, certain he has her pinned and defeated. Maddy bucks her hips upward and tilts, a move Oleg had taught her.

"Get your enemy off balance, and use that momentum," the weapon master had said.

Maddy plants a foot and continues to quickly shove her body upward with a grimace on her face. The vampire is heavy, but she manages to get him on his side and her right arm free. He shoves a hand against her chest and before he can push her away, Maddy jerks her arm forward, fingers clenched tightly around a stake. The vampire's yell is cut short as his body bursts into a thousand flecks of gray ash.

Maddy rolls to her feet in time to see Felix dispatch the two vampires he'd been fighting. More vampires emerge from the trees and Maddy's heart sinks. It's as if they are hiding an entire army in there. Felix runs forward to meet the onslaught, a yell of pure fury bursting from him. Maddy tightens her grip on her stakes, and starts to dash forward to help.

But an arm wraps tightly around her waist and in the next second, the battle scene before her blurs. Air rushes over her ears and her stomach dips at the incredibly fast movement. Low tree branches scratch at her legs and catch in her hair. Only seconds pass, but when the frenzied movement stops, Maddy finds herself surrounded by trees. Confusion clouds her mind for a moment. What happened? Her feet are planted on the ground and the world spins around her. She closes her eyes, fighting the dizziness. In the distance, she can hear shouting and fighting, but she's so far away and it doesn't make any sense. Then, clarity works past her muddled thoughts and she senses a presence behind her.

She's been taken by a vampire.

A scream for help tears up Maddy's throat, but the plea is cut short when a rough hand clamps over her mouth. An arm wraps around her in an iron grip that pins her arms to her sides, her back colliding with a strong body. Maddy's muffled screams cut off when she feels a sharp pinch on the side of her neck. At first, the sensation brings confusion. Then, she realizes the vampire is biting her.

Pure horror washes over Maddy. The vampire is drinking her blood. Her pulse quickens and her heart drums in her chest, pumping more blood into the vampire's mouth. Frantic, Maddy freezes. What is one supposed to do when in the clutches of a vile monster? Her thoughts race, a tangle of fear, disgust, and utter panic. She can't think straight, but something deep inside scratches for the surface.

A feather light touch whispers across Maddy's skin as the vampire's thumb strokes her cheek in a gesture that seems almost...intimate.

Maddy blinks at the sensation, and then the hunter she's been trained to be finally breaks through her rigid terror. She jerks her body in a violent twist and must take the vampire by surprise because he nearly loses his hold on her. His grip around her middle loosens a fraction. Maddy uses the opportunity to hook her left foot behind the vampire's leg, and steps backward. The vampire's mouth leaves her neck in a rumble of curses as he tilts, off balance.

Momentum which should have carried them both to the ground cuts short, a thud reverberating through the vampire and into Maddy. Leaves rustle overhead. She hasn't done anything except knock the vampire back into a tree.

Screaming against the vampire's palm, Maddy twists and turns her torso but the man quickly regains his grip around her ribcage. Her stakes are still clenched in her hands and, try as she might, finds herself unable to get the sharpened wood anywhere near the vampire's body. The inhuman strength he possesses is beyond anything Maddy can imagine, though she'd been warned. The man's grip won't budge again and Maddy finds she may as well have been fighting against steel wrapped around her.

Hot breath brushes against her skin and Maddy's heels tear into the ground when the vampire's fangs punch into her neck once more. Tears prick Maddy's eyes and roll down her cheeks. She doesn't stop fighting, but her restrained movements begin to slow. Her muscles grow watery and she finds she can no longer bear her full weight on her feet. A haze crawls through her mind and clouds her thoughts as the vampire pulls more blood from her body.

Maddy's legs buckle and her fingers grow weak. The stakes fall from her hands. The vampire loosens his grip and Maddy crumples to the ground. Her chest heaves with short, quick breaths and the edges of her vision crowd with black. Dead leaves crumple and poke against her cheek as she turns her head to watch the vampire walk away. He glances once over her shoulder. Maddy's heart thuds a beat faster. She knows his face.

Caleb?

Maddy squeezes her eyes shut against the encroaching darkness, trying to think. Caleb was here. Did he attack her just now? Nothing makes sense. Nausea churns in her belly. He isn't a vampire...is he? She opens her eyes again, but the face peeking back at her blurs beyond recognition. No. It couldn't be him.

Shadows swim through her vision and everything turns black. Maddy tries to move but she feels like she's sinking into the ground, the earth rolling beneath her in waves. She needs to get up. Run. But her strength is gone. Her eyes drift shut.

"Maddy?" It's Felix. "You're going to be okay."

His voice is strained, though she can't understand why.

Before she can ask, she in gives to the pressing shadows and lets the darkness take her.

CHAPTER 17

CALEB

The cool glass of the small vial presses against Caleb's palm as his fingers clench. A morsel unlike anything he's ever tasted fills his mouth. The glass threatens to break in his tight grip and with monumental effort, he loosens his fingers. Slowly, as if his very body were fighting against it, Caleb lets the blood spill past his lips and into the vial. It almost feels like a sin to waste such a delicacy.

The blood of Madeleine Grimes is decadent beyond compare. He wanted to drink and drink until he'd drawn in every last ounce of her. The monster within him snarls at the loss of such a feast even as it laps with pleasure at the taste still coating his tongue.

Caleb pauses and braces a hand against a tree, catching his breath. God, he hadn't been expecting Maddy to taste so good. She smells lovely, of course, but her blood... His fingers dig into the bark and he shoves away. He has to stop thinking about her, but it's so damn hard. The temptation to turn around and finish what he started makes his muscles tense and his head spin.

The blazing need burning him from the inside out is a

reminder of what he is now. That if he doesn't control it, he'll become everything his aunt Kenna fought to rid this world of.

In the distance, he catches the sound of the other vampires making their way to the predetermined rendezvous point. He glances at the bottle filled with dark crimson and grimaces at the cost of such a prize. He didn't want to hurt Maddy and he regrets he caused her not only pain, but such fear. He can still taste her terror and desperation to get away from him.

This time, perhaps he has gone too far. It was necessary to get her blood, but he nearly killed her. Bloodlust had been sinking her deadly claws into his very soul and for a moment, he'd wanted nothing more than to give in. Leaving Maddy lying on the forest floor makes him feel like a despicable coward, but there was nothing else he could have done but to flee. He'd already paused for too long, looking back at her to assure himself her heart was still beating.

Caleb draws closer to the others. He can hear their voices as they gather. His thoughts bounce once more to Maddy. Had she recognized him in that last moment? Only time will tell but he severely hopes he hasn't overplayed his hand.

A small clearing opens up in the forest. Morgan waits there, along with several others. Caleb jogs over to them and holds up the vial.

"Got it." Caleb gives them a triumphant grin, though guilt eats away inside of him.

Morgan takes the vial and examines it. The darkness of night has fallen, and the pale light of the moon reflects off the glass. He brings it close to his nose and inhales, then makes an appreciative groan.

"She still alive?" he asks. Caleb nods and Morgan lets out a low whistle. "You have better control than me. I would have drained her for sure."

The others crowd around, wanting to see what the fuss is

about. Caleb snatches the vial back from Morgan and tucks it into the pocket of his leather jacket. He looks over the others. Many of them are amped up, with excitement bright in their eyes. Taking down hunters has that effect on vampires, especially when those hunters are directly tied to the Order.

Caleb turns to Morgan. "How did it go?"

"We were unable to get Felix, though we did manage to kill a few of the Order members. Felix brought out some sort of strange chalice, and it made us retreat." His friend shrugs. "We lost some, as well. A couple fell to that girl of yours."

Caleb doesn't react, though he wants to snarl at Morgan to shut his mouth. Maddy isn't *his girl*, and yet he hadn't let the others catch the scent of her blood, and the thought of her lying back in the forest, suffering from blood loss, forms a knot in his chest.

"I thought you said she was a green hunter." A woman strides closer to Caleb, her black hair tied in a braid looped over her shoulder. A long, red burn traces down her arm where she was struck with a stake. "She doesn't fight like a newbie."

Caleb had watched Maddy take down a couple of vampires. His heart had leapt to his throat when one of his comrades had pinned her to the ground, but it was Maddy he had yearned to save, and not his brethren. He couldn't help but admire her fighting skills. She hadn't given up when he'd captured her, either. She'd fought until her body weakened beyond the point of resistance.

The female vampire—Caleb can't recall her name—watches him expectantly. He wishes the lot of them would leave already. He's responsible for this small group under the Master's orders, but that doesn't mean he wants them constantly at his elbow.

"I'm not sure," Caleb says. "Perhaps she has strong instincts, or maybe there's something in her ancestry that gives her an edge. That's precisely why I want a witch to test her blood. We need to know what we're up against." Unwilling to pique their interest about Maddy even farther, he jerks his chin. "You can head back. I'll have Morgan give you a call if something else comes up. Until then, lie low. Felix will have his hunters out on high alert after our attack."

None of them argue, and the leaves on the forest floor barely make a rustle as they dash through the trees. Only Morgan remains and he stares at Caleb with a curious expression.

"What?" Caleb snaps. Irritation leeches through his calm demeanor.

Morgan seems nothing but amused. "What is your fascination with the Grimes girl? Why does it really matter what her ancestry is? She's a hunter, Caleb. Worse, she is a hunter working under Felix. The only thing she needs to be is dead."

Caleb bristles at the thought and can't stop the glare he slices toward his friend. "She isn't just a hunter." The tree branches rattle overhead as a brisk wind howls through the night.

"What do you mean?" Morgan leans against a tree and flicks a bit of debris off his arm from the fight.

Caleb grows quiet for a moment, deliberating. There's something he's been keeping close to his chest and he has no intentions of divulging such information. Morgan is his closest friend, however, and as much as he wants to keep his secret, he decides now is the best time to share it. Especially if Morgan's starting to ask questions.

"Some time ago, a seer outside of Mercy City sought me out. I've always thought such people were ridiculous, but this was no mere fortune teller. She was the real deal and the moment I agreed to talk to her, I knew my path was about to be forever altered."

Morgan eyes him, then adopts a crooked grin. "Did she tell you that you would fall in love with a hunter? Man, that sucks."

Caleb snorts at his bad pun, and his poor guess. "No, nothing like that. She told me a girl would be recruited into the Order, and this girl would play a vital role in bringing about peace between the immortals and the hunters. Her destiny will also involve helping the vampires fight an ancient enemy of ours. The seer said the girl will come from a special legacy, and it is for this reason I'm insisting on getting Madeleine's blood checked out. I need to know if she's the one the seer spoke about."

A long stretch of silence settles between the two vampires. Caleb waits on his friend to scoff and tell him he's ridiculous for listening to a seer's drivel, but he doesn't. Morgan just stares at him. After a moment, he shoves away from the tree and approaches Caleb.

"Caleb, this doesn't sound like something the Master has approved."

A prickle of unease touches Caleb and he wonders if he made a mistake telling Morgan about the prophecy. Morgan is loyal to the Master, and Caleb isn't certain how strong his ties of friendship with the other vampire will hold if he thinks this is some sort of betrayal.

"That's because the Master doesn't know anything about it," Caleb says. He doesn't let a touch of worry enter his voice. He can't risk Morgan believing this is a bad idea. "I understand he wants to bring down the hunters, including Maddy. What if she is the one, though? What if she can stop all this fighting? Instead of snuffing her out with the rest of the Order, we need to bring her to our side."

Morgan's frame stiffens and he slowly shakes his head. Moonlight casts a shadow over half of his face. "We cannot disobey the Master's orders. I will not. He wants the Order brought down, for good reason I might add, and I intend to do whatever I can to lay waste to them."

"I'm not asking you to disobey him." Caleb pulls in a deep breath. "Not really. I'm asking you to give me time to check things out. He's being very shortsighted with his eyes on one goal: destroying the Order and everyone in it. But what if by doing so, what if by killing Maddy, he also destroys our greatest chance to survive what's coming?"

"But what's coming?" Morgan asks.

Caleb lifts his hand and squeezes his friend's shoulder. He can't tell him about the darkness Bryn had spoken of, not yet. There's too much risk involved. "Just, please, go along with my plan for the time being and keep this from the Master."

"He'll find out."

"Not if we keep going along with his plans, with everything except for Maddy. By the time we carry out what I have going on, the Master will have to acknowledge we've done the right thing. This could be our chance to get into his inner circle, Morgan."

Caleb's playing on his friend's desire for more inclusion in the Master's closest allies, but there's no other way. Morgan has to follow through with this plan, or it won't just be Maddy's life in jeopardy, but Caleb's, as well.

"Fine," Morgan groans, tilting his face to the sky. Then, he gives Caleb a small smile. "But you owe me. Big time."

"Deal," Caleb says. He brings the vial out of his pocket. "Now, let's go and see this witch."

CHAPTER 18

CALEB

A solitary light glows from within the house across the gravel lane. The steering wheel creaks beneath Caleb's fingers as he watches the witch's house. He doesn't like getting involved with a witch, but he has to know if Maddy is the one from the prophecy. Caleb pulls in a steadying breath and climbs out of the car. There are no other houses around. The witch seems to like her privacy. Most of them do. After being hunted for centuries for witchcraft, many of their kind have adopted a lonely life.

Morgan let the witch know to expect Caleb, but Caleb's friend had no interest in accompanying him to her home. Caleb dropped him off at the edge of town before following a country road out into the middle of nowhere. With the vial of Maddy's blood tucked safely away in his pocket, he hurries across the road and onto the covered porch. The weathered boards creak beneath his boots. There's no doorbell, so Caleb lifts his hand to knock. The door swings open.

A woman stares up at him with a shrewd expression. Her eyes are the brightest green he's ever seen, peering out from a sharp face.

"Galina?" Caleb asks.

"That's me." The witch steps back and wraps her long cardigan around her petite frame. Caleb guesses she's in her forties. "Hurry inside, you're letting in the chill."

Caleb follows the woman into her quaint house. The living room is furnished like any other, though potted plants sit on nearly every flat surface and even hang in baskets from hooks on the walls and ceiling.

"Herbs, mostly." Galina glances at her plants, then back to Caleb. "Among other things. I never know what sort of spells I will need to perform and I always like to be prepared." Her gaze sharpens. "You have blood you need me to test?"

"Yes." Caleb appreciates her bluntness. He doesn't have time for small talk, anyway. He draws the vial out of his jacket pocket. "Here."

Galina plucks the vial from his fingers and holds it up in the poor light. "This will do. Come, have a seat." She settles into an armchair and Caleb sits on the loveseat beside it.

The witch has set up a bowl, several lit candles, and a few jars of dried substances on the table before them. Caleb isn't certain what the bottles hold but he rubs his nose against the sharp scent the contents give off.

"Say nothing until I speak," Galina says. "I need to hear what the blood sings."

Galina uncorks the small vial and tips Maddy's blood into the shallow bowl. Caleb's throat burns and he tries not to think about the decadent taste. He swallows away the excess moisture that suddenly pools in his mouth. The witch grabs a pinch of a powdery gray substance that resembles ash and drops it into the blood. Strange words tumble from Galina's lips as she plucks a few dried leaves from another bottle and sprinkles them onto Maddy's blood. The witch closes her eyes and waves a hand over the bowl, still muttering some sort of incantation.

Caleb watches with rapt attention, waiting for something to happen. He holds his breath, in part so he can't draw in the delicious scent of blood, in part because he's not sure what he hopes the answer is. If Maddy is the child of the prophecy, what does that mean for her? For him? And if she's not, will Morgan insist it's time to kill her?

He still as he realizes her life is in danger, either way.

The witch's eyes suddenly open. "Ah." Galina blinks. "How very curious, and yet, I could have sworn I'd felt something strange in Creed."

"What is it?" Caleb leans forward. "What did you find?"

Galina's green eyes swing to Caleb. "This girl hails from a very special, and very rare, legacy, though I cannot see how this line will serve the Order."

"What do you mean by that?"

The witch peers back into the bowl and speaks quietly, almost as if to herself. "Nobody knew it ever existed. Such an ancestral lineage is rare, a legend, even." Galina blinks, then holds Caleb's stare. "Madeleine, correct? This Madeleine is descended from a medieval Romanian king named Dracula."

Caleb grows very, very still. Disbelief holds his tongue and steals his breath. After a moment, he slowly shakes his head. "That's not possible."

Every vampire, hell, every supernatural entity, knows of Dracula. He was one of the most formidable vampires ever known to mankind. There were even rumors he had been blessed by Lilith herself, the very woman who created vampires. Maddy can't possibly be descended from Dracula, because vampires can't create human life.

Galina straightens with a huff. "Are you calling me a liar? I'm a blood witch. I can read a person's entire genetic history with a single, crimson drop, and I'm telling you, this girl is descended from Dracula himself. If you wish to have a second opinion, you will need to obtain more blood from her and seek out another witch. I'm warning you, however, there aren't any other blood witches in this side of the country. You will have to travel several days."

"I don't want another opinion." More, Caleb doesn't want to hurt Maddy again. "I just don't see how it's possible. Dracula was one of the most powerful vampires in existence. How could he have descendants?"

The witch wiggles her fingers over one of the candles on the table, playing with the flame and making it dance. "Dracula was once a man, as are all vampires. Do you really find it so impossible he had women before he was turned and became a Lilith worshiper?"

"No one has ever heard of Dracula having any sort of family. It would be known if he had children."

"Not if his line was hidden." Galina still stares at the flames of the candles, the light flickering in her far away gaze. "Dracula's children would have been a liability to such a powerful being. They would have been used against him. I would not be surprised if the mother, or mothers, themselves kept the children hidden from him. So, his powerful line fell from existence in this world...until now. Madeleine is the heir of Dracula."

Caleb can barely fathom the witch's claim. Maddy is the descendant of Dracula, a vampire powerful beyond imagining. A smile comes to his face as he thinks of the seer's prophecy. Along with telling Caleb the girl would save the vampires, the seer had also mentioned the girl would hail from a hidden line. This is better than Caleb could have predicted. Fate has brought forth Dracula's heir to save them. He just wishes Maddy hadn't fallen into the hands of Felix and his hunters. Alarm beats through his heart. If Felix finds out who Maddy truly is, he will end her life.

"Do not be fooled by her delicate mortal shell," Galina says. "For Madeleine is more powerful than you know."

"How so?"

Galina eases back into her chair and folds her legs up onto the cushion. "Did you know, even before Dracula became a vampire, he worshiped Lilith? He called her Mother, and was a part of a huge satanic cult who worshiped Lucifer as the one true god, and Lilith as the heiress to the dominion of Hell and darkness."

Caleb shifts in his seat, restless, wondering if Maddy's okay, or if she's in danger from Felix. "I fail to see your point."

The witch clucks her tongue and her eyes flash with annoyance. "You vampires can be so impatient. I'm trying to tell you Madeleine has powers that have long remained dormant."

Caleb frowns. "What do you mean?"

"This girl possesses gifts that are one of a kind, and as such make her very unique." Galina lifts her hand and curls her fingers inward. "All she has to do is embrace them."

"You're telling me Maddy has some sort of magical powers, even though she's a human? Wouldn't that make her a witch?"

Galina lets out an exasperated laugh. "No. Witches may have certain gifts, but we must use herbs, stones, and other forces of nature to unlock and channel them. Madeleine has power in her very blood." She pauses and purses her lips. "Of course, that power does come from the gift of demons."

"What?" The word hisses up Caleb's throat and a fist of dread tightens in his chest. He thinks of Maddy and her beautiful face, her stubbornness, and loyalty to her friends and family. If she possesses the power of such vile creations, how long before it completely taints her soul? "Does this mean she's a demon?"

The witch is silent for a long moment as she watches a bead of wax slide down one of the pale candles. "No. The girl is not a demon. Her bloodline is gifted by demons, but she is not one of Lucifer's children."

Caleb scrubs his fingers through his hair. "I don't understand. How can someone have demon magic, and not be a demon?"

"Before Dracula was killed by the Van Helsings, he had been given a boon by a demon named Belphegor that his line would never end, and if ever his vampire lineage met an end, the other lineage would receive the powers they possessed. The vampire king has always held that power, so when the hunter, Kenna, slayed the King, all of the powers he possessed passed on to Madeleine, though the girl is unaware." The witch stands and peers down at Caleb with a shrewdness that makes him uncomfortable. "Tell me, have you tasted her blood?"

Caleb also gets to his feet. "Yes, I have. It was the only way for me to obtain some to bring to you."

Galina stares at him for several seconds. "Then you need to have a care, vampire. The blood which pumps through the veins of Dracula's heir is powerful, and you may have taken some of that power for yourself."

Caleb stills, hardly breathing. He's inadvertently tapped into some sort of dark magic by drinking Maddy's blood. Will it change him, or make him more powerful? He thinks back to his time with the seer and wonders if she had known. Fate was an often tricky woman, and Caleb hopes the path he has leapt on won't lead to his end, or Maddy's.

Galina breaks the silence. "A vampire, once a hunter, and a hunter, heir to a vampire, all tied together with magic gifted by demons." A wide smile lifts the witch's cheeks and shadows dance across her face in the light of the candles. "Things are about to get *very* interesting."

CHAPTER 19

MADELEINE

A mechanical hum fills Maddy's ears and something squeezes her arm nearly to the point of pain, then releases. The sound of a faint laugh follows and she cracks her eyelids open. Fluorescent lights bleach out the already pale color of the walls. In the distance, she catches the whoosh of an automatic door. Warmth pulls at her left hand and she turns her face, a soft pillow giving beneath her head.

Her mom is sitting beside her, clutching Maddy's hand even as her chin rests on her chest. A soft snore shudders through her. In the corner, Felix sits in a chair, watching a sitcom on the small T.V. near the ceiling. Maddy shifts uncomfortably in the hospital bed and Felix's eyes catch the movement.

"You're awake." Felix gives her a small smile.

Beside Maddy, her mom jolts. Then, she sees her. "Madeleine, oh, thank goodness." She leans over and gives her a gentle squeeze.

Maddy reaches over to hug her back, but her arm is tangled in the leads for a blood pressure cuff around her arm and a heart monitor on her finger. She grimaces at the sight of the I.V.

in her arm. Needles are at the top of her Least Favorite Things list.

"What happened?" Maddy licks her lips and rolls her tongue around in her mouth. God, she's thirsty.

Felix gets to his feet. "You had a blood transfusion. You're lucky to be alive. The others are in the waiting room." A tightness pulls at the corner of his eyes and a muscle ticks along his jawline.

The lines on the heart monitor beside Maddy's bed start to jump a little higher. "Is everyone okay?" Her mom squeezes her fingers.

"The Order lost three," Felix says. "Jess, Daryl, and Antonio."

Maddy's eyes burn. She didn't know them extremely well, but the loss still forms a knot in her chest. "And the vampires?"

"Many got away." Felix walks over and pauses beside the bed. "You managed to kill two. For a new hunter, that's very good."

"I'm so proud of you, sweetie." Maddy's mom gives her a smile, but the fear of nearly losing her daughter still carves a groove between her eyebrows.

Guilt sours in Maddy's stomach. "I should have been more prepared. They came so fast."

Felix grunts. "Yes, they did. I still don't understand how they found us, or how they got past the wards. We were very careful and those spells couldn't have been brought down by a vampire. None of the Order would have dared. I know my people, and every single one of you is loyal to our cause."

A nurse comes in and asks Maddy how she's feeling. She checks the monitor, adjusts the little clamp on Maddy's finger, then brings over a cup of water. Maddy drinks greedily, then sets the cup on the little table beside her. The nurse tells her she'll see if the doctor will allow her to have any food, then leaves, shutting the door quietly behind her.

Maddy's stomach growls at the mention of food, but she doesn't feel hungry. If anything, her stomach is rolling too much to be able to keep anything down. Her thoughts race to the fight with the vampires. She had felt nothing that indicated they'd broken the wards. One second Bryn and her crew had been leaving, and then...

Maddy gasps quietly. "Felix...I saw something strange right before the vampires showed up."

"Strange?" he asks.

"That Grail Keeper girl, Bryn, well, something seemed off about her to me, so I followed her outside. She took a knife and drew a line in the dirt, then left with the others. It was only a minute or so later that the vampires showed up."

Felix exchanges an uneasy glance with Maddy's mom. "That's not possible. The Grail Keepers would never ally themselves with the vampires."

Maddy shrugs. "That's what I saw."

"Did you see anything else out of place?"

A shiver ripples over Maddy and she wishes she had another blanket. The one draped over her is thin and smells a bit too much like bleach. She sits up straighter and her mom adjusts the pillow behind Maddy's head.

"Not there, but, well, there is this guy I'm suspicious about."

"What guy?" The tone in Maddy's mom's voice is sharp and her eyes narrow slightly. "You never mentioned any guy to me."

Maddy shakes her head. "I didn't think it was a big enough deal. I ran into him on campus, he dropped his wallet, and I chased him down." She pauses, hesitant, and even before she speaks, she realizes perhaps she should have said something sooner. "I thought I saw him again when I went to meet the rest of the Order for the first time, but I wasn't certain. Mom, remember when I went out with Cora? Well, she wanted me to meet her date, and it turns out it was this guy. He just seems... off, somehow. I swear, it feels like he's dating her just to get to me."

"What's his name?" Felix asks.

"Caleb."

The leader of the Order curses. "I know him." He eyes Maddy with a mixture of disbelief and annoyance. "Caleb is a vampire. And a very dangerous one."

Maddy's mouth pops open and ice collects along her veins. Her pulse beats in her ears, loud in the shocked silence of Felix's claim. Disbelief snatches her body and keeps her still, even as the bed seems to sway beneath her.

Caleb is a vampire.

"Oh, my God." Maddy's breath comes out in a wheeze and she presses her palm to her forehead. For days, she's seen him with Cora. Maddy has spoken with him, and been alone with him, and this whole time he's been the enemy. Even the first time Maddy saw Caleb after that initial run-in, he'd been awkward around that girl he'd helped when she'd tried to hug him. Had it been because he was tempted by her blood?

"I'm sorry." Maddy swallows against the lump in her throat. "I should have said something sooner, I just had no idea." How could she have? With the exception of being extraordinarily good-looking, Caleb had seemed like any other human being.

Felix shakes his head. "It isn't your fault. I knew Caleb was around. We have an unpleasant history and this isn't the first time he's slipped through my fingers. I should have known he'd go after our newest recruit."

The thought Caleb is not only a vampire, but trying to use her for information, makes Maddy nauseous. "I have to warn Cora." She glances around for her clothes. Her cell had been in the pocket of her jeans.

Maddy's mom squeezes her daughter's arm. "It's too dangerous. Cora cannot know about our world, Maddy. We'll get this sorted out, don't worry. First, you need to recover."

Recover. The word drags Maddy farther into the dangerous reality she's been thrown into. Her hand shakes as she reaches up and touches a bandage on the side of her neck. "I think Caleb is the one who bit me." Her vision had been blurring in those last seconds before she'd passed out, but something deep in her bones tells her it had been him. Maddy lifts her gaze to Felix. "Why didn't he kill me when he had the chance? I'm a hunter, and yet he left me there alive. I don't understand."

Maddy tries to piece together the thoughts and actions of Caleb, yet she can't. If he wanted to take her down, he'd had the chance. There was no possibility he'd be able to use her for information, anymore. Not after he'd nearly drained her of blood. Had he assumed she would lay there and die?

"I don't have any answers to explain his actions, but Caleb's intentions can only be vile. He's using your best friend to further his cause. Caleb serves the vampire Master, after all, and he'll be seeking revenge for what the Order did to his kind in Mercy City."

Maddy thinks about Cora's date with Caleb, and the way he'd reacted to the news of the missing girl. "Do you think he could be behind those who are missing?"

"Probably, sweetheart." Maddy's mom sighs. "We're lucky we found this out before it was too late."

Felix pulls a cell out of his pocket. "Yes. I'm going to tell the others downstairs to keep an eye out for Caleb. He may try to come here and finish what he started. We also need to make sure he stays away from your friend." He eyes Maddy. "Do you feel up to helping set up a trap?"

Maddy nods. "I'll do anything to keep Cora safe." Anger

sizzles through her at the thought of her best friend in danger at the hands of that conniving jerk.

"I'll speak with the others and return shortly. Then, we can make a plan. We'll lay out the trap, and when he falls into it, we'll end Caleb's life for good."

Felix leaves to meet up with the others downstairs in the waiting room. Maddy's mom busies herself with trying to flag down a nurse to bring in another blanket.

We'll end Caleb's life for good.

Felix's words echo in Maddy's mind, and as much as she wants to hate Caleb for being a vampire and for tricking her, the thought of watching a stake pierce his chest unfurls a deep sense of unease.

She sucks in a deep breath and forces the sensation down, along with any feelings she's foolishly developed for the man who stepped into her life.

Caleb's a vampire.

And that makes him the enemy.

CHAPTER 20

CALEB

The sharp scent of disinfectant burns Caleb's nose as he approaches the emergency room doors. He watches an ambulance, lights flashing and siren wailing, back up to the dock. The EMTs quickly unload the patient and wheel them inside. Caleb makes his move and dashes through the loading bay doors before another paramedic has the chance to see him.

He spotted one of Felix's Order members outside at the main entrance. He has people watching, which means he either expects another attack, or Maddy recognized him after all, and told Felix. Caleb bites down on the pain of regret. She would hate him now, making it that much harder to convince her of Felix's dark purpose.

Eyes and ears open to every little movement and sound, Caleb quickly makes his way over to a desk. He works on breathing as little as possible. Hospitals are too full of smells—antiseptic, fear...blood. He smiles at the older woman there. "Hello. I'm here to see my friend, Madeleine Grimes, and I'm afraid I've gotten turned around."

The woman opens her mouth to object, no doubt about to

ask if he's family, but her eyes unfocus as he compels her. A second later, she returns the smile and looks up Maddy's room number. Caleb thanks her then takes the nearest set of stairs to the third floor. Riding in the elevator is too risky when he doesn't know who may be waiting for him at the top. He eases the door open once he reaches the third floor and peeks out. Nurses and other hospital staff walk across the shining floor, and one patient is taking a walk, wheeling his IV stand along with him. There's no sign of the Order.

Caleb pulls out a ballcap he has in his car and puts it on, then keeps his eyes toward the floor as he makes his way over to a desk. A woman in purple scrubs stands behind it, peering down at a stack of release papers. Caleb glances at the papers and sees Maddy's name at the top. The woman must be her nurse. He clears his throat.

As soon as the woman looks up at Caleb he leans forward and captures her gaze, reeling her in. "Hello." His voice is pleasant, but devoid of much emotion as he compels her. "You're Madeleine Grime's nurse, yes?" The woman nods. Caleb glances around, but no one is paying them any attention. "Good. I want you to tell me if you've heard anything strange from her room, such as an odd conversation."

The woman doesn't look away from him, ensnared as she is in his stare. "I was going to give her more water and I heard her and the man she is with talking about setting a trap for someone."

"For who?"

"Caleb. Maddy and the other man are setting a trap for Caleb."

Caleb grinds his teeth together. Felix had gotten to her too quickly. "What else did you hear? Do you know where the trap is?"

The woman shakes her head. "No."

"Thank you so much for your help." Caleb offers her a bright smile and turns away, breaking his control over her. The nurse finishes gathering papers for Maddy, none the wiser.

Remaining on the third floor is risky. Order members could spot him any second, but he has to get to Maddy and tell her what Galina revealed to him. Before he can even begin to search for her room, a sudden sharp tugging sensation ripples through him. He closes his eyes and curses.

The Master is summoning him.

Caleb has no choice but to leave. He makes his way back to the stairwell and gives Morgan a call.

"Morgan, I need you to get over to the hospital. I've been summoned. Maddy and Felix are making some sort of plan for a trap. I need you to follow them when she's released and see if you can find out where they plan to spring it. Let me know as soon as you find something out." Caleb ends the call and tries not to wonder if Morgan let the Master know about what Caleb had confided to him. He needs to have someone to trust in this lonely existence that's been forced upon him, and if that can't be Morgan, he doesn't know who.

Caleb's been to the vampire safehouse only once since coming to Creed from Mercy City, and he hadn't seen the Master then. Instead, one of his inner circle had met with him to give him instructions. Now, a pair of vampires flank him as he walks into the nondescript building. Inside, Caleb is swiftly taken down a set of stairs. Cool air kisses the back of his neck as they descend. Once at the bottom, he's led through a door and what he finds sends goosebumps scattering over his arms.

The smell hits him first. Fear, pain, and hopelessness blend together with the scent of sweat, filth, and blood. Cells line the long stretch of hallway and he peers at them from his peripheral as he walks.

Humans.

Caleb recognizes them as those who have gone missing. Then, Aubrey, the girl he'd known before, sees him. Recognition flutters across her face and she lurches to her feet.

"Help me." Aubrey's hands wrap around the bars, her face smeared with dirty tear tracks. "Please. Please, help."

It takes everything in Caleb not to react. He may have the shell of a monster, but inside, he doesn't want to harm others more than he has to. He can't help these humans, however. It's too risky. He wants to ask one of the Master's men flanking him why the humans are here, but they reach the end of the hall and Caleb is shown into another room. The two who lead Caleb down leave, and a single man turns to face him as the door shuts at Caleb's back.

The room seems to grow colder and quieter as Caleb comes face-to-face with the Master.

With light blond hair, average height, and plain features, he looks...ordinary. One would never think he's the Master of immortal beings who survive on blood, that is, until they saw his pale eyes. Power and viciousness have hardened them to stone, cold ice. Caleb bows his head in a show of respect.

"I have come," he says.

The Master doesn't greet him, but steps closer, hands folded behind his back and face fixed into an impassive mask. "I have received credible information that you are trying to glean some information about this new family Felix came into contact with. What do you know of this girl that has kept you so enthralled with her life?"

Caleb's mind whirs into overdrive. It could have been any of the vampires Morgan and himself work with who has told the Master, but if it was Morgan, then the Master knows much more than he's letting on.

"I'm not sure of my find," Caleb says. "But I will know soon enough. When I confirm my findings, I will inform you immediately." He places a hand on his chest and bows his head again. "I do not wish to disappoint my Master."

The Master stares at him for an achingly long moment, and Caleb begins to worry the vampire leader won't be satisfied with his answer. Eventually, the man nods. "Very well. See that you do not disappoint me, youngling."

Caleb fights a grimace at the word "youngling", but it merely means he is a younger vampire.

"Felix and his band of hunters are still alive, even after what he did to your friends back in Mercy City. Why is this?"

A bead of sweat trickles down between Caleb's shoulder blades. The Master is disappointed, and that is a very dangerous thing. Caleb tilts his chin up, unwilling to show fear in the face of his unmerciful leader. "I led an assault on their second safe house. We managed to kill a few of the hunters, but Felix has possession of some sort of mystical chalice. It drove the rest of our party away before we could finish the Order off."

The Master peers at Caleb, a frown weighing down his lips. "Did you see this chalice?"

"Unfortunately, no. I was busy pursuing one of the hunters, but one of my team members saw it."

The ancient vampire paces across the room to a table. Lanterns flicker overhead and he flips open a book, then gestures for Caleb. Inside the book is a drawing of a chalice, plain, but with an inscription etched onto the silver surface.

"I believe it is the Chalice of Solomon, an object King Solomon used to control demons." A flicker of something moves in his pale eyes. "Its power stretches farther, however, and can be used to control vampires along with any other supernatural creature."

Caleb doesn't respond, pretending to be mulling over the

information when he's actually shocked. Control every super-natural creature in existence? The Master is talking of untold power. Power that could change the world as they know it.

The Master's nostrils flare, the only sign of his excitement. "We will take this chalice from Felix's hands and use it to achieve vampire domination," he orders sharply.

Caleb nods even as he's reeling. "I'll see to it, Master."

Vampire domination. It's a world his aunt Kenna dedicated her life to stopping.

"Do so quickly." The Master snaps the book shut and it emits a plume of dust. "I will use the chalice to collect the blood of those I sacrifice."

Hesitating, Caleb glances over his shoulder, then back to the Master. "Do you mean the humans in the cells?"

The Master chuckles darkly. "Of course not. The prisoners are not sacrifices. They have a much more current use. I intend on creating human enslavement camps where our kind will feed on human blood without the need for secrecy or fear of a stake in their hearts. Humans are nothing but blood bags for vampires, and they must be treated as such." He lays a hand on Caleb's shoulder, the closest thing to affection the young vampire has ever felt from his Master, and turns him toward the door. "Over time, we will expand to the entire world, and with the Chalice, that will only happen quicker. With its power we will be able to control the other supernaturals and make them do our bidding."

Caleb nods again, throat tight as he takes in the Master's cruel intentions.

The Master shoves him lightly toward the door. "Go. Bring me this Chalice."

Caleb reaches for the door, feeling cold in a way he never has before.

"And Caleb?"

He turns to face the Master. "Kill the girl."

After a quick bow, Caleb leaves. His heart hammers as he walks past the pleading, crying prisoners. *Kill the girl.* The command hadn't latched onto his heart with an iron grip, so the Master hadn't used his full power to give the order. Caleb can technically disobey, though it will mean his life if he does so. He hurries up the stairs and draws in a deep breath when he steps outside into the crisp air, washing away the scent of fear clinging to his nostrils.

Caleb's pocket vibrates and he pulls out his cell to find Morgan's name lighting on the screen. He swipes his thumb across.

"Yeah?"

"I did as you asked. They're laying the trap at 34 Chancellor Avenue."

"Thanks." Caleb hangs up, but his phone immediately buzzes again. This time, it's Cora. Caleb pauses. Maddy must not have spoken to her friend, but why? Curious, he answers.

"Hey, Cora. How's it going?"

"Good!" She hesitates. "Actually, there's a party tonight and I was wondering if you wanted to come and hang out with me? It's at 34 Chancellor Avenue."

He blinks. Felix works fast. And he's willing to use Cora as bait.

Cora laughs nervously into the silence. "It's fine if you're busy—"

Caleb unlocks his car and climbs in. "Sounds great. I'll meet you there."

"Great," breathes Cora. "I'm looking forward to it."

They say their goodbyes and he pulls away from the curb, leaving the vampire safehouse behind. Caleb lowers his shoulders as he flexes his hands on the steering wheel. He can still hear the screams of the human prisoners echoing in his head and he heads straight into a trap.

He can feel the line he's been balancing on for so long beginning to fray beneath him.

CHAPTER 21

MADELEINE

An electric energy sparks in the room, making Maddy want to fidget. She crosses her arms over the charcoal top of her dress to keep still. The room is massive, with a sleek dance floor underneath a spray of lights. Tables line the edges, laden with food and drinks. Music thumps in her chest from the speakers in the corner. Beside her, Cora nods her head to the beat. Maddy has to admit, Felix's ability to throw together a party as a cover-up is spot on.

Maddy leans over to speak to Cora. "Thanks again for inviting Caleb."

Sparks of light dance off the subtle shimmer of Cora's seafoam dress. A smile brightens her face. "Of course. I've been wanting to see him, anyway. We've both been so busy so it's been a while. It was nice of your taekwondo instructor to throw such an awesome party." She glances at Felix, who's standing in the corner with Kai and the twins, Laura and Matthew. Oleg and Oliver are around, as well, ready to close in on Caleb as soon as he steps into their trap. Cora turns her attention back to Maddy, and a touch of disbelief pulls down her lips. "Even if it is kind of strange."

Maddy shrugs a bare shoulder, then adjusts the thin strap of her dress. Beneath the soft fabric, stakes are strapped to her thighs. "He's been friends with my mom for years, so it isn't like he's just a taekwondo teacher."

"Why do you want to meet up with Caleb?"

"He promised me something and he's late getting to it." Maddy's excuse is bland, but it's the best she came up with on short notice. "I'm going to corner him tonight. It's no big deal."

Cora tilts her head. "What is it?"

The music picks up tempo and Maddy sways her hips, grinning. "I hope you're ready to wear those shoes out." She points at Cora's feet, hoping to hell the deflection works.

Cora twists her ankle, studying the same silver shoes she'd worn on the date with Caleb. "I don't know about that. Dancing isn't my forte." She quickly scans the room. "I'm going to go freshen up before Caleb gets here, okay?"

Maddy watches her friend hurry off and sighs with relief. Thankfully, Cora's distracted and didn't press the issue regarding why Maddy really wants Caleb at the party. Felix and the others drift out of sight, as is the plan. It wouldn't do for Caleb to walk in and see members of the Order standing in the crowd. Maddy helps herself to a drink, moving subtly to the music as she waits. She doesn't know any of the people here. Most of them appear to be college students. More people arrive, demonstrating the power of posting an invite on social media. Maddy's about to look away when she spots who's at the back.

Her heart skips faster as their target walks in out of the night.

Caleb's eyes immediately swing to Maddy and she wonders if he can hear her heart thundering in her chest. Even at a distance, his gaze traps her. Does things to her.

He walks smoothly through the crowd, then pauses in front of her with a smile. "Hello, Maddy."

Maddy takes in Caleb's appearance. He wears his usual dark jeans and a tee that fits snuggly, drawing attention to his hard stomach and sculpted shoulders. The sight of him makes her mouth dry, though it should be fear quickening her pulse, not appreciation.

Especially when he's a vampire.

She returns the smile and does her best to act as if nothing is out of the ordinary. She can't let Caleb know she's aware of what he really is. "Hi. Cora will be back soon. She's looking forward to seeing you."

"I'm happy for the invite." Caleb's stare drifts down her body, over her favorite black dress, then back up to her face. "You look amazing."

The back of Maddy's neck heats and she clears her throat. "Wait until you see Cora. She's beyond adorable." She wants to kick herself. She needs to keep Caleb away from Cora, not urge him to hang out with her. The tempo of the music draws her attention and she jerks her head toward the dance floor. "Want to dance?"

A grin lifts one corner of Caleb's mouth. "You're a lot less snarky than usual." He takes Maddy's hand and leads her out onto the dance floor.

Maddy screams at herself to get it together. Caleb is likely already getting suspicious with her sudden change in attitude toward him. Just as she starts to get into the groove of the beat, the music changes, smoothing out into a slow song. Caleb peers down at her with a mischievous spark in his eye, like Maddy's the one caught in a trap instead of him.

Slowly, Caleb wraps an arm around her waist. The press of his touch is warm through the fabric of her dress and her breath catches slightly as he draws her closer. More couples merge onto the dance floor, but Maddy pays them no mind as Caleb expertly swirls her in a circle. He's a magnificent dancer, his steps smooth and precise.

A little laugh bubbles up her throat as Caleb spins her again. She's never danced like this before and she finds she's actually enjoying it. Her stomach swoops when he dips her, eliciting another laugh, and Caleb smiles widely.

"You have a beautiful smile," he says.

Maddy's cheeks warm at the compliment and she glances down. The music shifts to another slow song, and Caleb and Maddy sway together. His fingers lightly draw circles on her lower back and Maddy tilts her face toward him. He has such kind eyes, beautiful eyes, but when her gaze lowers to his mouth, she suddenly remembers the pain of his fangs sinking into her neck.

Caleb is a vampire. He's meant to draw her in with his perfect looks and smooth words. He's probably compelling her. How else could he have her forgetting everything so easily? Maddy mentally shakes herself and focuses on the plan.

There's still no sign of Cora. One of the Order members likely distracted her to give Maddy time alone with Caleb. The vampire suddenly leans in closer, and for a second, Maddy could swear he inhales deeply. It should be terrifying after everything that's happened, but it's...sexy. Then, his warm breath brushes over her ear and raises goosebumps down the side of her neck.

"Maddy, I need to talk to you in private." His whisper tickles over her skin.

Maddy can't believe her luck. He's playing right into their hands. "I know where we can go," she says, telling herself the breathlessness simply works into her plan.

She weaves through the crowd on the dance floor, Caleb a step behind her. The music switches to another fast song and the crowd cheers as the lights overhead flicker to bright colors.

Maddy pulls in steadying breaths as she leads Caleb to the opposite side of the building, away from the party-goers. Ahead, light creeps underneath a closed door. "It's quieter on this side of the building. We can talk in private."

The hinges creak slightly as Maddy opens the door. She steps inside and lifts her chin, heart hammering. Her steps carry her halfway across the room, Caleb close behind her, when the door slams shut behind them. Swiveling, Maddy watches as the Order members quickly fan out, ending any chance of Caleb escaping.

Caleb's eyes lock on Maddy. "You shouldn't have done this," he says. He stuffs his hands in his pockets, seemingly unbothered by the hunters glaring at him. Caleb glances over his shoulder to the Order members. "Especially since they don't know who exactly they've recruited."

Maddy steps away, her stomach tied in knots as she moves around, closer to her brethren. She did the right thing, she tells herself. Caleb's a monster. Her role as a hunter is to make sure others are safe from him.

"Well, well. I finally have you in my grasp, Caleb." Felix steps out of the corner of the room. His stare is cold as it fixes on the vampire. "I may have failed to kill you all those months ago in Mercy City, but now I can finish the job. In fact, the wait has only made it sweeter."

Caleb straightens, his own glare laced with steel and fury. "Kenna would be ashamed of what you've become, Felix. Hatred has made you blind."

"Ashamed of what I have become?" Felix barks a laugh. "I think not, scum. Kenna was responsible for killing your kind, because the vampires were trying to feed the world to demons. You are the one who should be filled with shame and regret."

For a few seconds, Caleb stares at the hunter. Then, he nods. "I can respect that. However, you're the one who broke away from the real Order and killed innocent vampires back in Mercy City. That cannot be forgiven."

Felix scoffs. "No creature who feeds on human blood can be called innocent. The Order, and The Knights Templar before them, were created for one purpose—to eliminate the vampire kind from the face of the earth. We almost succeeded, too, when they were put to sleep in the late 1600s." The hunter stalks closer to Caleb. "It was darkness who called to your kind and woke them up."

Maddy watches the exchange in rapt silence. Caleb doesn't look at her, but she could swear his feet shift toward her a fraction.

A sneer twists Caleb's face, and his voice grows low and dark. "Yes, and that same darkness has caught your attention, hasn't it?"

Felix's nostrils flare, but he remains silent. A shiver runs over Maddy, and a warning latches onto her soul. Unease swirls around her, but she can't figure out why.

Caleb lifts his chin. "The Order doesn't execute unless in war. I deserve a trial." His stare never wavers from Felix. "I certainly have some things I'd like to bring out into the open."

"A trial?" Felix snarls. "You deserve no such thing. You will be beheaded and staked at sunrise."

Caleb's eyes suddenly swing toward her. "Is this what you want?"

Maddy blinks and takes a half-step back. She swallows, glancing quickly at Felix before returning to Caleb. "You're a vampire, and you've most likely killed a lot of people." God, she almost sounds like she's trying to convince herself. She swallows the regret trying to rise within her and hardens her voice. "You're probably the one behind the disappearances. Tell me, did you kill them all?"

The hunters of the Order tense as Caleb leans forward. More

than one has a stake in their grasp. "I am not behind their disappearances, nor did I kill them." He straightens. "They are still alive, if you want to know the truth. The Master is planning something deadly, but if you let Felix kill me, you'll never know what it is."

Maddy purses her lips, mulling over Caleb's claim. "You almost sound as if you want to help us. Why should I trust you?"

"What makes you think you can trust Felix?" Caleb gives Maddy a hard smile. "Why trust someone who split from the true Order and has taken it upon himself to purge the world of vampires and any other supernatural creature who stands in his way?" He shakes his head slowly, though his eyes stay locked with Maddy's. "You don't know the entire truth about these people, and they don't know the truth about you. If they did, do you think they would actually stand by you? No, they would have you in chains at my side."

The strange prickling warning drags Maddy's heartbeats faster as her eyebrows draw together. "What are you talking about?"

"Drivel." Felis's face pales with anger. "He will spit out anything to convince you to let him go. I'm not waiting for sunrise. You die now, filth!"

A laugh rolls through Caleb''. "Is that so? Tell me, Felix, did you know Madeleine Grimes is descended from Dracula himself?"

The room stills, and Maddy can hear nothing but the pulse drumming in her ears. Dracula? It can't be. "You're wrong," she says. "I'm a hunter. I'm not...I'm not descended from a vampire."

Felix doesn't move for several seconds. Then, he reaches into his coat and draws out a silver chalice with strange markings etched onto the surface. "This is the Chalice of Solomon, and under its power, I command nothing but truth to fall from your tongue." He holds the chalice toward Caleb. "Speak, creature. Do you speak the truth about my young hunter?"

Caleb pulls in a deep breath, flicks a quick apologetic glance at Maddy, then speaks loud and clear. "Madeleine Grimes, the young woman you have recruited into the Order, is a direct descendant of Dracula."

"No." Felix's voice is little more than a growl. "This cannot be." He lowers the chalice.

Maddy is stunned by the wrathful glare he settles onto her. "I didn't know." She shakes her head. "It doesn't matter. I'm not one of them." She sends a pleading look to the other hunters, but the young men and women she'd been training with and had fought with, now stare at her as if she is something nasty they've stepped in.

"I will not have a hunter in the Order who belongs to that accursed line of kings." Felix faces Maddy fully now, and his body nearly trembles with rage. "I will not have such a vile descendant *breathing*."

Maddy steps away from him, unconsciously drawing closer to Caleb. What does Felix mean?

"Cut this abomination down, before such wickedness spreads."

The hunters step forward, and Maddy's throat tightens on a scream.

CHAPTER 22

CALEB

Too fast. The energy in the room shifts much too quickly and Caleb has mere seconds to make a move.

Maddy's heart stutters in shock as her fellow hunters turn on her and a strangled scream erupts from her. She retreats backwards, nearly running into Caleb. He grabs her firmly around the waist and whirls her out of a massive hunter's grasp. Maddy's legs fly up and her left foot comes into contact with the chalice in Felix's hand. It flies from his fingers and hits the floor. Caleb tenses. He can make a run for it, get the chalice, and flee. But Maddy...

The hunters yell, driven on by Felix to get what he calls an abomination. Maddy's heartbeats thrum like a hummingbird's wings as she stands behind him. Determination and fear mingle together as he pulls in her scent. A quick look over his shoulder finds her glaring with a stake in her hand at a female hunter. The Order is ready to shred her to pieces.

How could their loyalty shift so quickly? Disgust pulls Caleb's lips up into a snarl and he flashes his fangs, standing protectively in front of Maddy.

"See how he protects his own?" Felix's features have fixed into cold steel.

Maddy's heartbeats quicken at Caleb's back, and he can taste her shock and anger like acid on his tongue. One of the hunters flash forward and Caleb closes the gap between them. The room is a blur and in the next instant, the neck of the lithe hunter snaps between his hands. Maddy gasps, but her humanity and unwillingness to hurt someone who should have been her friend have her frozen in the center of the room as the woman leaps for her. Caleb wheels around, grabs Maddy's wrist, and yanks her backward. The hunter's stake barely misses her mark. Caleb releases Maddy and riding the momentum, he swings his fist through the air. His knuckles collide with the female hunter and her skull gives beneath his supernatural strength. She hits the floor with a thud and her stake intended for Maddy falls from her limp fingers. A blond male hunter fills the room with an enraged scream.

Caleb's chest tightens with a wrath of his own. These hunters are twisted, corrupt. Who the hell would slaughter an innocent simply for her bloodline? His body snaps forward, and he shifts to the left and right, avoiding the swinging stakes. He takes down the blond who closely resembles the dead female across the room, and then another young male. Only the massive hunter and Felix remain, the latter watching him from the corner with eyes burning with fury.

"Caleb!" Maddy hollers his name.

Caleb flicks his stare from Felix just in time to find a stake whistling through the air toward him from the large hunter. He releases a vicious, feral snarl as the stake pierces the wall behind his left shoulder. That will be the last thing the man does.

His muscles bunch and he springs forward.

Vampire and hunter collide. The hunter's back hits the floor,

Caleb's knee pinning him hard on the chest. Pure adrenaline and instinct race through his veins as his fingers constrict on the hunter's neck. The man tries to pull a stake from a holster on his thigh but Caleb presses the heel of his boot to his arm, nearly crushing the man's bones.

The hunter doesn't last long before he stills beneath Caleb's grasp. The room is quiet aside from Maddy's quick breaths. Caleb lurches to his feet, spinning to face Felix, only to find the head of this faction of the Order is gone. A quick glance shows he's taken the chalice. Caleb swears beneath his breath and turns to face Maddy.

Her face is pale and she is very purposefully avoiding looking at the dead hunters in the room. She looks like she's trying to hold her breath even as she breathes fast.

"We need to get you out of here." Caleb steps toward Maddy and she retreats, tightening her grip on the stake. He lifts his hands. "I'm not going to hurt you, Maddy. I swear."

Slowly, reluctantly, Maddy lifts the hem of her dress and slides the stake back into the holster strapped there. Caleb tries to keep his stare from sliding up the exposed skin of her thigh before the fabric falls back down. Now isn't the time to remember how she felt in his arms on the dancefloor.

"Come on." Caleb grabs her wrist and pulls her from the room.

"Wait." Maddy's feet plant and she tugs her hand free. "Just wait a second." Her shoulders rise in a deep breath and she tilts her face up to stare at him. "You saved my life."

Caleb glances away. "It's fine. No big deal." He blinks in surprise when Maddy throws her arms around his neck and buries her face against him.

"Thank you," Maddy whispers. "Thank you for saving me. I can't believe Felix turned on me like that. I just don't understand."

Relief softens Caleb's muscles as he realizes just how fortunate they both are. He's pleasantly surprised by Maddy's sudden affection and he wraps his arms around her. "You'll be okay now. I promise." Softly, slowly, he presses a hand to the back of Maddy's head and wonders when she became someone he couldn't bear to lose.

"Maddy?"

The two break apart and look down the stretch of hallway. Cora stands there, watching them with wide eyes. Maddy's breath catches, then she glances between Cora and Caleb.

"Cora...it's not—"

Cora's nostrils flare. "Don't. Don't even say it's not what it looks like. Felix told me there was something down here I had to see. How could you betray me like this?" She turns and runs back toward the party.

Maddy takes off. "Cora, wait! Let me explain."

Her friend doesn't listen, and she dashes into the crowd of party goers. Caleb follows, gaze sweeping the room for Felix but the hunter is nowhere to be seen. Maddy's still in danger. Felix won't let her life continue so easily, especially after the death of his hunters. Maddy weaves quickly through the crowd on the dance floor, still shouting for Cora. By the time she makes it outside, a pair of taillights are already disappearing down the road.

Maddy stands in the middle of the street and throws her arms up in the air. She turns to find Caleb watching her from the sidewalk. "We need to go after her." She jogs over to him, heels clicking on the pavement. "You have to help me convince her that what she saw didn't mean anything."

A cool breeze blows between them, snagging Maddy's raven hair and sending her scent swirling around Caleb. He picks up her unease, and a trace of attraction that explains her quickening pulse.

Caleb draws in a deep breath through slightly parted lips, trying to ignore the scent of her blood, as well. He looks down the street where Cora disappeared, then back to Maddy. She's peering up at him with her beautiful big eyes, and he can't bring himself to look away as the truth falls past his lips.

"I can't tell Cora it meant nothing, because that wouldn't be exactly true."

Maddy's head jerks back a bit. "What do you mean?"

"You said it yourself. I've only been going out with Cora because I needed to get close to you." Caleb rubs the back of his neck, already feeling the anger building up in Maddy. "I mean, I care for Cora. She's a sweet girl, but I'm not really in love with her or anything."

Caleb wants to tell Maddy that he's beginning to care for her, more deeply than he realizes, but Maddy closes the distance between them and gives him a shove in the chest so hard, he stumbles backward.

"You bastard." She seethes, her fingers clenching at her sides. Anger comes from her in hot waves that burn Caleb's nose. "You used her. You *used* my best friend, and now Cora is pissed at me."

"I didn't mean for that to happen." Another blast of icy wind gusts around them and Caleb realizes Maddy doesn't have her jacket. Goosebumps rise across her hunched, bare shoulders. "It's cold. Let's get inside and talk, okay?"

Maddy clenches her teeth and glares at him like she wants to punch him with one of those clenched fists at her side. Caleb has to admit, he likes her fire.

"I'm not going anywhere with you." Maddy presses a hand to her neck. "God, you *bit me*, Caleb. Is that how you found out about my lineage?" His silence gave her the answer. "What makes you think I want to talk to you after you used me like that? You violated me!" A shiver wracks through her.

Caleb stuffs his hands in his pockets. "I had to know, for your sake and mine."

"I don't care," Maddy snaps. She crosses her arms, likely more in an attempt to ward off the chill than due to anger. "Felix turned on me because of what you found out. I was doing great with the Order, and now Felix despises me. You not only used my friend, and used me, but you told Felix the truth, knowing full well that I would be kicked out of the Order." Her face drops to the sidewalk. "It was so damn humiliating and now they're dead."

"Maddy..." Caleb reaches for her. She doesn't understand. They would have found out about her heritage eventually, and they would have killed her regardless. He has to make her realize this was the only way to protect her.

"No." She takes a step back from him. "Get away from me, Caleb. I don't want to see you again." She falls quiet as she pulls in a shuddering breath. "You saved me in there, and you made me realize how cruel and blind Felix can be, but what you've done...it's too much. You're just as bad as the rest of them."

His hand falls to his side. His shoulders drop. What can he say? Maddy's right. He's just as cruel and uncaring as the hunters. He did what he could to find out the truth about Maddy, even if it meant using her best friend. He stalked her, bit her against her will, got her kicked out of the Order, and killed those she likely considered friends.

Maddy wheels around and storms off toward her car. Her name is on his tongue, but he doesn't call out. It wouldn't do any good. She's made up her mind about him, and guilt keeps him silent.

Caleb watches as she pulls away from the curb and tears off down the street. He did what was necessary...

But was the price too steep?

CHAPTER 23

MADELEINE

The road blurs in front of Maddy and she rubs a hand across her eyes, letting out a growl of frustration. Everything has gone wrong. Cora's mad at her, and Maddy's standing with the Order has been severed. She shakes her head, trying to dispel the image of the other hunters lying dead on the floor. Caleb killed them, and while she despised his actions, she also knew that he'd merely been protecting her.

Realizing she's grateful he saved her life makes her even more aggravated. What he'd done had been necessary.

She pulls over into the parking lot of a gas station and sits with her hands clenched on the steering wheel. Her breaths shudder in and out, and there's a knot in her chest that seems to grow tighter with each passing moment. She still can't believe Felix turned on her so quickly. She didn't know anything about her bloodline. Why should it matter who her ancestors were? She was a hunter. She wanted to kill vampires. She'd proven herself.

She leans forward and rests her head on the steering wheel, hating the tears tracking down her cheeks, but not bothering to wipe them away. Now, however, she's not so certain. Caleb's a vampire, and he saved her. Are there other vampires like him? He'd mentioned the slaughter of innocent vampires to Felix. How many have been staked by hunters who had done nothing to them?

Maddy's head spins. Her breath feels like sandpaper. Caleb and Felix and Cora and the dead hunters whirl around in her mind until she wants to scream. Joining the Order had given her purpose in a life where she'd felt like she'd been drifting, untethered. Now, that has been stripped away and her friend-ship with Cora is in jeopardy. A large part of her even regrets that Caleb will no longer be in her life. After several minutes, she finally wipes the remaining tears from her cheeks and lifts her chin.

"I've got this." She straightens her back and pulls back onto the road. "I can handle this. It's going to be okay." Her pep talk does nothing to smooth the edges of uncertainty clinging to her, but she heads home, regardless. Right now, repeating those words gives her mind something to do.

Maddy glances at Cora's house before she turns onto her home street. There are a few lights on, one of them being Cora's bedroom light. Maddy's tempted to stop by, but shakes her head. She knows Cora, and time to calm down is what she'll want. Plus, Maddy needs to go home and try to figure out her next steps. Her house isn't far and she's relieved to see her mom's Jeep in the driveway. She'd half-expected her mom to be out looking for her after the night's events.

A sharp breeze tugs at Maddy's dress as she steps out of the car. She'd been so upset during her confrontation with Caleb, she'd forgotten her jacket at the party. Crossing her arms, she bumps her car door shut with her hip, then hurries up the steps. She grabs the door knob, but when she turns it, finds it is locked. Maddy's eyebrows pinch together. Her mom rarely locks the door if she's home.

Maddy bangs her fist on the door. "Mom? It's me."

"Are you alone?" Maddy's mom's voice is muffled through the door.

"Uh, yeah? Let me in. It's freezing out here."

Her mom opens the door and flicks a quick glance behind Maddy. "All right, hurry up."

Maddy shuffles past her mom and rubs her arms. "What's the deal?"

Lines of worry etch her mom's face and her lips turn downward. Even her ponytail is a little droopy. "I was talking to Felix."

Maddy's heart jumps. "Felix? Is he here?" She leans around her mom, trying to spot the leader of the Order.

"No." Her mom walks toward the kitchen and Maddy follows. "He called. I just got off the phone with him." A teapot starts to whistle on the stove and she turns off the burner. A cup with a tea bag inside is already waiting on the counter. "He told me you betrayed the Order. He said you sided with a vampire and had the man decimate the hunters. Felix said you let him slaughter your own people."

Shocked into silence, Maddy says nothing as her mom pours hot water into the mug. For a moment, neither of them speak. Her mom watches steam curl up from tea that smells like chamomile. Finally, she turns, eyes wide.

"Maddy, please tell me that isn't true. All of those hunters, people you knew, are dead. You tried to stop them from being killed, right? Felix is just mistaken."

Maddy glances at the kitchen window and stares at her reflection. Her features do nothing to hint at the turmoil tearing her apart inside. Slowly, she pulls in a steadying breath and turns back to her mom.

"I did let it happen. I didn't try to stop the vampire from killing them."

Maddy's mom blanches. "God, Maddy. Why? Your own people. You're part of the Order. You're trained to kill vampires. Why would you allow this to happen?"

"Why?" Maddy's nostrils flare. "They were going to kill me, mom. Felix ordered the hunters to take me down."

Face paling, Maddy's mom lays a hand on her chest. "Kill you?" she whispers. "Why?"

"Because of our bloodline." Maddy narrows her eyes. "Did you know we're descended from Dracula?" Judging by the stunned look on her mom's face, Maddy guesses she was ignorant of the fact. "Caleb told Felix, then Felix ordered the others to kill me."

"Caleb?" Her mom tilts her head. "Hang on. Isn't he the one Cora has been dating? He's the one who bit you?"

The sting of betrayal pierces Maddy's heart all over again. "Yes, he is. He was using her to get to me. He knew about my ancestral line, and for some reason, he wanted to help me. He let me walk him right into the trap we'd set for him, risking himself, and then he confronted Felix. He said Felix has broken away from the true Order. Then Felix used some sort of chalice to get Caleb to tell the truth. That's when he found out I was a descendant of Dracula. If Caleb hadn't killed the other hunters, I'd probably be dead right now."

Maddy's mom looks like she wants to give Maddy a hug, but she clutches her mug of tea instead and holds it tightly between her hands. "I had no idea Dracula was in our bloodline. I still can't believe Felix would try to have you killed over such a thing. It isn't as if *you* are a vampire." She takes a tentative sip of her hot tea. "What did the vampire mean, Felix had broken away from the real Order?"

"I have no idea." Maddy shifts, bearing weight on her left hip. Her feet are sore from the heels she was wearing. "And honestly? I don't even care to know. I'm done with the Order, and with vampire hunting. It's only led to one huge disaster and I don't want any part of it. I'm done with it all."

"Maddy." Her mom reaches out and squeezes Maddy's shoulder. "Don't say that. You're a hunter. It's in your blood, and it doesn't matter what Felix or that vampire say. You have a purpose to keep humans safe. No matter what happened tonight, we'll get this figured out. It's just a big misunderstanding."

"I don't think it is." Maddy shrugs her mom's hand away. "Caleb couldn't lie about my ancestral line. Felix loathes me, and now even Cora hates me because..." She pauses, realizing she's said too much.

"Why?"

Maddy glances at her mom. She can't exactly tell her mom she had been getting feelings for a man who turned out to be a vampire. Maybe she even still has feelings for him. Her emotions are such a mess, she isn't even sure what to think anymore.

"It's nothing." Maddy sighs. "It's been a long night. I'm going upstairs to change."

"Are you sure you don't want to talk about this some more?" Maddy's mom asks. "Or I can fix you some tea and we can just sit quietly and watch a movie if you like."

Maddy gives her mom a tight smile. She's trying, but Maddy just isn't in the mood to be comforted. "Thanks, but I'm going to pass. I just need to go upstairs and unwind." Before her mom can argue further, Maddy retreats to her bedroom.

Once inside, she locks her door and crosses to one of her windows. She peers outside but can see nothing but the light glowing from her neighbors' windows. Felix could be out there, watching and waiting to attack her again. Maddy closes her curtain. Surely, with his Order in shambles he wouldn't make a move against her just yet. Hell, for all she knows he's taken off and won't return.

Bitterness burns up Maddy's throat. Felix trained her as a hunter, then discarded her as if she were nothing but a piece of garbage. Clearly, she wasn't fit to serve whatever agenda the Order leader has in mind. He used her just as much as Caleb. With an angry shake of her head, Maddy yanks open a drawer on her dresser. She pulls out a pair of leggings and then a long-sleeved shirt.

She wiggles out of the dress, then holds the silky fabric in her hands. Despite the outcome, she'd actually enjoyed the party for a moment. Dancing with Caleb had certainly been a surprise, and was far more enjoyable than she should have allowed. Maddy closes her eyes, recalling the smooth expertise of Caleb spinning her around, and the touch of his hands on her, drawing her close.

A growl rolls up Maddy's throat and she tosses the dress into a corner. The dance with Caleb had meant nothing. It was just another way to try to get to her. She gets dressed and just as she flops down on her bed, her cell phone buzzes on her bedside table. She picks it up to find a message from Cora.

I can't believe you did that to me. You knew how much I liked him.

Maddy quickly taps out a reply.

It's not what you think, Cora. There's a lot more going on that I can't tell you about, but I wasn't doing anything with Caleb.

The reply is almost instant.

Our friendship is over. Don't call or text me. I don't want to hear from you.

Maddy drops her phone on the table and clenches her fists in her hair. Cora is angry, and understandably so, but she can't just throw away years of friendship. Maddy gets to her feet, then puts on socks and ankle boots. She isn't having any of it.

Once she explains things to Cora, her friend will come around. She'll tell Cora she has no interest in Caleb. He means nothing to her whatsoever.

All she has to do is ignore the lie coiling inside of her like a wicked serpent.

CHAPTER 24

CALEB

Dark shadows and cool night air keep Caleb company as he lingers beneath a tree across the street and watches Maddy's house. He followed her after she left, afraid Felix may have gone to her house. He's seen no sign of the traitorous hunter, but that doesn't mean Maddy is safe. Felix is a determined man and if he wants the young woman dead, then he won't stop until she's six feet under. The head of this twisted faction of the Order told Cora where to find Maddy at the party. He'd driven a wedge between Maddy and her best friend on purpose. Caleb wouldn't be surprised if Felix turned Maddy's own mother against her, as well. So far, nothing seemed amiss inside the house.

A light flicking to life upstairs draws his attention and for a brief moment, he catches sight of Maddy staring out of the window. He tenses, glancing around. She's making herself an easy target for a bullet, or even an arrow. In the next moment, her curtain closes and her silhouette draws away. Caleb loosens a breath. In his pocket, his cell vibrates. He pulls out his phone to find a text from Morgan asking if he's okay. Caleb told him he is, and that the trap failed. He also says to let the

Master know several hunters are dead and that he's on Felix's trail.

Lies. How many is he going to stack up before they tumble down and crush him?

He's lied to Cora and Maddy, the Master, and even himself. First, he told himself he didn't want to have anything to do with Maddy, and now he was standing guard outside of her house. If he thinks he doesn't care about her, that she's just a curiosity or a means to an end, then he's a bigger fool than he realizes.

He cares for Maddy in a way he wouldn't have thought possible, and he'll be damned if he lets anything happen to her.

"You have some serious stalker vibes going on."

Caleb jumps. He twists to the left to find Bryn approaching him, a little bounce in her step and a grin of triumph on her face at having caught him off guard.

"Geez, Bryn, you nearly gave me a heart attack."

The young woman tilts her head, staring at his chest. "Is that even possible?"

Caleb glowers. "What are you doing here?"

"It's a nice night for a walk, don't you think?" Bryn zips her jacket up a bit more, then rolls her eyes. "Obviously, I have something important to say. You need to get Madeleine on your side."

"On my side?" Caleb lets out a hollow laugh, thinking of the hateful glare in Maddy's eyes right before she stormed off and left him on the sidewalk. "I don't think that's going to happen any time soon."

Bryn joins Caleb's side and faces Maddy's house. A shadow passes by a window downstairs, back and forth. Maddy's mom is pacing and the sight puts Caleb on edge. Is she going to turn against her daughter, or is she trying to figure out a way to get Maddy out of this mess?

"You need her with you sooner rather than later. She needs

to be on your side *now*." Bryn tilts her chin to look up at Caleb. "The darkness is only extending its influence on the earth. I can feel it. It's well on its way to creating a place more chaotic than when the Sins were released into the world."

Caleb scoffs, but it's quiet and lacks the disbelief he's trying to put out. "You sound like one of those lunatics with end-of-the-world signs, spouting doomsday prophecies."

"This isn't a joke." Bryn grabs the front of Caleb's jacket and jerks him around to face her, her eyes fierce. "What do you think is going to happen when the darkness starts influencing things on a grander scale? Ancient enemies will awaken to walk the earth and there will be nothing you or me or any other supernatural being with good intentions will be able to do about it. It's the prophecy of the obsidian, and it is unfolding before our eyes."

Caleb raises his hands and Bryn releases him. He turns back toward the house, peering at Maddy's window. "I don't know what you expect me to do. Maddy doesn't want to see me again. She hates me."

"Hate is good," Bryn says. "Hate is passionate, and people don't easily forget that depth of a feeling. Whether she hates you or not, Maddy will soon have no choice but to accept who she is, and who you are. She'll need to accept it if we are to stop this darkness."

Caleb sticks his thumbs in his pockets and ignores the sharp breeze carrying the icy scent of the coming winter. "This darkness, what else have you found out about it? We know Felix is dabbling in it, but I'm not certain if he's the source. From what I saw of him, he's just going off the deep end with his heretic notions for the new Order he wants to create."

"I haven't been able to pinpoint the source." Unlike Caleb, Bryn feels every ounce of the chill of the night. She crosses her arms and bounces on her toes in an effort to generate warmth.

"But I know someone who may know what to do about the darkness. I'm not sure if they will help, but I don't see that we have much of an option right now."

Caleb hesitates. The last thing he wants to do is leave Maddy without protection, but she's at home with her mom. They're both hunters, and he's seen Maddy in action. She's more than capable of taking care of herself. He nods slowly, then peers down at Bryn. "Take me to them."

"I'm parked down here." Bryn turns and heads down the sidewalk. "This person knows more about the obsidian than I do."

The pair approach Bryn's silver car. "Where are we going?" Caleb sinks down into the passenger seat and shuts the door.

Bryn turns the ignition then cranks the heat. She holds her fingers in front of the vent for a moment, quietly complaining about the cold. She answers as she pulls away from the curb. "We're going to Mercy City. Well, outside of it, anyway."

Houses pass by as they leave town, and then Caleb watches as forests and fields flash by. In the near distance, he can see the glow of Mercy City, but Bryn turns off the main highway. Shortly after, gravel crunches beneath her tires when they take a small country road. Caleb squints, trying to pick out their destination in the darkness. They round a curve and hug the base of a hill before the terrain opens up into a field. Caleb spots a building and when Bryn draws closer, the headlights wash over the structure of a large farmhouse.

Caleb climbs out of the car and studies the building. The house has definitely seen better days. The white paint is peeling off the siding, leaving the house a weathered gray instead of whitewashed. One of the shutters is tilted sideways and there are more than a few cracked panes of glass in the windows. A section of the roof on the covered porch sags downward, the beam supporting it broken. Caleb even spots a hole in the right wall, the edges charred from flames. There are no lights on inside, and the farmhouse looks cold and desolate.

"Lovely place," Caleb says dryly.

Bryn sits on the edge of her car's hood. "It used to be. The recent war left it damaged and uninhabitable. The Grail Keepers used to stay here, but they've since moved out and left the old place abandoned."

"Are we meeting with the leader of the Grail Keepers?"

"No." Bryn frowns toward the house. "Reign has other things on his mind."

"Then, who?" Caleb asks.

The wind answers him, and he turns toward a sudden whooshing sound in the night. His muscles coil and his gaze sharpens as a winged figure suddenly swoops in from the darkness. The female's luminous white wings spread wide and she drops daintily to the ground. She folds them behind her back and regards Caleb indifferently. The woman is gorgeous, with blonde curly hair and big blue eyes. Of all things, she's wearing a miniskirt with leggings underneath.

Bryn pushes away from the car. "Thank you for meeting us." She gestures at Caleb. "This is Caleb, and he wants to help Madeleine."

The angel strides closer to him. He stands his ground, but being around other supernaturals puts him on edge. Angels and vampires don't have the greatest history, especially after his kind sided with demons.

"My name is Gabby." A bright smile lifts her cheeks, but there is a fierceness sparking in her blue eyes. "And if you bring any harm to my friend, Maddy, I promise you, vampire, I will personally see to your painful, tortuous end."

hoping she'd be able to take her by surprise and not give her a chance to leave. Unfortunately, it's Cora's mom who opens the door, which means Cora may have already spotted her and sent her mom to send her off.

"Maddy? It's late, are you okay?"

Maddy glanced at the clock on the wall over Cora's mom's

shoulder. It was nearly ten at night. "Sorry to stop by so late. I was wondering if I could talk to Cora."

Her mom steps to the side and lets Maddy into the living room. Maddy sighs at the warmth and the scent of something sweet and spicy. Cora's mom has been baking during the day, no doubt.

"Cora came home from the party in tears, but she wouldn't talk to anyone about what happened. I'm worried about her."

Maddy looks down. "That's my fault. There was a misunderstanding and we had a fight. Cora told me not to call or text her, but I want to make things right between us."

Understanding lights in Cora's mom's eyes. "Ah. I see. Of course, you can go on up. I'm sure you two will work things out. I'll be in the living room if you need anything."

Maddy tramps up the stairs to Cora's room. She used to share it with her older sister before she moved out. Her sister's name is still on the door. Maddy knocks, but there's only silence. She purses her lips and wonders if the door is locked. Barging in on Cora won't help the situation, however, so she knocks again.

"Cora? It's Maddy. Please, let me in."

There is a pause. "Go away. I told you I don't want to talk to you. I don't want anything to do with you." Cora's voice is thick, evident she's been crying.

Maddy's chest squeezes at the pain she's causing her friend. "Please, just open the door so we can talk." Her throat burns. "Even if it's the last time we do, I need to speak with you."

There's a pause, and she holds her breath for its entirety. Then there's footsteps and slowly, Cora opens the door. Her eyes are red and her face is pale, but her jawline is hard as she clenches her teeth. "Fine." She swings the door open wider and crosses the room. Cora doesn't sit at her desk or on her bed, but stands in the middle of her carpet and crosses her arms. "Go ahead. Tell me why you thought it was a good idea to betray your best friend."

Maddy closes her eyes for a brief second and pulls in a breath through her nostrils, fighting down her angry retort. She reminds herself that Cora is hurt and lashing out. She can't mean what she's saying.

"I didn't betray you, Cora." Maddy hears Cora sniff and when she looks over at her friend, there is cold disbelief on her face. "I didn't."

"It sure looked like you did." Cora shook her head. "I saw you. There's no point in denying it."

"You don't understand. Something happened and Caleb comforted me. That's it. It didn't mean anything." Maddy's heart beats faster mentioning the embrace with Caleb. It meant nothing...hadn't it? She tries not to think about him standing protectively in front of her, or the dance they'd shared, or how now, even trying to hate him and cast him away, something inside of her mourns the loss of what could have been. Maddy swallows. "I want nothing to do with Caleb."

Cora wipes a tear from her cheek and finally sits on the bed. "You know what? I don't think you're done with Caleb. I've seen you two together, so don't worry, I'm not going to come between you two any longer."

Maddy opens her mouth to protest, but Cora cuts her off.

"Remember in the beginning when I asked you if you liked Caleb or not? I offered then to back out, but you insisted you didn't have feelings for him. You should have said something then instead of letting me date Caleb with false hope. You let me grow feelings for him, knowing you liked him." Cora sniffs. "It isn't just you, either. The entire time we've been dating, it's always felt like Caleb has an eye for you. No matter where we went or what we were doing, it always seemed as if you were never far away, like Caleb was hoping to run into you or something."

Maddy bites the inside of her cheek, hating Caleb for coming between her and her best friend. He'd played with Cora's feelings and now it's falling back on Maddy in the worst way possible. There has to be a way to fix this. Maddy can't lose her place in the Order, her role as a hunter, and Cora all in one night.

Cora's shoulders rise and fall in a shuddering breath. "I know you, Maddy. I probably know you better than anyone. I can tell you're attracted to Caleb even if you deny it. I see it on your face and the way you look at him. I think I've always known, but I was hoping it was just nothing. I guess I should have listened to my gut." Her eyes are wide as she peers up at Maddy. "I just really wish you would have told me from the start and been truthful. I really like Caleb." Cora squeezes her eyes shut and presses a palm to her forehead. "And I know that he's at fault, too. If he was hung up on you, he shouldn't have led me along."

A stretch of silence settles between them. Maddy stares at the carpet at her feet, trying in vain to come up with something to say that will soothe the hurt in Cora's heart. Maddy knows Caleb has been watching her, and she wishes more than anything he hadn't involved Cora, but the damage is already done. She just wants to fix things between them. She has to convince Cora that getting involved with Caleb isn't something Maddy wants to do.

Except she knows such a claim could very well be a lie. She hates Caleb for what he's done, and yet, can she really dismiss him forever, after what he did for her in that room?

"Caleb shouldn't have led you along, Cora, but I swear I had nothing to do with it."

"Somehow, I don't quite believe that." Cora's eyes flash as

she flicks a glance at Maddy. "Caleb is practically a stranger, and his dishonesty and betrayal don't sting nearly as much as yours."

Maddy takes a step closer to her friend. "Cora, I'm sorry. I—"

"Don't." Cora lurches to her feet. "I don't want an apology from you, Maddy. You were my best friend, but we're done. You and Caleb have something going on together. I know it. You've been hiding things from me, and both of you have been playing around with my feelings." Cora's voice is tight as a single tear rolls down her cheek. "I'm going to text Caleb and end things with him. I also need a break from you. Don't call me. Don't text me. I don't even want you waving at me on campus. Just...just leave me be for a while. I just need some time and maybe later we can work things out."

Hurt coils in Maddy's chest but she nods. "I understand. I really hope you change your mind. You're my best friend, Cora. I'd do anything for you. This wasn't supposed to happen, and there are things going on that are complicated, but I'm working them out." She pauses. "I know you need space, but if you want to talk, I'm always here for you. Besides, it's going to be totally weird not having my coffee buddy in the mornings."

Maddy smiles, hoping the mention of their daily meet-up at the café on campus would lighten the mood, but Cora just stares. Maddy's shoulders slump slightly.

"Okay, well. I'll go." Maddy turns to the doorway. "See you around." She peeks over her shoulder but Cora isn't even looking at her anymore.

Defeated, Maddy plods downstairs, tells Cora's mom goodbye and heads out of the door. Maddy's throat burns and her eyes sting. She'd been certain she was going to work things out with Cora, and now, her situation is even worse.

She draws her jacket closer as she steps off the porch and

glares up at the sky. It's beginning to sprinkle and the cold rain only worsens her morose mood. She starts down the sidewalk and suddenly, the hairs raise on the back of her neck.

A shiver scatters through her.

In the next instant, a crash sounds behind her. Maddy whirls around, facing Cora's house. For a split second, a silhouette passes over one of the front windows, then disappears. With her heart in her throat, Maddy rushes back to the house, jumps onto the porch, and shoves the door open.

Nothing but silence greets Maddy as she steps inside. "Hello?" Something draws her attention at the corner of her eye and when she turns, she finds Cora's mom lying on the floor.

She hurries over and drops on the floor beside her. She shakes her shoulder, then notices something on her neck. Slowly, she tilts her head to the side and fear spikes her pulse. Fang marks. Thankfully, the woman is merely unconscious, but Maddy leaps up on high alert.

"Cora!" Maddy takes the stairs two at a time, then hurries to her friend's bedroom.

The room is a mess. A lamp is knocked over on the bedside table, and part of the comforter has been dragged to the floor. Papers flutter from the desk as a breeze blows in through the open window. There's no sign of Cora. Maddy can scarcely breathe as her pulse hammers in her ears.

Her best friend has been taken by vampires.

she'll surely cut him with if he doesn't find a way to help Maddy, and keep her safe in the process. Things are getting deeper than one hunter with a remarkable bloodline, however, and Caleb's beginning to find he's juggling the fates of many lives in his hands.

"We have an obsidian problem," he says.

Gabby glances between him and Bryn. "I beg your pardon?"

"It's true." Bryn steps closer to Gabby. "I know it is."

Gabby slowly shakes her head. "No, that isn't possible." Her wings curve around her for a moment, blocking the wind. She peers over her shoulder at the house. "Let's get inside and talk. My legs are freezing."

Caleb follows the two women into the old farmhouse. The hinges creak on the door and the floorboards groan beneath his steps. Gabby's wings rustle together before disappearing, magically hidden. Caleb shuts the door behind him as Bryn plops down in an armchair. A plume of dust billows up around her. Gabby wrinkles her nose at the remaining seating in the small living room and opts to stand. Caleb settles his back against the door, watching and waiting.

"Tell me what you know." Gabby's attention swings to Bryn, who shifts on the squeaky cushion.

"Potentials have found that it was Arielle's touching of the obsidian that broke the vampire's spell." Bryn flicks a glance to Caleb. "And part of the obsidian's powers were siphoned off by a mysterious organization."

Gabby lifts a delicate eyebrow. "An organization? Who?"

"We're not sure," says Caleb. "And they're refusing to show themselves."

Bryn casts an annoyed glare at him for interrupting. "These people are using darkness to influence events in the world, creating chaos that could have the potential to spiral into wars."

"War." Gabby clicks her tongue and props a hand on her hip, lips downturned. "We can't have that. You don't know what this organization is up to, aside from attempting to cause mayhem? What are their reasons?"

"We're not sure yet." Bryn leans to one side, then the other. Finally, she sighs sharply and stands. "Awful chair. This organization is up to something, but we don't yet know what. All we know is the darkness of the obsidian is being wielded, and if it continues, ancient monsters and legends will start waking up, and we all know those beings should stay long buried."

Gabby paces, muttering. "Monsters. Legends. Demons. All manner of vile and destructive forces will spin back into existence. We're strong, but I'm not certain we have the numbers to hold back such a tidal wave of darkness."

Caleb eyes Gabby as she walks back and forth across the small space. The wind outside blusters against the house, making the cracks in the window panes whistle. It sounds like screams to Caleb, and it makes him think of the captives hollering for help in the Master's stronghold.

The Master's plans are maniacal, and Caleb's beginning to wonder if he's being influenced by this same darkness as Felix. Both of them are diving head first off the deep end. How many more will be lured into the chaos festering in the earth?

"We know the source of the darkness must be coming from the obsidian," Caleb says. "But is there any way the obsidian can be stopped? If we can halt the obsidian, we can keep the darkness from spreading further."

Gabby stops pacing and sighs. "Don't you understand? The obsidian's powers come from the energy of the Creation itself. It was powerful from the very start." She opens her mouth to speak, but pauses at a crinkling sound.

Bryn has taken a piece of hard candy out of her pocket and pops it in her mouth. She balls up the wrapper and flicks it into a corner. Both Gabby and Caleb are staring at her.

"Sorry," Bryn says. "I literally haven't eaten anything all day."

Caleb's lips quirk as he catches the sound of Bryn's snarling stomach.

"Anyway." Gabby draws out the word with a flicker of annoyance on her face. "Back when the world was young, Lucifer created a bright white light, which ultimately became the Grail. Michael, in turn, created a darkness. Uriel siphoned the darkness and placed it in a dark stone, then broke it into seven pieces."

Beside the dusty chair, Bryn nods. As a Potential in the Grail Keepers, she is well-versed in such mythology and legends.

Caleb props a heel against the door at his back, then crosses his arms, trying to ignore the sound of the candy clacking against Bryn's teeth. "So, this dark stone was the obsidian. If it was broken, how is it now a problem?"

"You really should brush up on your history, Caleb." Bryn shares an exasperated look with Gabby.

The angelic woman jerks her head to fling back some of her blonde curls, then lifts her chin. "I rebuilt the stone."

Caleb adopts a flat tone. "You rebuilt the stone, which is capable of wreaking such darkness? Ah, why?"

"It was the only way I could stop Michael. In order to trap him in an alternate dimension, I had no choice but to rebuild the stone and use its energy to create another dimension and trap him inside of it. I then buried it deep in a crypt."

Caleb stares at Gabby with even more suspicion than he'd felt when his eyes first fell on her. She's a dangerous powerhouse wrapped up in a pretty little package. Gabby is a friend of Maddy's, however, and he has to trust this woman.

"Then how is the darkness leaking into this world," Caleb asks.

"Arielle," Gabby says. "She brought the stone back to Earth and it might be how some of the obsidian's powers separated from the original stone."

Caleb doesn't know who Arielle is, but it doesn't matter. The current situation does. "Okay, so how do we defeat this darkness? Find the obsidian and destroy it once and for all?"

Gabby walks over to one of the windows and peers out into the night. Rain begins to fall, peppering against the tin roof of the porch with hollow clinks. "No. Unfortunately, the darkness is a primordial force. We cannot destroy it altogether."

"Great." Caleb lets his head fall back against the door. "So, you're saying that we and the rest of the world are pretty much screwed, then?"

"That's not what I said." Gabby still stares out into the dark night, as if she were waiting for an answer. Finally, she turns to face Caleb. "If we can find this darkness, I can divide it and bury it once more. It will be dangerous and more difficult than you can imagine, but it's our only option."

Caleb looks to Bryn for an opinion, but she merely shrugs a shoulder. The phone in Caleb's pocket vibrates. He takes it out and glances at it to find an incoming call from Cora. Unwilling to give her an explanation right now, he decides to ignore the call and puts it back in his pocket.

"I'm going to work on finding out who could possibly be behind all of this." Gabby glares at Caleb. "May I have a word with you in private?" Before waiting for an answer, she turns and walks through a doorway leading into the kitchen.

Caleb follows her inside. The kitchen is just as derelict as the living room, with a cracked bench and cabinet doors hanging on their hinges. His nose wrinkles at the musty smells clinging to the place. Gabby closes the space between them and drops her voice.

"I need you back in Creed. I've been receiving some disturbing reports regarding the disappearances. They are not merely falling victim to young and hungry vampires. Kenna was my friend, and if you want to honor her, then you will ensure that whatever your kind are planning doesn't happen."

It's a tall order. For Caleb to stop the plans from unfolding, he would need to take down not only the Master, but all of his loyal followers, as well. He thinks of the captives, screaming and drenched in fear.

"I promise I'll do what I can." Caleb's phone begins to buzz again, but this time he leaves it in his pocket. After he leaves this place, he'll give Cora a call and end things. It wasn't fair to her to keep her hopes up any longer. He hates himself for it, but he got what he needed out of her.

Gabby nods. "See that you do." She pauses, dropping her gaze to Caleb's pocket as it lets out a solitary buzz. "Popular guy, aren't you? I'm going to speak with Bryn and see if we can join together in the search." Her eyebrows lower. "And you need to make sure you keep Maddy safe. She's a special girl, and my earlier threat isn't to be taken lightly."

Gabby stalks back to the living room and Caleb yanks his phone out of his pocket, hissing through his teeth in irritation. He swipes his thumb across the screen and opens the text from Cora. His breath catches as he reads.

Caleb, it's Maddy. I need you to call me back. It's an emergency.

Exiting out of the messages, Caleb quickly taps the alert for the missed call from Cora's phone, calling back. What could be wrong? Has Felix found her? His fingers clench the phone tightly. After one ring, Maddy answers.

"Caleb?"

"Yeah, it's me. What is it? Are you okay?"

"No. I need you." Maddy's voice shakes on the other end and her breath hitches as she gathers herself. "I need you to meet me outside Cora's house. She's been taken by vampires."

"I'm on my way."

Caleb is already moving past the two women in the living room, and without an explanation, he dashes out of the door and tears into the night.

CHAPTER 27

MADELEINE

Maddy doesn't hear anything but suddenly, a presence is behind her. She whirls, fingers tight around a stake. Caleb stares down at her, his hand clenched around her wrist. He looks pointedly down at the tapered wood an inch from his chest.

"Nice reaction time, but how about you not slay the help, hm?"

Maddy jerks her arm free and shoves the stake back in the holster. "What have you done with Cora?"

Caleb doesn't answer. He reaches toward Maddy as if he wants to touch her face and she can swear there's a touch of concern in his eyes. For a brief moment, she sees the man who had saved her from the wrathful hunters. Then, she thinks of Cora and the hurt he caused. She takes a step back.

With a sigh, Caleb drops his hand. "I didn't take Cora. You know that, or you wouldn't have used her phone to call me. Besides, I've been in Mercy City. I have an alibi, if you'd like to speak with her."

Maddy's eyes narrow and her jaw works as she chews on a retort. It shouldn't bother her one bit to hear he was off in

Mercy City with some other woman, but for some reason, it does. "Well, then, it was your group of vampires who abducted her. Where is she?"

"Keep your voice down." Caleb glances around the dark street. Cora's house still has a few lights on and none of the neighbors seem to notice the couple standing outside. "What about her mom?"

"She'll be fine. She was bitten but her heartbeats are strong. I think she just passed out from the shock." Maddy crosses her arms. "Are you going to tell me what happened? I know you had something to do with this. Is this your way of getting me to join your vampires or something?"

Caleb holds a finger up to his lips but Maddy is having none of it.

"Stop telling me to be quiet. Everyone is either asleep or doesn't care."

Caleb bears his teeth and the sight of his fangs makes Maddy's heart jolt. In the next instant, he's whirling around with a snarl tearing up his chest. A man leaps out of the shadows, sidesteps around Caleb's swipe, and collides into Maddy. Her back hits the pavement and the air whooshes out of her lungs as he lands on top of her. She groans and tries to wiggle out from underneath the stranger.

"Devon?" Caleb watches the man kneeling atop of Maddy.

Cold trickles through Maddy's veins when she realizes the man astride her is a vampire. He looks over at Caleb. "You were taking too long. He wants her dead. You were given orders, Caleb."

He wants her dead. Maddy peers at Caleb with wide eyes and betrayal stings her heart anew. All this time he had been trying to get a hold of her to kill her? Why save her from the hunters, then?

The two men stare at each other for a moment, and when

the vampire, Devon, looks back at Maddy with a growing grin, Maddy sees Caleb stare pointedly at her thigh. Her stake is there in the holster. Her breath quickens and she puts on a show of struggling beneath the man, who does nothing more than chuckle at her feeble attempt of escape.

Maddy's fingers close around the stake and when she tilts to the side like she's trying to throw the vampire off, she draws it out. Caleb is suddenly behind the vampire and he grabs his shoulders and pulls him back into a more upright position. She curls up and shoves the stake into the vampire's chest. Ash erupts in the air.

Maddy coughs and scoots backwards. "That is so gross." She climbs to her feet, wiping the speckles of gray from her jacket. Her gaze swings to Caleb. "Why did you do that?"

Caleb peers down at the ash, then turns his palms over and stares at them blankly. "I let you kill him. He was in my group. Morgan must have sent him." He shakes his head. "I can't deal with this right now." He stalks forward and grabs Maddy's arm. "We need to get out of here."

"Let go of me." Caleb releases her and Maddy glowers. "I'm not going anywhere until you tell me what is going on. Was he the one who took Cora?"

Caleb shakes his head. "It isn't safe out here. They could be watching the house. And before you ask, no you can't go home right now, either. Your mom is a hunter. She'll be fine. They want you. Please, let's just go somewhere so we can talk."

Maddy bites her lip, deliberating. If there was one vampire stalking in the shadows, there could be more. As much as she hates to admit it, Caleb's right. Plus, he just helped her. "Fine. There's a gas station around the corner with a twenty-four-hour diner attached. We can go there." She stalks off down the street.

A few seconds later, Caleb hurries to her side. "Hey, are you okay?" His voice is quieter, softer. "I mean, did he hurt you? That was a pretty hard hit."

Maddy's chest feels like it's been hit with a hammer and she knows she has bruises forming on the back of her shoulders. "I'm fine." She peeks at Caleb from the corner of her eye. He stares at the road as they walk, with his hands shoved in his pockets and his lips pressed into a hard line. He's clearly upset and she wants to ask if the vampire she'd staked was a friend of his, but she stays silent.

The warm air of the diner carries the scent of coffee and fried food. Maddy heads toward a booth in the corner and slides in. Caleb takes the seat across from her. A waitress comes over and sets down a pair of laminated menus.

"Anything to drink?" she asks.

Maddy doesn't bother looking at the menu. "I'll take a coffee, please." Her stomach is rolling too much from nerves to even attempt to eat anything.

"Sure thing, hon." The waitress looks at Caleb but he just shakes his head. "I'll be right back."

As soon as the waitress walks away, Maddy leans forward. "Spill."

Caleb runs a hand through his hair. "I don't know why Devon was there, unless he was looking for you, and I don't know if it was him and the others I know who took Cora but I know the Master is likely behind it."

The shock hitches Maddy's breath. The vampire Master is powerful and someone to be feared. "Why would the Master want Cora? Is it because of me?"

"Possibly." Caleb pauses as the waitress walks past. His voice drops even lower. "But it's more than that. The Master is behind the kidnappings. He wants to...he wants to use humans as nothing more than a food source for vampires. You know, keep them captive and use them whenever he or any other vampire likes. His lunacy is spreading, and he plans on taking over the world with his crazy idea. He's as extreme as Felix. There are enough vampires out there who will support him, too, if he isn't stopped."

Maddy feels like she's going to be sick. Cora was possibly being held captive as nothing more than a food source?

"Hey." Caleb reaches across the table and grabs Maddy's hand. The gesture surprises her and she finds herself squeezing his fingers back. "Maddy, I promise you we will rescue Cora." His thumb feathers across her skin for a moment before he releases her as the waitress returns with her coffee. For a brief second, Maddy wonders if Caleb would've kept holding her hand. Then she wonders if she would've held on even tighter.

She lets out a shaky breath and grabs three packets of sugar. She tears them open and dumps them into her coffee. She adds two tiny cups of creamer next, then stirs it. The coffee is still piping hot and burns her tongue, but she takes a few sips regardless. It settles like acid in her stomach.

She looks back up at Caleb. He's watching her with an expression she can't quite place. It's something between pity and determination. "I know where the prisoners are being held, but we have to be careful."

Maddy's head jerks up. "You know where they are?" Her hands squeeze the cup. "We can just storm the place and get Cora back."

Caleb sits back against the booth with a hard laugh. "You, me, and what army?"

Maddy's shoulders slump. Without support from the Order, Maddy's alone. Her mom might help, but even then, can the three of them go up against who knows how many vampires? There's no guarantee Caleb will continue to fight against his own kind, either. Maddy has a suspicion he only let her kill Devon to save her life.

"We have to do something," Maddy says. She'll never forgive herself if something happens to Cora. She's only in this mess because of her.

"There is a way to help." Caleb leans forward, resting his arms on the table. "You can learn how to tap into your own powers."

Maddy chokes on her sip of coffee. Coughing, she wipes her hand across her mouth. "What? I have no powers."

"You do." Caleb peers around but there's no one near enough to hear their quiet conversation. "Dracula's line possesses a gift. When Kenna slayed the King, those gifts passed onto you, Maddy."

Several seconds of silence pass. She taps the side of the cup. "No. I don't want any sort of power or gift from that legacy."

"Not everything supernatural is a bad thing." Caleb reaches out again and rests a hand on Maddy's forearm. "You could save Cora, and the rest of them. Just think about it, okay?"

Maddy looks from Caleb's face to his hand on her arm. Part of her wants to grab his hand and feel the warmth and comfort of his grasp. "Fine. But there has to be another way." Surely not everything comes down to her unknown, untapped powers.

Caleb sighs. "We don't have a lot of time. The Master said something about sacrifices, but for that, he needs the Chalice of Solomon." His hand slides from Maddy's arm as he straightens. "Felix has it. I think the Chalice is our one chance at controlling the vampires. If we get it, we can use it to free Cora and the others, even without your powers."

Maddy nods slowly. She'd seen Felix with the silver chalice a couple of times, and had only guessed at what it could do. "I have no idea where Felix is. He's too smart to go back to one of the Order safehouses. He could have fled town for all we know."

Caleb folds his arms and stares out of the window beside

him. "I wouldn't worry about that. We need to be ready, because I guarantee we haven't seen the last of Felix."

Maddy watches his pensive, handsome face. There are layers to his words, she can feel it. Just like she knows without a doubt he's telling the truth.

This is more than just Felix's hatred for vampires.

His grudge with Caleb is personal.

CHAPTER 28

MADELEINE

Maddy zips up her jacket, the taste of coffee still on her tongue. Before she heads outside, she leaves the area dedicated to the diner and heads toward the counter of the gas station. After a moment of deliberation, she picks a pack of soft, chocolate covered mint candy. She doesn't turn to see if Caleb is waiting for her. His stare is settled on her like a cloak. Only after paying for the candy does she meet his gaze.

"Ready?" Maddy says. She isn't entirely sure what they should be ready for. Until they find Felix, they can't move forward with their plans to stop the Master, and save Cora and the others. The only reason Maddy isn't going in, guns blazing, right now is because Caleb managed to convince her that the Master would do nothing with the humans until he had the Chalice in his grasp.

The two head outside and into the night. Maddy shivers as she unwraps the small bag of candy.

"My car isn't too far from here." Caleb pauses. "It will be warmer in there."

Maddy peers down the street that would lead her home, but home isn't where she wants to go right now. Her mom isn't waiting up for her, assuming she's with Cora. She knows Cora's mom will wake, soon, however, and call the police and probably Maddy or her mom. Being home would be best...

Yet she turns to follow Caleb, her body deciding long before her mind.

True to his word, Caleb's car is only a block away. He opens the door for Maddy, then rounds the front and climbs in. It purrs to life and he immediately starts pushing buttons and turning knobs to get the heater going. Warmth spreads under Maddy's legs.

"I've always wanted a car that had seat warmers." She pops a piece of minty chocolate into her mouth, chasing away her coffee breath even though she really shouldn't care.

"Anytime you need a ride, all you have to do is call me."

Caleb's statement makes Maddy's heart pick up pace. It sounded as if he plans on sticking around. She also realizes she doesn't have his number, which is why she called him on Cora's phone. "I don't have your number."

"I have yours." Caleb had the grace to look chagrined. "I got it off Cora's phone. I'll text you later so you have it."

Maddy wants to be angry that he'd taken the liberty of searching through Cora's contacts, but that feeling seems to be fading fast. Sure, she's cautious, but also curious.

"You know about my bloodline." The plastic bag crinkles in her hand as she digs out another piece of candy. "How?"

"A witch told me, but I already knew you were special, Maddy." Caleb's leather jacket creaks as he turns in his seat. "I knew it from the moment you barreled into me outside the café."

Maddy rolls her eyes. "I bumped into you, I didn't barrel." She chews the chocolate up, then stuffs the rest of the package in her pocket. "What do you know about my legacy?"

"Not much other than what I've already told you. You are

the descendant of Dracula. The last one, or you wouldn't have gained his power. Which, by the way, I still think you should learn how to use."

Learning how to use some kind of ancient vampire magic forms a knot of unease in Maddy's stomach. Moving away from the subject, she asks another question. "You mentioned that Felix wasn't part of the true Order. What did you mean? I thought his group of hunters *are* the Order?"

Caleb leans closer to Maddy. "After Kenna's death at the hands of vampires and demons, a schism formed in the Order. While most of the members stayed with a man named Marlowe, others sided with Felix."

Maddy wishes she knew more about the Order's history, but now that she thinks about it, Felix never seemed inclined to reveal much to her. She'd always put it off as him being busy or wanting her to focus on physical training. No wonder he wanted to hide it, since he was involved in essentially breaking up the true Order.

"Something is bothering you." Caleb doesn't ask, but simply states, watching her closely.

Narrowing her eyes, Maddy says, "Are you...are you smelling my emotions? I was told vampires can do that."

A crooked grin lifts his cheek. "We can, and I am. We can sense so much more, too." His gaze drops to her chest, then back to her face. "Am I making you nervous? Your heart is racing."

Maddy swallows. Is Caleb making her nervous? She studies him, realizing they've both leaned closer to each other. The space between them is tense and electric. This isn't right. Maddy's supposed to be angry at him. She's supposed to hate him. Caleb is a vampire. He bit her. No matter how hard she tries, however, she just can't see him as the enemy.

"I just wish I knew more." Slowly, Maddy leans away.

"About the supernatural world, and our history. I followed Felix blindly without a question as to the why or when or how things got this way."

A flash of anger sparks in Caleb's eyes, though it isn't directed at Maddy. "It was his duty as the leader to inform you of such things. Instead, he's been building an army of blind hunters who do nothing more than follow orders." A sharp sigh blows through his nostrils. "He's only growing worse. Some kind of mysterious organization has lapped Felix up and has influenced him with the obsidian's darkness, making him more hateful than he'd already been. Perhaps that hate is why he succumbed so quickly."

Maddy peers out into the night, watching a car turn a corner in the distance. "Do you want to destroy Felix, or the whole Order?"

Caleb grabs Maddy's shoulder, drawing her attention back to him. She notices a wrinkle of concern between his eyebrows. "I don't want to destroy the Order, Maddy. I have nothing against the members, especially given that I once trained to be a part of it."

Maddy's head jerks back. "What?" She blinks and studies the man beside her. There's no doubt he's a vampire. She'd felt his fangs. Back in that room at the party, she'd *seen* his fangs as he'd snarled at the hunters. If Felix had cast her away simply for being descended from a vampire, there is no possible way any part of the Order would have accepted Caleb. "But...how? You're a vampire."

A hard smile presses on Caleb's lips. "Do you think I was born this way?" The smile softens as sadness creeps into his features. "I'm Kenna's nephew."

"Wow," Maddy breathes. She isn't the only one with a legacy, it seems.

"Yeah. She raised me, you know. My dad died and my mom

didn't cope. Kenna also trained me to become a part of the Order."

Maddy found herself leaning closer to Caleb again, drawn in by his story. "If you were supposed to be a part of the Order, then how are you..."

"A monster?" Caleb's voice bites sharply in the quiet car.

"I don't think you're a monster." God, Maddy should. She should condemn him for likely killing humans, and definitely for killing the hunters, but any fault she'd found in him is quickly breaking away.

Caleb watches her for a moment, as if he's trying to detect a lie. "I was turned in retaliation for Kenna killing the Vampire Masters and the King."

Maddy reaches out and takes Caleb's hand, squeezing his fingers before she has time to realize what she's doing. "That's awful. I'm so sorry."

"After Kenna's death, even though I was turned, I'd planned to retaliate against the vampires and created a group to stage a coup but Felix killed all of them and I lost my chance."

Realization dawns on Maddy. "That's why you hate him."

"One of the reasons." Caleb scoffs. "The guy always was a bit of a prick, to be honest."

Maddy falls silent and stares at her hand holding Caleb's. He'd wrapped his fingers around hers as well, and now neither of them seem willing to let go.

"Now I'm a vampire and I have no choice but to obey the Master."

Maddy peers up at Caleb to find his jawline hard and could swear she hears him grinding his teeth. "You don't have to follow the Master. You can still strike against him. Once he's gone, you'll be free of his hold for good."

Caleb gives her a small smile. "I wish it were that easy. The only way I can see that happening is if we get our hands on the Chalice of Solomon."

Maddy wants the Chalice so she has a chance to save Cora and the other humans. Now, it seems, she has another person to save, as well. "We can do it. We'll find Felix and get the Chalice."

"We?" Caleb glances down at their interlocked fingers, then back up at her.

Maddy nods, and smiles. "You know, it's kind of funny. You were raised as a hunter, but became a vampire, and I was supposed to be a hunter, but am descended from Dracula. We're both off track."

He angles his head, the shadows caressing the strong lines of his face. He looks dangerous...yet sexy. "Or we're both on the right track."

The space between them grows smaller, and Maddy breathes in the leather-and-sandalwood scent that is Caleb. His blue eyes are fixed on hers and her pulse quickens. Her stare flicks to his lips and she licks her own, wondering what it would be like to kiss him. Startled by the thought, she withdraws her hand from his but Caleb catches her wrist. Slowly, he presses her palm to his chest and she can feel the heat of his body through his shirt.

"I'm glad you don't think I'm a monster." Caleb reaches up with his other hand and gently hooks his fingers behind her neck. His thumb brushes just below her ear, drawing goosebumps across her skin.

Caleb's intention is plain. Maddy knows he can likely smell her attraction to him, and the growing need to be closer to him pulsing in her veins with each rapid beat of her heart. He waits, however, giving her time to withdraw.

The last shreds of doubt Maddy had clung to fall away.

Though his actions may have been faulty, the intentions behind them were true. He saved her. He's been trying to save her.

Maddy closes the space between them, and Caleb's mouth is suddenly on hers. He doesn't claim her roughly, instead his movements, his mouth, are soft and gentle. Achingly sweet. He's still uncertain.

And yet, she's never been more sure.

Maddy's fingers curl into his shirt, holding him there in case doubt makes him want to back away. His mouth moves on hers, becoming her new center of focus. So hot. So spellbinding. So freaking delicious. Her neck and chest heats, butterflies wing in her stomach, and her pulse hammers in her ears. She's never been so affected by just one kiss.

Caleb's breath catches and they break apart. For a split second, Maddy feels his thumb press a fraction harder on her neck, feeling her pulse...and the blood pumping there.

She stills, unsure at the feelings the knowledge sparks. She's not scared. She should be, but she's not. In fact, the passion spikes even more.

"I won't hurt you, Maddy," Caleb promises softly.

Maddy nods. "I know you won't." She draws him closer again, claiming his mouth in another kiss.

This one far longer and deeper.

CHAPTER 29

CALEB

The taste of Maddy's kiss lingers on Caleb's tongue as she sits back against her seat. He's full of her scent, the attraction, the pleasure, the need...and her blood pumping below her delicate skin. His throat burns with the desire to taste that sweet nectar again, but he shoves the instinct to bite down. A flush brightens Maddy's cheeks and she gives Caleb a shy smile. It's the most adorable thing he's ever seen. He swallows. In a sexy kind of way.

It only reinforces the importance of taking Felix's slimy existence out of the equation.

"I want to take you somewhere." Immediately, Maddy's eyes widen and Caleb realizes his mistake. After their kisses, she's jumped to the wrong conclusion. He hurries to elaborate. "It's about Felix."

"Oh." Her lashes flutter and he's not entirely sure what that means. Is she relieved? Or disappointed? "What about him?"

"I have no idea where to find him, but I know he'll have gone underground. As far as we know, most of his hunters in this area are dead so he's a target. Felix will be hiding and it won't be easy to find him."

Maddy's head falls back to the seat. "And without Felix, we can't get the Chalice. Without the Chalice, we won't be able to stop the Master and save Cora. So, what do we do?"

"Do you trust me, Maddy?" Caleb's voice is quiet and he waits to scent a lie.

"I do." There's nothing but truth and determination in her beautiful face.

Caleb smiles. "Good. I want to take you to Galina, the witch. She's the one who revealed your bloodline to me." He hasn't yet told Maddy about the prophecy from the seer. She'd gone through so much just in the past twenty-four hours. Telling her she is destined to bring peace between the hunters and the immortals could be a bit of a stretch on her sanity at the moment. "Felix won't be found by normal means. It could take months to track him down and we don't have that kind of time. A witch, however, might be able to find him in other ways."

Maddy is silent for so long, Caleb is certain she'll refuse. "I've never met a witch," she says with a shrug. Then she smiles, her mocha eyes twinkling with the spark that drew him in from the first moment they met. "I guess it could be a learning experience."

"She lives outside of Creed a little way, but it won't take too long." Caleb shifts his car into drive and pulls away from the curb.

The ride is silent, and while Caleb wants to talk with the beautiful woman he kissed minutes earlier seeing as they've gone and complicated things—not that he can bring himself to regret it—but he lets Maddy have her peace and quiet. No doubt she has much on her mind. She perks up a bit as Caleb pulls up to the house he'd visited only days before. Maddy climbs out of the car and waits for Caleb before the two head up the gravel path to the witch's home.

Caleb lifts a hand to knock but the front door swings open

before his knuckles hit the wood. Galina stares at him, her hair in a loose braid and her gaze impatient.

"You again," she states. Her eyes flicker over to Maddy. "I've already told you what I know about the girl."

Beside Caleb, Maddy bristles, no doubt at being referred to as "girl" as if she's not really here. "We're not here to talk about me. Caleb has a favor to ask you."

The witch swings her door open wider with a sigh. "Very well."

Caleb gestures Maddy inside then closes the door behind them. Galina settles down on her chair. A silver and gray cat lounges on the back, eyeing the newcomers sleepily and flicking her tail once.

"Sit." Galina points to the small couch across from her.

Maddy sinks onto one of the creaky cushions, her thigh brushing up against Caleb's. He hides a smile, realizing perhaps Maddy is not so blasé about seeing a witch as she appears.

Galina's cat stretches, then crawls down into her lap. The witch begins to run her fingers through his long hair. "What is it you need?"

"A locator spell," Caleb says. "I have a wayward hunter I need to find."

"Felix, I presume?" Galina lifts an eyebrow. Caleb nods and the witch grows quiet. After several beats of silence, she speaks. "I can do it, but I will require you to do something in return for my services."

Maddy stiffens beside him and gives him an uneasy look. Caleb presses his lips together and turns to the witch. "This doesn't involve Maddy," he states flatly.

"I need nothing from her." Galina's fingers scratch behind the cat's left ear. "Only from you, vampire."

Caleb considers her words carefully. Making a deal with a witch is a binding contract. Once he agrees, he will be hard pressed to refuse. Many witches speak an oath so heavy, only death would free him. "What is it you'll require from me?"

Galina's cat hops down onto the floor as the witch leans forward. "In return for finding Felix for you, I would have you make an unbreakable pact. I need help getting information about a young boy named Alex." She points at a portrait on the wall between a set of hanging plants. It's of a boy in a nice shirt and a small smile on his face. A locket hangs on his chest, a pentagram etched on the surface. It's a strange portrait for a witch to have in her home, and the necklace was even stranger on the boy. Caleb wonders if he's perhaps a warlock. They are rare, but not completely unheard of in the supernatural world. The boy doesn't seem to be a relation to Galina, though he could be.

"What happened to him?" Maddy is staring at the portrait of Alex, as well. Then, she glances down to find the witch's cat rubbing against her shins. She smiles, reaches down, and lifts the animal into her lap. The cat begins purring loudly, butting her head against Maddy's palm.

"He was taken by vampires." Galina, too, peers at the portrait. A slight frown pulled down at the corners of her mouth. "I have tried to find him, but he seems to have been blocked from any spell reaching him."

Maddy pauses stroking the cat. "I'm sorry. Is he your brother?"

"No." Galina sighs and settles back against her chair. "I believe Alex was the very first boy who was abducted."

Caleb pinches his chin and stares at the witch, noting she didn't answer exactly who this young boy is, but also knowing Galina won't tell him if she doesn't want to. "What makes you think I can find him?"

"Do not play daft with me, vampire. I know you serve the Master, in one way or another. You can get close to him."

Maddy and him share a look, the cat leaping from her lap as if it wants no part in this decision. Then Caleb nods. "All right." Locating Felix is their priority, no matter what. "I'll find Alex for you."

The witch grabs a small box from a table beside her and flips open the lid. There's a small, slender knife inside. She takes the dagger then grabs a small glass jar of dried leaves. Galina uncorks the top and Caleb wrinkles his nose at the pungent smell. He watches as the witch takes a pinch of the leaves and sets them in a shallow bowl. Next, she lights the leaves on fire with a flick of a match.

Galina takes the knife and holds her hand out for Caleb's. "Quickly, before the flames burn out."

Caleb gives the witch his hand and with a sharp nick, she draws blood from his finger tip with the blade. Then, she does the same with her own. Beside him, Maddy leans forward, watching with rapt attention as the witch mutters strange words, squeezing her blood and Caleb's over the burning leaves.

A shiver shakes through Caleb as the pact sinks into his bones.

"It is done," Galina says. She wraps a small bandage around her finger and offers one to Caleb, but he shakes his head.

The witch stands and walks over to a set of shelves on the far wall. She searches for a minute, then grabs a small, black velvet bag. After returning to her chair, she scoots the bowl over she used to bind the pact. The leaves are burned, but the smoke and scent still linger in the air.

Galina loosens the drawstrings on the bag. "The answer will be clearer if you both steer your thoughts to finding Felix." She closes her eyes and upends the bag.

A collection of small animal bones tumble across the surface of the table. Caleb hears Maddy swallow, but other than that, she shows no reaction. Galina leans down, peering at the bones with a wrinkle of concentration etched in her forehead. Her hand hovers over the display for a few minutes as she mutters to herself.

Finally, she straightens. "Felix is in an abandoned building off the highway that connects Creed to Mercy City." The witch's cat peeks over the edge of the table and attempts to paw at what appears to be a miniscule femur bone. Galina quickly scoops up the pile. "I believe it is his new headquarters for the Order he is rebuilding."

Caleb stands and Maddy follows. "Thank you, Galina. I will find Alex for you. We really appreciate your help."

Galina opens her mouth, but whatever she was going to say, she seems to change her mind. Instead, she gives a single nod and turns her attention to the cat.

"That was...different." Maddy peers at the house over her shoulder as they walk back to the car.

Caleb lets out a chuckle. "Dealings with witches are always interesting."

"You deal with witches often?" Maddy asks, watching Caleb over the top of his car.

"No, thank God." Caleb and Maddy climb into the car. "The less I have to deal with a witch, the better."

Maddy fastens her seatbelt. "What are we going to do now?"

"First, I'm going to take you back home."

"What?" Maddy twists in her seat. "I can't go back home. We have to work on finding Felix and saving Cora." Her voice rises, panic ringing through.

Caleb pulls out onto the road and speeds from the witch's house. "I know, and we will, but you can't keep going like this forever. I don't grow tired easily. You do." Her anger stings his nostrils. "And I need you to speak to your mother. Ask her about

Alex for me. She was investigating the disappearances, right? Maybe she knows something. I'll look into it, as well, but we need to try to cover as much ground as we can."

"What are you going to do?"

The steering wheel creaks as Caleb's fingers tightened over it. "I'm going to take care of Felix and get the Chalice."

CHAPTER 30

CALEB

The phone buzzes in Caleb's pocket as he waits beside the deserted road and he sees Morgan's name on the screen. He quickly swipes his thumb across the surface. "Hey." His tone is short. He'd tried to contact Morgan over three hours ago and never got a reply.

"Sorry, man. The Master has me busy. I got your message and sent some of the guys to meet up with you, but I can't get away right now. They should be there shortly. Any luck with the girl?"

Caleb opens his mouth to reply, but hesitates. Morgan said he was doing something for the Master, and it isn't something Caleb's aware of. Something about that makes him suspicious. And right now, Maddy's at home, out of harm's way. He's going to keep it that way. "No, not really. I'm putting more focus on finding the Chalice."

"How's that going?"

"We'll see, I guess." Caleb leans against the side of his car. "You sure you can't get away? I could really use you." Whatever Morgan is doing for the Master, it can't be good. Why is he being so secretive? Worry prickles through him. He likes

Morgan, and respects him. He's a good friend, a good fighter, and is loyal. Perhaps too loyal. Caleb isn't certain what the future holds, but he doesn't want Morgan too wrapped up in the Master's favor.

Morgan falls quiet on the other end for a moment. "I can't. Sorry, Caleb. The others are on their way, though. I sent the best fighters."

"No problem. You be careful." Caleb spots a car approaching in the distance and recognizes it as one of the members of their usual crew. "Looks like they're here."

"Good," Morgan says. "I'll talk to you later."

Caleb ends the call and the other members step out of their car. They line up in front of him, waiting. "All right, here's the deal. I found a location outside of Creed where Felix seems to have holed up. To my knowledge, he's alone, but likely has plans to bring in other members of the Order so we need to act quickly. Our main goal is to retrieve the Chalice. Our Master wants it for sacrifices. If you find it, bring it to me immediately."

The other vampires nod, talking about how easy it will be to take Felix down without his hunters there to protect him. Caleb climbs back into his car and hopes they're right. Although, what to do after he gets the Chalice is the real concern. He can't turn it into the Master, but the others will raise the vampire leader's suspicions if they notice Caleb holding onto the magical object without turning it in. He speeds away toward the end of town, the other vehicle tailing him. He'll face that problem when he gets to it.

Caleb drives a few miles, then pulls over. The others climb out of their vehicle. "We'll go on foot from here," he tells them. "He's in an abandoned building about a mile up the road."

He'd already checked out satellite images on his phone and had found what appeared to be a large, abandoned house off the highway. Eagerness ripples over the others and the same electric energy laces Caleb's muscles, as well. There was just something about a hunt, especially with such a target as Felix, that makes him feel more alive.

Leading the way, Caleb jogs a distance off the road and then breaks into a run. His steps eat up the ground in a blur and in mere minutes, he stops. The others gather around and the group stare at the house. A single light shines inside. Caleb watches a moment, but doesn't see a flicker of movement. Perhaps Felix is sleeping. He gestures toward the house, and the team of five break up and rush off in different directions. Caleb runs right for the front door. The moment he hears glass pop in the back, he shoves it open.

His gaze sweeps left and right as he walks in. The light is coming from a single lantern in the living room. The flame is low and he can smell the oil burning along the fat wick. He can hear the subtle steps of his fellow vampires, but doesn't catch the breath or heartbeat of Felix. His eyes narrow, noticing the complete lack of evidence that there is anyone here. There are no discarded shoes on the floor or coat hanging by the door. Caleb can't even pick up the lingering scent of the despicable man anywhere as he walks into the living room.

Felix may have been here, but he isn't any longer.

"Damn," Caleb growls under his breath. He walks farther into the living room. Another lantern sits on a table beside a dusty couch. He lays a finger on the glass globe. Humans wouldn't feel the miniscule warmth, but Caleb can sense it lingering on the glass. Papers are scattered on a table in the corner, a few of them having fallen to the floor. A single, leather glove sticks out of the cushion in a chair near a fireplace with dying embers.

Felix left in a hurry, and judging by the lantern, it hadn't been too long ago. No more than an hour, most likely. The rest of the crew come in from somewhere in the back.

"Search the house and premises," Caleb orders. "Perhaps we can find some indication where Felix has disappeared to." The team disperses and Caleb wanders over to the papers. There's nothing too extraordinary about them. Most of it is a list of weapons inventories and a few hold several people's contact information. They're no doubt people Felix is looking to recruit into the Order. Floorboards creak as Caleb leaves the living room and heads down a hall. He pushes doors open one at a time, peering into a bathroom followed by a couple of bedrooms. The second one has a crumpled blanket on the bed and a pile of discarded clothes on the floor. Felix had spent at least a few hours' rest here.

"There's nothing here," one of the others call. "I can't find anything."

Caleb blows out an irritated breath. "All right, let's go." As much as he despises the idea, he may just have to go back to Galina and trade another favor for a second location spell.

One of the team walks from the kitchen and Caleb catches a slight clinking sound. He glances down and freezes, then holds up his hand.

A trip wire.

Down the hall, another young man walks through a wire.

"Stop!" Caleb calls. "Don't move. There are trip wires." It's a miracle no one triggered any until now. Cold washes over him when he hears a rhythmic clicking. He looks up, finding tiny wires running along the edges of the walls and ceiling. Then, he finds the red, blinking lights coming from above the ceiling fan.

Bombs. The entire place is rigged to blow.

"Out!" he shouts. "Everybody out!"

Caleb reaches a window in three steps and hurls himself through it. Glass shatters and as soon as he rolls to the ground, a blast deafens him. He covers his head, shouting as the explosion propels him through the air. Pieces of debris hit his back as the heat of the fire blows over him and he lands heavily on the unforgiving ground. Frantically, he digs his fingers into the soil and crawls away. After several feet, he flips onto his back.

The entire house has been destroyed. It's barely a shell, its remains scattered in a wide circle. Flames dance high into the sky, almost jaunty in their celebration of the total destruction. Caleb listens for the shouts of the others, but aside from the crackling of fire and the groan of the settling, ruined timbers, he hears nothing.

Caleb climbs to his feet, his ears ringing as he blinks at the roaring brightness. He approaches the building with caution, calling out to the others. His eyes begin to sting in the smoke and his throat burns at the acrid smell of melting plastic and char. No one answers as he circles the entire house, face warm from the heat of the flames. They're all gone. All dead in the fire. Guilt burns in his stomach at their loss, but a small sense of relief works through his shock that Morgan hadn't been able to come with him, after all.

Caleb's phone begins to buzz in his pocket and he jogs away from the smoke and pop of burning timber before drawing it out. He looks at the screen. An unknown number is calling him and he quickly answers.

"Hello?" His voice is breathless and he swallows at the rough, dry sensation the smoke has left in his throat. There's no answer. "Listen, whoever this is, it's not the best time."

"Are you sure about that?"

Caleb's breath hitches at the familiar voice.

"Felix," he seethes.

"That's right, Caleb. I do hope you enjoyed my little surprise, though it's disappointing it didn't quite have the effect I desired. You are certainly one slippery bloodsucker."

In the background, Caleb swears he hears a muffled voice. Someone's struggling to speak and when the person finally calls out his name, horror washes over him. It's Maddy's voice. "What have you done?" His tone is low, dangerous, and drenched with the promise of pain.

"Oh, don't worry." Felix doesn't seem the least bit bothered by the threat in Caleb's voice. "The little traitor and her mother will be just fine...as long as you bring me the Master's head."

Caleb's heart sinks at the impossibility, but he says nothing.

"And Caleb? Nice try attempting to get the Chalice from me. That is one thing you will never get your hands on." Felix pauses, then clicks his tongue. "You better hurry, boy. Time is running out and my patience is growing thin. Bring me the Master's head, or Maddy's mother will be telling you of her daughter's slow, painful death."

The other end of the line goes dead and Caleb roars into the early morning sky. His mind works feverishly as he tries to come up with a plan. After a few minutes, he takes a deep breath and looks down at his phone.

He'll save Maddy.

No matter what.

Which means he has a few phone calls to make.

CHAPTER 31
MADELEINE

The bite of the handcuffs dig into Maddy's wrists as she pulls against their hold. Her teeth grind together, her face wrinkling with effort, but it's no use. They won't break, and neither will the thick metal bar they're wrapped around. Her shoulders ache from her arms being pulled back and the time spent trying to break free. She lets out a breath and straightens her legs. The concrete floor is cold, even through her jeans, and it makes her shiver.

Across from Maddy, her mother hasn't moved. Dried blood coats the right side of her head and tangles in her hair. Her chest rises evenly, however, and the sight brings Maddy a small hope.

She lets her head fall back against the hard wall and curses herself for being so careless. It wasn't as if she had been expecting an intruder in her home, much less that it would have been Felix, himself. Caleb had dropped her off and Maddy had crept quietly into the house, not wanting to wake her mother. She remembers the way her stomach had dropped when she saw the man who should have been her leader and mentor holding a knife to her mom's throat. Blood dripped onto his arm from the wound on her mom's temple, evidence she'd put up a fight.

Fearing for her mom's life, Maddy saw no other choice but to surrender. Felix had gagged and bound them, then grabbed the phone out of her pocket and made the call to Caleb. Afterwards, he covered their heads and brought them to this place, wherever it was.

Maddy peers around the dark space, again seeking some sort of clue as to where they could be, but there is nothing save concrete all around, and a single metal door to the right. Her eyes have adjusted to the lack of light and the cool, damp scent of the air reminds her of the basements she's been in before. Somewhere in the room, she can hear the quiet drops of water from a leaky pipe, but other than that and the sounds of her pulse in her ears, there's only silence.

Hours pass in quiet worry and useless struggle. Maddy's mom moans a few times, shifting slightly, but doesn't fully wake. Suddenly, the door opens, hinges creaking, and Felix steps in.

Maddy glares at him. "Let us go."

He sniffs in response and shuts the door behind him. "I think not."

"Please." Her breath shudders in. "My mom is hurt. She needs a doctor."

"Your mom is a hunter and is capable of handling such injuries. Besides, I can't very well let my insurance run free, can I?"

A light flares to life, buzzing and flickering for a moment before settling into a quiet hum. Maddy squints at the sudden brightness. Her mom stirs again.

"I haven't seen your new friend, despite my threat." Felix wanders farther into the room, the heels of his boots scuffing against the dirty concrete. "Perhaps I overestimated his fondness for you, though considering he killed several of my hunters to protect you, it's unlikely."

Maddy clenches her teeth and pulls on the handcuffs. "Leave Caleb out of this. He can't defeat the Master alone. It's suicide to ask such a thing of him."

Felix peers down at her, folds his hands behind his back, and gives her a wicked smile. "My dear, why do you think I asked such a thing of him? There is no doubt in my mind Caleb will go up against the Master in an effort to protect you, and when he does, the Master or his loyal followers will shred him to pieces. I'm hoping for two birds with one stone, to be honest."

"You..." Her heart is in her throat at the thought of losing Caleb. She shakes her head. Everything Felix has said or done regarding Caleb seems so extreme. "Why do you hate him so much?" Her words are quiet, almost to herself, but Felix hears them.

"I know who Caleb really is, girl. I know him to his marrow." Felix walks away from her, but continues to speak as he studies a spider crawling up the wall. "He is the nephew of Kenna DeVoe. Did he tell you that? He was destined to be a hunter, and was a potential member of the Order. Now he is nothing more than an abomination. If he was truly devoted to the Order, he would know that a monstrosity such as himself doesn't deserve to live on the earth." Felix smacks his hand against the wall with a sharp slap. Then, he slowly moves his hand away, revealing the spider smashed against the concrete. "Caleb has embraced his vampirism, and for that I want him dead."

Maddy's eyes flick to her mom for a moment, but she has grown still again. God, she hopes her mom will be okay.

Felix wipes his palm on his pants. "Of course, his newfound beastly nature isn't the only reason I despise him. Caleb and I used to train together, you know. We trained under Kenna, as equals. We were both capable fighters and surpassed every challenge the great Kenna DeVoe could throw at us. I was always better than he was, though. Smarter. More patient. Caleb reacted too quickly, preferring to dash headlong into problems. He would have made a good hunter, I'll admit, but he wouldn't have been an adept leader. I asked Kenna to let the legacy of the Order pass to me should she meet her end, knowing the risks she was taking and unwilling to let the Order be without authority and leadership. She refused my offer. Kenna insisted that the mantle would be passed on to Caleb, despite his shortcomings."

Maddy glares over at Felix as he continues his jealous ramblings. From what she knows of Caleb, he would have made an excellent leader in the Order.

A dark chuckle sounds from Felix. "I suppose that irritating problem solved itself, didn't it? Caleb got himself turned. But I wasn't even her plan B. Instead, she left a declaration that put Marlowe in charge instead." He shakes his head, grumbling under his breath. He finally turns to face Maddy. The fluorescent light humming on the ceiling leeches the color from Felix's face, making him seem even more cruel and cold. "What else could I do but separate from that Order and create one of my own? They were weakening, and making poor decisions. I saved our cause. Mine is the real Order. We are the ones saving humanity from monsters like Caleb. Do you hear from the other Order? No, because they are no longer adept in doing what needs to be done in this world."

Maddy scoffs and draws her legs up as Felix narrows his eyes at her. If he comes near enough, she plans on sending a sharp kick at him. She imagines how satisfying it would be to see him crash into the hard concrete. He'd surely retaliate, and she'd take it with a smile on her face. But Felix doesn't draw closer, just glares.

"What about the kidnappings?" Maddy sits up as straight as she can given her restraints. She refuses to look cowed in front of Felix. "It seems to me a fearless vampire hunter such as yourself, and his new almighty Order, would have been able to put a stop to the abductions. Your efforts have gone largely unnoticed. Your Order has failed. Even my friend, Cora, was taken."

Felix clicks his tongue. "It really is a shame about your heritage, Maddy. You have a fire inside of you. Your determination to save those people and your willingness to do what is necessary would have made you an excellent member of the Order."

"You're the one who kicked me out," says Maddy. Not only that, he tried to kill her.

He lets out a sigh and eyes her with pity. "The terrible truth cannot be ignored. Your dark lineage will always make you closed to the Order."

All respect Maddy had for Felix evaporates. She used to think he was good leader, a wise man, and a strong hunter. The man she sees before her is nothing more than a jealous, conniving, selfish person.

"Your new Order isn't the only Order in existence," Maddy says. "The true Order is still out there in the world." Maddy isn't certain if she still wants to be a hunter, but the thought that perhaps the other Order may accept her despite her bloodline gives her a small sense of hope. Although, even if they didn't take her as a hunter, she still has to try and find a way to contact them to tell them about the deranged man staring down at her.

Felix throws his head back and laughs. Behind him, Maddy's mom lifts her head for a moment before it lolls to the other side. A small mutter comes from her lips before she's silent again. "You will never be leaving here again. No rescue will be coming for you, Maddy. This place will not be so easily found and it is heavily protected with magical wards."

"Caleb will find me." Maddy lifts her chin. "You told him to bring you the Master's head."

"I won't have him meet me here, foolish girl. I doubt very much he will survive, anyway."

Maddy's throat constricts, but she refuses to let her despair crack across her face. Caleb is strong, and smart. He will find a way to bring Felix down. She glances at her mom and worry resurfaces.

"You can't just leave us down here."

Felix circles around Maddy's legs as if he senses she would like nothing more than to give him a good kick. He crouches down beside her shoulder, an excited light in his eye. "Oh, I won't leave you in the basement forever. In fact, there's a room I've been preparing for you and your mom upstairs."

Maddy's eyebrows pull together. Why would he throw them in a basement, only to end up treating them like guests? Goosebumps scatter across her skin and she shivers. Something isn't right.

"You see," Felix continues. "I have big plans for the both of you. I work for a certain organization, and they would very much like to study you both."

Unease sours in Maddy's gut and she leans away from Felix. "Study us?"

"Yes. You and your mother are both descendants of Dracula, though for whatever reason you gained his ancestral curse. The people I work for wish to see what sort of powers they can extract from you."

Extract. The way Felix said it instantly makes Maddy think of being strapped to a bed with sharp instruments made for cutting through flesh.

Felix pushes to his feet. "Try and get some rest, Maddy. Tomorrow, the real work behind my true purpose begins."

She watches him stalk out of the room and shut the door firmly behind him.

Maddy wants to scream. For a brief second, she considers whimpering.

How can she save Cora or Caleb or anyone when she can't save herself?

CHAPTER 32
MADELEINE

Maddy begins to wonder if perhaps darkness would have been better. Felix left the light on and for hours the fluorescent bulbs have hummed and sputtered, casting flickering shadows in the corners and giving Maddy a headache. Her mom woke a few hours earlier, though neither of them speak now. Too wrapped up in her own mind, Maddy sits with her head against the concrete in silence.

Caleb has saturated her thoughts. If she doesn't try and get out, she knows he'll likely do something reckless. It seems absurd that the man would risk his life to save her when they hardly know each other. Not long ago, they'd barely even tolerated each other, but something had changed. Maddy's attracted to him physically, sure, but despite Caleb's vampirism, she knows he's a good guy who deserves a second chance. After all, he hadn't signed up to become a vampire. He'd been forced to become what he is now, and as far as she's seen, he's still determined to do what's right in this world. A few of his methods are skewed, like the crap he'd pulled with Cora, but deep down, Maddy has no doubts he will do the right thing.

Unfortunately, the right thing in this situation means Caleb going up against the Master. Maddy doesn't know much about the leader of the vampires, but if he's in that position, he isn't a decent or forgiving leader. Only someone cruel and cunning could earn the position of Master. Caleb won't win against such a person, especially considering the Master has a hold over all of those who follow him. Caleb will have no choice but to obey any command he's given. How close will he be able to get before the Master realizes Caleb had bad intentions? Worse, Maddy's certain the Master will likely have guards or the like with him.

She needs to get out of this place. She doesn't want Caleb risking his life to help her. If she can get to him first, she'd have the chance to stop him from doing something stupid. Besides, Caleb going to face the Master alone was never the plan. They were supposed to be in this together. The thought makes her chest tighten. A hunter and a vampire, trying to save the world as one. It's nearly poetic.

A sharp sigh blows through Maddy's nose and she peers around the dank basement. Nothing about this is poetic. Though she has already done so countless times, she studies the room. There is a crack on the left-hand wall that runs from the concrete floor to the ceiling. The ceiling is made up of large lightweight tiles and she wonders if she were free if they would be able to break through them to the ductwork or something.

The door on the right wall hasn't been opened since Felix visited, so Maddy isn't certain what's on the other side of it. She doesn't know if they're in a house, an office building, or a type of warehouse. There are no windows, and no outside sounds can be heard to give her a hint of where this place could be. Maddy lets out a growl and yanks against the handcuffs. They scrape and clank against the pipe, drawing her mother's attention.

"Maddy, take it easy."

"Take it easy?" Maddy's voice rises to a shrill pitch. "How can I take it easy? We're prisoners and Felix is going to use us in some sort of twisted experiment with whatever this mysterious organization he's wrapped up with, Mom. How can I possibly take it easy? We need to get out of here." She glares at the concrete walls. "Wherever here is."

Maddy's mom peers around. "You know, the more I think of it, the more I realize I may know where we are."

Eyes narrowing, Maddy wonders if her mom is delusional. How could anyone know where they are beyond a square concrete basement? "How can you possibly know that?"

"You watch your tone with me, Maddy." Her mom gives her a stern look before she eyes the door. "It isn't so much as me recognizing this place physically, but more of a feeling. Intuition, perhaps."

Maddy loosens her arms, her hands numb from fighting against the cuffs. "Okay, so where are we?"

"The Order used to have a hideout much like this underneath an old factory in Creed. There were a bunch of concrete rooms that had once been used for storage when the factory was still open, but the Order used the rooms to hold prisoners for questioning. Kenna decided to abandon the building in favor of turning her focus on Mercy City." Her mom pauses for a moment. "If I recall correctly, she also used to train a couple of initiates in these rooms where they would be free from distraction. I didn't know her well, she was like royalty among the Order and the hunters, but I do recall seeing her with a young boy with blond hair." A small smile touches her face. "Yes. It's coming back to me. I remember he complained about the smell of the basement rooms."

Maddy's heartbeats quickened. "Caleb," she says. "The boy you saw was most likely Caleb, her nephew. He's the one I told you about, the one who has been helping me and the vampire

Felix wants dead." Desperation leaks into Maddy's voice. "Mom, we have to get out of here. He'll try and do what Felix asked of him to save me. I can't have his death on my conscience." Worse, Maddy fears what his death would do to her heart. "Is there anything helpful you remember about this place? Maybe a way out?"

Maddy's mom's gaze drifts from the door, up to the ceiling, then down. Her lips purse as she stares at the floor. "If I'm correct about our location, and I'm certain I am, then there are sewers underground that connect with the city's drainage system. There would be an access point in the basements some-where." Her eyes narrow. "And I think I know where we can find it."

Making their way through a sewage system isn't something Maddy's keen on, but she'll do anything to get out of Felix's grasp before Caleb does something reckless. "Sounds like a great plan, Mom, except for one thing." Maddy clanks her hand-cuffs against the pipe at her back. "How are we supposed to get out of these? Even if Felix does come back, I highly doubt we'll be able to steal the keys off him."

Maddy's mom hesitates, testing her own cuffs, then sighs. "There is a way, but you won't like it." Regret wrinkles her fore-head as she stares at her daughter. "It will be painful."

"What is it?" Maddy asks slowly.

"I know a sure way to get out of handcuffs." She pauses. "I was hoping it wouldn't have to come to this. We'll need to dislocate our thumbs and squeeze our hands out."

Maddy swallows. "I don't know how to do that."

"I'll talk you through it." Her mom glances at the door. "But we'll need to hurry."

After quick instructions on the process, Maddy pulls in several breaths. She maneuvers her hands in the position her mother told her, then begins to work her thumbs. At first, she doesn't think it will be possible, and her stomach churns with bile at the thought of what she needs to do. But she grits her teeth and pushes on the base of her thumb, digging into the joint.

Pain explodes through her hand and dark spots dance across her vision as her thumb pops out. Consciousness threatens to leave her, wanting no part of this. Her mom's voice filters through the agony, encouraging her, though her own voice is tight with discomfort. Pushing through, Maddy quickly dislocates her other thumb. It takes everything she has not to cry out.

After a moment of agonizing shifting, she pulls her hands free. Bile rises up in her throat at the sight of her disfigured hands. Squeezing her eyes shut, Maddy grabs her thumbs and manipulates them back into place with painful pops. Her head swims again and she only holds onto consciousness because most of the pain ceases. Residual throbbing pulses through her hand and bruises wring her wrists, while her muscles ache along her shoulders from having her hands behind her back for so long. The need to vomit is overwhelming.

But she's free.

Drawing in steadying breaths, Maddy pushes to her feet, her backside numb from the hard concrete. Across the room, her mom is already standing, looking as pale and ill as Maddy feels.

"We need to go." Her mom massages her wrists as she walks to the door and listens. "I don't hear anything but Felix could return any moment."

Maddy joins her mom by the door as she slowly pushes it open. The rusty hinges are loud in the quiet and Maddy holds her breathing, hoping Felix isn't close enough to hear. There's no way she wants to have gone through dislocating her own thumbs just to get caught. Fighting right now would be agonizing.

Her mom creeps out of the room first and Maddy follows. They step into a long hallway. Overhead, exposed pipes and ductwork crisscross along the ceiling. There are other rooms with closed doors, and as they make their way down the hall they pass a couple of stairwells leading up.

"Over there," her mom whispers.

The two make a right at the end of the hall and in a small alcove is a hatch in the floor. Faded painted letters say "Caution: Sewer" on the wall beside a square metal door.

Maddy pulls in a deep breath. "Let's do this."

She bends down and grabs the handle. It takes a few tries but she finally gets it to turn. Her hands throb with pain and her muscles burn as she lifts the hatch with her mom's help. A metal ladder descends into darkness and Maddy's heart races. There's no other choice, however. Felix may not be alone in this place and if they venture upstairs, they could be spotted. He won't give them the chance to escape again.

Maddy swivels around and begins her descent, avoiding using her thumbs even as she discovers how important they are. After she's a few rungs down, her mom follows. All light is cut off when the metal door is closed and Maddy freezes for a moment.

"It's all right," her mom says. "Let your eyes adjust. There will be lights farther down. The city's sewage system has to be kept up to code, even under abandoned buildings."

Trusting her mom is right, Maddy continues down the ladder. Finally, her feet hit a solid floor. After a few moments, her eyes adjust enough to see a vague light in the distance. They hurry along the curved cement walls, the echoes of their steps swallowed up by the shadows. Maddy cringes when she hears the scurrying of rats, but she's thankful the only smell is that of stagnant water from the trench to their right, and not the putrid smell of waste.

As they draw closer to the light, keeping an eye out for a ladder leading up to the street, Maddy prays she isn't too late to save Caleb from taking on the Master.

If she is, Caleb will most certainly walk into his own death.

CHAPTER 33

CALEB

A string of curses tumble from Caleb's lips as his car roars down the road. The smell of smoke clings to him and though the destroyed house is far behind him, he can still see the blazing fire that consumed the other vampires burning behind his eyes. Anger roars through him at what Felix had done.

Caleb shouldn't have let Maddy return home. He should have kept her with him until he had taken out Felix. Instead, he let Maddy stroll straight into a trap. He smacks the steering wheel and pulls in short, quick breaths through his flaring nostrils. He has no way of reaching Felix beyond the address the man of the Order gave him. Calling the number back had done no good. He merely received an automated message that the number was no longer in service. Caleb tried Maddy's number, as well, and reached nothing but her voice mail.

He doesn't care what it will take. He's going to save Maddy and make sure she's safe. Felix will not hurt her. He's going to pay with his life for merely considering harming the young woman Caleb is growing to care for, even when he shouldn't. Felix demanded Caleb give him the Master's head, and he sees no other choice but to do just that. It will take time, however, and he doesn't know how long the twisted hunter will give him to complete the task.

After leaving the destroyed house, Caleb makes a bee line for the Master's stronghold. As he pulls up outside of the house, however, doubt begins to creep inside. He'll need to be careful. Crafty. He needs to act as if there's nothing out of the ordinary, which shouldn't be too hard. Most of his life has been a lie since he became a vampire. He climbs out of his car, locks the door, and heads toward the vampire sanctuary. There are two sentinels outside and one starts to step into Caleb's path.

"It's all right. He can go inside."

Caleb turns to find Morgan approaching. His friend smiles at him, then takes in his appearance. Smudges of ash and debris coat Caleb's face and clothing.

"What happened to you?"

"I need to speak with the Master." Caleb eyes Morgan curiously. What gives him the authority to tell the guards he's allowed to enter the house, when Caleb doesn't have it himself?

Morgan nods at the men flanking the door as they pass. Once inside, he leans down and speaks quietly. "Thanks to you, I got promoted. The Master saw the work we were doing and said I had great potential. I appreciate your support more than you know."

Caleb presses his lips together but says nothing. If Morgan is getting further into the Master's good graces, it will only be harder to get him out again. There's nothing he can do about that at this point in time, however.

"I need to speak with him," Caleb says. "Where is he?"

Morgan leads Caleb down a hallway and to a set of double doors. Another pair of guards stand watch and this time, Morgan doesn't give them orders. After Caleb announces he's here to speak with the Master, one of the guards goes inside the room and returns a moment later.

"Go on." He opens the door to let Caleb through, but Morgan remains outside.

The room is furnished like any sitting area, though the furniture is rather dated. The Master sits behind a desk and stares at Caleb over steepled fingers. Despite his plain features and pale hair, he exudes an air of fierce power.

"I see you don't have the Chalice, Caleb." The Master lets out a long-suffering sigh. "That is very unfortunate."

Caleb walks closer but pauses on the rug in the middle of the room. He needs to take out the Master, but despite his looks, the vampire is ancient and experienced. The guards would be alerted to any scuffle and Caleb wouldn't be surprised if the leader of the vampires had others nearby to come to his aid. "I took a team with me to where I'd gotten word Felix was hiding. When we arrived, it was evident he was there not long before, but unfortunately, he'd rigged the place with explosives. I was the only one to survive." At that moment, Caleb realizes just how suspicious that looks. He clears his throat. "I'm ready to go after him again immediately, with your permission."

The Master stands slowly, and though his voice is even, wrath unfolds around him like a shadow of death. "You dare return here to ask for a second chance after your failures? How is it so many of my vampires cannot stop one single man? Are you so weak?"

Caleb starts to shake his head, but lifts his chin instead. "Even a strong man can be outwitted by a snake. Felix is slippery, but he will be caught. I promise you that." A hard edge seeps into his voice, but it is not for the satisfaction of the Master that Caleb makes his vow, but to save Maddy's life.

The confidence rings clearly in his words, and the Master gives a single nod. "I'm glad to see you are still eager to end the man's life. I was beginning to have misgivings about your intentions, Caleb." He rounds the desk, hands folded behind his back. "I do not want my sacrifices delayed and I want that Chalice."

"I'll get it."

The Master stares down at Caleb with merciless eyes. "I am giving you twenty-four hours to return here with the Chalice and news that you have taken care of Felix and the Order in Creed. Fail me, and I will put a bounty on your head and you will be nothing more than ash in two days' time."

Caleb nods mutely, but inside, he's raging in frustration. Two ultimatums, and no way to accomplish either one. He can't save Maddy without bringing Felix the Master's head, and the Master wouldn't trust him until he ends Felix and brings the Chalice.

"To ensure you will do what is necessary, I am sending someone from my trusted circle to supervise you on your mission." The Master snaps his fingers and a figure emerges from the shadows. "Caleb, you know Silas, yes?"

Caleb flicks a glance at the man who is one of the Master's assassins. He wears all black, except for his short, sandy hair. The man has eyes sharp as a hawk and gray as a cold winter sky. Caleb has seen the man a few times, but has never spoken with him, much less worked with him. It will be like teaming up with a wolf.

"Silas." Caleb inclines his head respectfully. The man barely regards him.

"Kill Felix," the Master says. "Bring me the Chalice, prefer-ably filled with that young hunter girl's blood."

Caleb nods and turns, leaving with Silas. Morgan is nowhere in sight when he exits the room and he doesn't spot his friend when he makes his way back to his car, either. He unlocks the doors and Silas slips in the passenger seat before

Caleb can speak to him. Shaking his head, Caleb rounds the front of the car and climbs in.

Silas stares out of the window. "Where are we going?"

Caleb turns the ignition and shifts the car into drive. "I have to find Felix, and the only way I know how to do that is to speak with a witch." Regret and unease prickle through him as he heads down the road to speak to Galina for a third time.

The witch is nothing short of irritated as she opens the door to find Caleb there. Her keen stare takes in Silas and she quirks an eyebrow at Caleb.

"I need your help. Felix slipped away and I need to find him again." Caleb shifts ever so slightly, stares directly at Galina, and mouths "get rid of him". He widens his eyes, hoping she understands.

If Galina catches Caleb's meaning, she doesn't give any indication. She opens the door and rolls her eyes. "Do you expect me to keep doing spells for free? One of these days, vampire, I may just have to exact a heavy price from you."

Caleb mutters as if in irritation, going along with the show so they don't raise Silas's suspicions. Obviously, Galina doesn't want the man knowing about the deal she'd made earlier with Caleb about finding the kidnapped boy.

"A location spell, is it?" The witch grabs a wooden box, something Caleb knew she didn't use for the previous spell. "I just need a bit of this." She grabs a pinch of some sort of blue powder in her fingers, then whirls and blows it directly in Silas's face.

The Master's assassin jerks once, then collapses onto the floor. His eyes are wide and glassy, and his body still. Galina steps over him and shuts the door, whacking the back of Silas's head. Caleb leans over, eyeing the vampire.

"Is he dead?"

"No. But he'll remain in this frozen, unconscious state until he is given the antidote, which I do not possess. I'll bury him in the backyard under my maple tree."

Caleb shakes his head. "Remind me never to piss you off."

The witch makes her way over to her chair, ignoring the fact her cat is walking on the frozen vampire. "I suppose you really do need a location spell? What happened to Maddy?"

Caleb gives the witch a quick run-down of the events that transpired since leaving her house earlier. Afterward, Caleb sits with his knee jostling as he watches Galina start the location spell. Her eyebrows knit together, however, and after a few minutes, her cheeks puff out in a sharp sigh.

"Felix is blocked. He must have realized how you have found him previously. The location is warded, no doubt."

Caleb pushes to his feet and runs a hand through his hair. What is he supposed to do now? If Felix's location is warded, then he won't be able to find Maddy, either. "I need to go. I have to figure this out, somehow."

"Sometimes it's okay to let things figure themselves out." Galina's lips quirk ever so slightly. "I'm sure you'll know what to do soon." She pauses, then grabs a piece of paper and scrawls out a name and number. "Take this. Ask her for information regarding Alex's disappearance. Don't worry about your friend over there. I'll take care of him."

Caleb wants to shudder at the wicked promise in her voice as he takes the slip of paper. Feeling helpless and at wit's end, he leaves the witch's house. As soon as he reaches his car, his phone buzzes. He pulls it out and his heart jumps when he reads it's an unknown number, just like when Felix called him.

"Felix," he growls.

But it isn't the revenge-filled hunter on the other end.

"Caleb? It's Maddy." Her breath is short and voice tight with strain. "I need your help."

CHAPTER 34

MADELEINE

Bouncing on her toes beside the road, Maddy glances with worry at her mother. "Are you sure you don't want to go to the hospital?" Dried blood still cakes the side of her face, though Maddy's given her a hair tie from her wrist so her mom can tie her mess of hair back.

"And tell them what, exactly?" Maddy's mom presses her fingertips to the wound from her scuffle with Felix. "I'll be fine, Maddy, don't worry."

Maddy wants to argue, but a car is suddenly speeding down the road toward them. It screeches to a halt and Caleb steps out. Before Maddy can so much as utter a thank you, he's standing in front of her with his hands on her shoulders.

"Are you all right?" He looks her up and down, then inhales, drawing in her emotions.

"I..." Maddy is taken aback by the intensity of Caleb's concern. She starts to give him a reassuring smile, then notices her mom's tense stance. The hunter in her has come out and she stares at Caleb with distrust. "Mom, this is Caleb. He's my friend."

Caleb inclines his head. "Mrs. Grimes. Felix will likely be looking for you. We need to get you two out of here."

Maddy nods, and Caleb's hand drops from her shoulder, fingertips brushing the back of her hand before the three hurry to the car. The inside is gloriously warm and Maddy can't help but let out a sigh as she lets her body melt into the heated passenger seat. Behind her, her mom slides in and closes the door. Caleb pulls away and the engine roars as he tears off down the road.

"I was afraid you were going to try to take down the Master," Maddy admits. "I'm glad you didn't."

Caleb peers over at her for a second before his eyes flash back to the road. "I would have, Maddy. I wanted to after I got that call from Felix. I went to the Master but he is too heavily guarded. Without the Chalice we don't have any hope of bringing him down." A muscle feathers along his jaw and he sniffs. "The Master has given me one day to retrieve the Chalice and kill Felix and the Order, otherwise he's putting a bounty on my head. I won't last long after that."

"I wouldn't let that happen." Maddy reaches over and squeezes his hand. She senses the sharp stare her gesture brings from her mother.

Caleb gives her a small smile. "I appreciate that, but regardless, it creates a complication for our original plan to rescue Cora and the others. One day may be too short of time to corner Felix again and retrieve the Chalice."

Maddy sits back against her seat and holds her hands toward the vents. Buildings flash by and soon, they pass the edge of town. "We've tried finding Felix and taking him down. I'm not sure we can do this on our own, Caleb. Even with the three of us, he's too smart and too determined to win."

"She's right." Maddy's mom leans forward in the back seat. "By now, Felix will have called in his followers from Mercy City and other places. He won't be alone and getting past those defenses will be nearly impossible."

Caleb slows his car and pulls into a parking lot outside of a lone dollar store. It doesn't look like it's frequented nearly as often as the one further in town. A lone employee puts out her cigarette and heads back inside with a bored expression, expecting customers.

A crooked smile lifts Caleb's cheek as he twists in his seat to look between Maddy and her mom. "I had a feeling Felix would be calling in some friends. After he tried to blow me up—"

Maddy pulls in a sharp intake of breath. "He *what?*"

"He tried, Maddy. Obviously, he didn't succeed."

Maddy's mom nods at Caleb. "Go on."

"Anyway," Caleb says. "I knew Felix wouldn't feel safe any longer, not with us making such efforts to track him down. He needs the protection and strength of his followers, so I contacted some of my own people."

Maddy opens her mouth to ask who he means, but then notices Caleb's attention has gone to a line of cars pulling into the parking lot. He steps out of his vehicle, and Maddy and her mom join him on the other side. A black car is in the lead and rolls to a stop near them. Maddy glances at Caleb for a clue as to who may be inside, but he's merely looking on with a small smile of triumph on his face.

A man and woman step out of the black car at the front. Maddy eyes them closely as they approach. The man is tall, and a bit broad in the shoulder. His corn-colored curls flop over his forehead, almost intense blue eyes. At first, Maddy thinks perhaps he's a vampire, but she doesn't get that sense from him. He shakes Caleb's hand.

"I'm glad you called, Caleb."

Caleb turns to Maddy. "This is Maddy, and Mrs. Grimes."

Maddy's mom nods her head, watching these two just as closely as Maddy. "Abigail will do."

The man gives Abigail a polite smile, but his attention swings back to Maddy. "My name is Marlowe. Caleb's told me about the situation here regarding Felix, and the Master." Marlowe gestures behind him to the line of cars. "We are the real Order. Kenna DeVoe entrusted our sacred organization to me. Felix, obviously, had his own ideas about what the Order should be."

So this is the Marlowe Felix ranted about. The one that Kenna was smart enough to trust.

"Felix is insane," Maddy says. She wants to be excited to meet the real Order, except she can't help but wonder how they will react when they learn she has the bloodline of Dracula pumping through her veins.

Marlowe chuckles, a deep and jovial sound that comes from him so naturally, Maddy has the feeling the man enjoys a good laugh. "That he is. Imagine learning one of your new hunters has the lineage of Dracula, and then casting such strength away rather than embracing it?" His smile deepens when he sees Maddy blink in surprise. "Felix broke off from the true Order to follow the path of extremism. Our true purpose, and you, are his loss."

"You...you don't mind about my lineage?" A balloon of hope swells in Maddy's chest. She hadn't realized just how much she wanted to be a hunter until the opportunity was taken from her. Now, she may just have another chance.

"No," Marlowe says. "I do not. I believe in a modern approach, as do those in the Order. While the Master needs to be dealt with, I know not all of his followers are guilty." The man squeezes Caleb's shoulder, emphasizing his claim. "There are those who are merely trying to do the right thing, or have no choice but to follow the Master's orders."

Caleb nods and the tightness at the corner of his eye makes Maddy's heart squeeze. He is one of those followers who has no choice but to do as the Master commands. Maddy can't imagine losing her freedom of choice to do what she thinks is right. But it's not just that for Caleb. He used to be one of the Order. In fact, would he have taken up Kenna's mantle rather than Marlowe?

"Felix, on the other hand, has the belief that every vampire should be executed." Marlowe peers at Maddy. "As evident with your situation, his extremism is getting out of hand. He follows the old ways, not the direction Kenna wanted the organization to be going forward. All things must change and adapt, or else they will crumble."

The woman who accompanied Marlowe laughs. "Don't get him started on making grand speeches or we'll be here all day." She's extraordinarily pretty. Her flame red hair flows over her shoulders in perfection, the morning sun picking out highlights of amber in the strands and her body is built like a goddess, both curvy and athletic. Green eyes take in Maddy, her mom, and Caleb, though Maddy sees her gaze linger on the man beside her a bit longer.

"This is Rachel, my girlfriend," Marlowe says, his face softening. "She's also one of the smartest and fastest hunters I've ever had the privilege of knowing."

Rachel rolls her eyes with a smile. "The second smartest hunter. And definitely not the hottest," she says, her eyes teasing. She moves from Marlowe's side and approaches Caleb. "Gabby says hi."

Maddy's lips part. "Gabby?" Surely, Rachel doesn't mean her friend. "What does she look like?"

"Like a blonde angel in a miniskirt." Amusement coats Rachel's tone.

"You know Gabby?" Maddy turns to Caleb, already

narrowing her eyes. If she finds out he was dating her, too, she's going to lose it.

Caleb raises his eyebrows, no doubt surprised at the rising anger coming from Maddy. "I met her briefly. I've only spoken to her one time."

"Caleb, we defs need to chat." Rachel loops her arm through Caleb's and the two walk off separately.

Marlowe doesn't seem bothered and has already begun to chat with Maddy's mom. Perhaps his girlfriend is just one of the overly friendly types. Maddy, however, watches Caleb and Rachel with unwavering interest. Jealousy prickles through her, and the sensation is surprising. She cares about Caleb, but until that moment, she didn't realize just how fast she was falling for the handsome vampire.

One who seems to be determined to take unimaginable risks and fight for her.

CHAPTER 35

CALEB

Maddy's stare follows Caleb as he makes his way over to a secluded section of the parking lot. None of the other Order members have gotten out of the vehicles save for Marlowe and Rachel, no doubt awaiting instructions from their leader. Relief sighs through Caleb when Rachel removes her arm. He never is comfortable with physical contact, though there are exceptions. He peeks over at Maddy, who quickly finds her shoes apparently very interesting. Caleb hides a smile. Curiosity, he'd expected, but he's fairly certain, even from this distance, he can scent jealousy. The thought pleases him.

"I spoke to Gabby on the way here," Rachel says. She tucks her hands in the pockets of her long coat and brings her shoulders in. The wind bites at their back and the morning sun does little to chase away the chill. "She thinks she might have a spell to siphon off the remaining vials of obsidian this secret organization has taken, but she still hasn't found anything on the organization itself."

Caleb curses under his breath. Even if they take down Felix and the Master, the mysterious organization has him worried.

What if they take down two enemies, only to have a larger, more sinister one rise up in their stead?

"Yeah, these pricks have hidden themselves well, however..." Rachel pulls a piece of paper out of her pocket. "Gabby wanted me to give you this. If you manage to find the headquarters of this organization, you should draw this rune on the obsidian's container."

Caleb takes the paper and studies the rune scrawled across it. It looks like a capital Z with two straight lines criss crossing either end of its tail. "What will this rune do to the obsidian?"

"Contain it, until Gabby can get it taken care of once again." Rachel shrugs a shoulder. "Other than that, there isn't much we can do. The obsidian is dangerous, and no one in their right mind would want to mess with it."

Caleb scoffs. "That's the thing, isn't it? Lunatics *do* have their hands on the obsidian." He folds the piece of paper and tucks it in his back pocket, along with the number Galina had given him. That had certainly been an interesting phone call, and one he hopes doesn't come back to bite him. "I'll do the best I can. If we can take Felix and the Master out of the equation, maybe this organization will finally show their face and we can make our moves against them."

Rachel nods. "The rest of the Order members are on the organization's case, as well. We'll get this figured out." She glances over at the rest, then smirks at Caleb. "I think your girlfriend misses you."

"She isn't my girlfriend."

Rachel chuckles and pats Caleb on the shoulder. "Whatever you say, vamp."

Caleb's lips press together as Rachel walks back toward Marlowe. He flicks a glance at Maddy, who is standing with her arms crossed as tightly as she can get them across her chest. Her legs are pressed together and her shoulders are hunched.

She's doing her best to make it obvious she wasn't just staring at him and Rachel.

As Caleb approaches he shucks off his leather jacket. "Here." He wraps it around her shoulders. "You look like you're about to freeze to death."

Maddy's heartbeats quicken. "Thank you." She slides her arms in the sleeves and laughs when her fingers fail to poke out of the ends. "It's huge."

Rachel catches Caleb's eye and lifts an eyebrow, an "I told you so" smile playing on her face.

"She seems friendly," Maddy murmurs under her breath. Her facial expression gives nothing away, yet Caleb can sense the jealousy within her. His first instinct is to say something snarky, or perhaps tease Maddy a little, but he realizes he doesn't want to risk hurting her feelings.

Instead, he grunts and shrugs his shoulders. "She's okay, I suppose." He shifts around Maddy a bit, blocking the cold wind. Behind her back, Maddy's mom, Abby, looks away from Marlowe as he speaks to her. She eyes him with a hint of suspicion, before speaking with the Order leader again. Caleb leans down to whisper in Maddy's ear. "I don't think your mom likes me very much."

Maddy peers over her shoulder, then turns back to Caleb with a smile. "She spent her life as a hunter, and under Felix, no less. Of course, she has her reservations about you, but at least she's trying. She'll get over it."

"Reservations regarding vampires is a good quality to possess." Caleb reaches up and shifts the collar of his leather jacket farther onto Maddy's shoulder where it had begun to slip. "Maybe that's something you should keep in mind, Maddy."

"Are you talking about yourself?" Maddy asks. "Because I'm

not afraid of you. You're a good person, Caleb. I appreciate your help and friendship more than you know."

Friendship. *Ouch*, Caleb thinks. But then he notices how close Maddy is standing to him, how he's certain when he slid his jacket onto her shoulders that she inhaled his scent, and he can still see the flash of jealousy in her eyes as she peered at Rachel. God, that kiss they'd shared, too...he's never felt so lost in the touch of woman's lips on his. Whatever this is between him and Maddy, they're surpassing the bounds of friendship. Caleb just wishes he knew if it was something Maddy truly wants. Has she really thought this through? After all, he isn't so certain she should be falling for a monster such as him.

"So, what did Rachel have to say?" Maddy asks.

Caleb clears his throat, chasing away the errant thoughts about his relationship with Maddy. If something is to unfold between them, it needs to wait until after their work is done. Distraction isn't something either of them need at the moment.

"She was telling me about the obsidian." Caleb rubs at the back of his neck. "I'm not sure about this darkness. It has me worried. From what I know, once it has a hold of you, it doesn't let go. It will spread and spread, until chaos and corruption bloom at every turn. It's bad enough to think perhaps the Master is involved with the organization harboring the obsidian, but I have a feeling some of that darkness has its clutches on Felix, as well. He's always been an extreme bastard, but he's pushing things farther than even his logical mind would have in the past."

The leather jacket creaks as Maddy does her best to fold her arms with the bulk of the sleeves. "I guess we'll find out soon enough." Her eyebrows slant together. "Are you sure you want to do this? The real Order is here, now. We have enough hunters with us to track down Felix and get the Chalice. It's too risky for you to be involved in case the Master catches wind of what you are up to."

A car door slams and one of the Order members trots over to Marlowe. He speaks to him quietly, then Marlowe nods and waves toward Caleb and Maddy. "We have his location. It's time to take Felix down once and for all."

Caleb looks down at Maddy, wishing he could untangle the thoughts shifting in her mocha eyes. "To answer your question, yes, I want to do this." Her arms are hidden in his jacket sleeves, so he reaches up and touches her cheek. "I'm not staying out of this, Maddy. I'm going to remain at your side, and see this through to the end."

CHAPTER 36

MADELEINE

Felix hasn't fled the location he'd used to hold Maddy and her mother captive, but instead has rallied his nearest followers to him. The old factory squats against the wind, the cement walls stained with rivulets of brown. Marlowe and the others park down the street, while Maddy waits for the order with Caleb and her mom at her side. The atmosphere sparks with eagerness.

Everyone is ready to end this.

"You look good dripping in weapons," Caleb murmurs as he leans in.

Maddy glances down. She's returned his jacket, and instead wears one a member of the Order had let her borrow that fits a little better. Despite being mostly trained to use stakes, she's been given knives for this particular mission. At least the maneuvers are largely the same. Although she'd hardly say she's dripping in weapons, she does have knives tucked into sheaths on her thighs and one up each sleeve.

"I'm ready as I'll ever be," she says, trying to smile.

Caleb looks fit for a fight as well, though he holds no weapons other than his speed and strength. Maddy can't help but wish she had such abilities, sometimes. At least these are just humans they're going up against. The thought gives Maddy pause as the members of the Order climb out of their vehicles. Can she really fight against fellow humans? Those who have sworn to fight dangerous vampires just like she has?

Caleb's hand squeezes her shoulder. "This will not end in bloodshed, Maddy. We are here for Felix only. Perhaps, like your mom, the others have simply been misguided. For all we know, they think Felix is getting his orders from Marlowe."

"But just in case, keep your wits about you, okay?" Rachel winks at Maddy and goes to join Marlowe's side.

Maddy can't decide if she likes Rachel or not. Especially when all she knows about her is that the woman is confident and beautiful. Marlowe raises his hand, and once he has the attention of the Order, he begins to walk toward the building. The very air tightens with tension.

There are few windows and only a pair of metal doors on the front. Two groups of the Order split off and go around the sides. Marlowe, Rachel, Maddy and her mom, and Caleb remain in the front with a couple of the other Order members.

The moment the others are gone, they rush toward the front doors on quiet steps.

Hours before, Maddy was held captive in this place. Felix had claimed they were preparing a room where experiments would be performed on her and her mother. She's safe now, with Caleb and the Order, but she can't help the shiver that trickles down her spine. Caleb reaches over and gives her fingers a brief, reassuring squeeze. She admits it has its advantages that he's so in tune with her emotions.

Marlowe tests the doors, but they're locked. He turns to Caleb and gives a nod.

"Time to knock and say hello." Caleb steps back several feet, then charges straight at the doors. His shoulder rams into them and with a loud snap of the lock and groan of metal, pummels through like a battering ram. The boots he wears scuff the floor as he slides to a stop.

Maddy raises her eyebrows. Caleb continues to surprise her. She knew he was strong, but damn. One door stands open, while the other lands against the floor, hanging on to life by a bent hinge.

Shouts echo through the building and the team takes off. Hallways and rooms make the place a maze, but Marlowe seems to know where he's going. Caleb also assists in directing, listening closely to the shouts and alerting them where they are coming from.

They push through another set of doors and into a large room. Boxes line the edges of one wall, a few of them tumbled to the ground. There are tables and chairs, too, and people dash and fight around them.

Maddy's instincts kick in and she jumps into the fray. Felix is in the center of the room and his hunters protect him fiercely. Caleb never drifts far from Maddy's side, and the two fight almost seamlessly. A tall, lanky hunter attempts to make a grab for Maddy and she sweeps a leg out, making him fall onto one of the tables. Caleb picks up a chair and throws it against another opponent. The man hits the floor with a thud and doesn't get back up again.

The room is full of shouts and crashes as the two Orders collide. Maddy's muscles burn, still sore from being handcuffed and her fists explode with discomfort with each punch after the thumb dislocation, but she perseveres. She catches her mom's eye and the two of them grin at each other. Strange as it seems, they were both made for this, destined to fight for not only humankind, but all supernatural entities.

Felix has gathered a good force, but there isn't nearly enough to resist the true Order. Clearly, he hadn't expected

Marlowe and his band of hunters to side with a vampire and Dracula's heir. The fight is intense, yet brief. Maddy holds a knife to a woman's chest but the hunter freezes. She's staring at the center of the room and Maddy follows her gaze.

Two of Marlowe's hunters hold Felix, and Marlowe himself is facing him with a stern frown on his face. "Stand down. Your leader is taken."

For a moment, no one in the room moves. Then, members of Felix's Order begin to drop weapons and step back along the wall. Maddy lowers the knife as the woman glares at her and steps away. Caleb takes Maddy's arm and pulls her closer to Marlowe so they can keep a closer eye on Felix.

"Felix, you have aligned yourself with evil." Marlowe's voice booms, void of the joviality Maddy had witnessed earlier. "As such, you have compromised the Order and created a rift among our kind with your extreme propaganda."

"Propaganda?" The word hisses past Felix's lips. He bares his teeth, and the madness inside of him rises farther to the surface. "What of your beliefs? You think that vampires should be allowed to walk the earth? I will die before I allow such a scourge to wander the world." He jerks his chin toward Caleb and settles a flinty glare on the vampire. "Rabid monsters like him need to be put down."

Maddy steps forward. "Not all vampires are guilty."

A sneer twists Felix's face. "You've fallen for one and think the rest are innocent, do you? Tell me, Madeleine, do you think Cora will understand? How many vampires do you think she's fed by now? Yes, I bet her neck has been nearly rent apart by this point."

Maddy pulls in a sharp breath, hand dropping to her knife, and steps forward. Caleb wraps an arm around her waist and draws her back.

"Easy," he mutters in her ear.

Felix's hunters along the wall murmur and Maddy doesn't need to look at them to feel the hatred in their stares. They don't understand, but hopefully soon, they'll break free of Felix's hold. "If you truly care about the people the Master has taken, then you'll give us the Chalice so we can save them."

Marlowe takes a step closer to Felix, and the man fights against the hold the true hunters of the Order have on him. "Do it," Marlowe says. "Tell them where to find the Chalice."

"I'll die first before I let the likes of *him* touch such a precious object." Felix stares at Caleb as if he wishes he could burn him to a pile of ash with merely a look.

A young man steps away from the wall on the right. He doesn't appear to be older than fifteen or sixteen. The other hunters beside him glare, but remain silent.

"I know where Felix hid the Chalice." The other hunters behind him mutter, but no one speaks up.

"Silence!" Felix spits.

The young hunter peers at Marlowe. "I didn't know we weren't really in the Order."

Maddy's chest tightens for the boy who had only been following orders. Marlow gives him a smile. "The true Order will welcome you, and any others who put Felix's lies behind them, with open arms. For now, tell them where the Chalice is hidden."

"Second floor. There is a corner office on the left side of the building. It's locked in a drawer in the desk."

Marlow turns to Maddy and Caleb. "Go and get it."

Maddy nods and hurries from the room. She prays they still have time to save Cora. Caleb grabs her hand and yanks her into a run. Her boots thump against the stairs as they go up to the second floor. Maddy's reminded of the time on campus when she tried to follow Caleb. He'd gotten up the stairs in the administration building so quickly and she chuckles at the memory.

"What's so funny?" Caleb asks.

"Nothing." They reach the second floor and race to the corner office on the left-hand side. Just as the young man had said, there's a desk on the opposite wall.

Caleb flashes across the room and by the time Maddy reaches him, he's already jerking open a locked drawer. The Chalice rolls into the side of the drawer and Caleb grabs it. Then, he takes his phone out of his back pocket and snaps a picture of the object.

"What did you do that for?" Maddy asks.

Caleb doesn't answer. "Come on, we need to hurry."

Suspicion curls in Maddy's stomach but she holds her tongue as they quickly head back to the room where Marlowe holds the false Order.

"We're taking you back to Mercy City," Marlowe says, still eyeing Felix with derision. "There you will be tried for your actions under the new age Order rules designed by Kenna. The old ways are being disbanded, and it is time for you and your followers to learn." He nods at his men holding Felix. "Take him and the others away."

Marlowe is silent as Felix and his followers are escorted from the building. Once the last of the hunters are gone, he turns to Maddy and Caleb. "You have the Chalice, Caleb. Use it to free the captives from the Master. You must be quick. Time is running out. Some of the Order members will help take the vampire Master out, but you need to be wary. If he's also influenced by this dark organization, he will be unpredictable."

Caleb nods, grip firm on the Chalice.

"I'm coming with you," Maddy says.

"Like hell you are." Caleb shakes his head. "It's far too dangerous. You can't stroll into a nest of vampires, Maddy."

Maddy's mom steps forward. "Maddy, maybe he's right. You are a new hunter. You're not ready yet."

Maddy scowls. "Cora's in captivity, and it's partly my fault. I'm going and no one is going to stop me."

Caleb stares at her long and hard, then sighs. "Fine, but you need to do exactly what I say. And trade those knives in for stakes. You're going to need them."

CHAPTER 37

MADELEINE

Maddy studies the stake in her hand, picking out the details of the wood grain on the smooth, tapered surface. The wider end has been wrapped in leather to improve the grip of the hunter who uses the weapon. Marlowe had given this stake and one other to her from his own holsters.

"It's not far." Caleb glances down at the stake. "I've seen you in action before. You'll do fine."

"I'm not nervous." Maddy puts the stake in a holster on her thigh. She should feel nervous, but aside from the shiver of unease "the spooks" are giving her, she's mostly filled with excited anticipation. Hunting vampires is her purpose, and while she knows there are innocent ones like Caleb, not all of them hold such regard for the survival of humans. Marlowe doesn't seem to mind about her bloodline, so she's planning on fully embracing her role. "I'm ready to do what needs to be done."

Caleb peers in the rearview mirror. Behind them, another car with the Order members Marlowe had sent follows them. "Yeah, well, we're heading to the Master's lair. It won't be easy to take him down, Maddy. He has vampires that have a vast amount of experience. They are quicker, stronger, and far deadlier than I. Don't be reckless."

Maddy sniffs but her retort dies in her mouth as Caleb slows his car and pulls over on the side of the road. There is no sign of the Master's lair anywhere.

"I don't want to drive up too close. He'll know we're there as soon as we enter the building, and the less of a surprise we can give him, the better."

The Order members park behind Caleb and climb out of their car. He jerks his head farther down the road. They follow his lead and soon, he points, indicating the place where the Master is holed up. Maddy stares at the building, bile burning her throat as she thinks of her best friend trapped somewhere beneath the brick and mortar of the Master's home.

Caleb draws Maddy behind a row of large, tangled bushes, and the others follow. They keep their distance, watching the area for any hint of movement.

"I'm going to take the Chalice inside," Caleb says. "Wait here until I get things sorted."

"No. I'm going with you."

Caleb barks a humorless laugh. "Maddy, they aren't just going to let me stroll in with a *hunter*. They'll either kill you on the spot, or take you down to the cells and kill me for insubordination. The Master is expecting me to bring him the Chalice. No one will stop me if I'm alone."

Maddy bites her lip and looks away. She doesn't like the idea of Caleb going in alone. After all, what was the point of her and the Order members coming if Caleb is going to try and make this a one man show? She knows his plan is logical, but she just wishes she can remain at his side.

"Caleb, I have a bad feeling about this. Are you sure this is the only way?"

He rubs his hand back and forth over his hair. "It's the only way I can see right now. We can't go charging in without the guards stopping us at the front door. I can get in without a fuss. I'll take care of the Master, and it will weaken the resolve of the others. Once he's taken care of, I'll let you guys in to help take control of the situation."

"Fine." Maddy agrees, but with reservation. "Please be careful. You can't fight off everyone alone."

"I know. I just want to keep you safe." Caleb lifts a hand and presses his palm to Maddy's cheek.

Warmth spreads from Caleb's hand and Maddy leans into his touch. She lays her hand over his, holding him to her as she looks up at him. Her chest tightens, and her heart beats faster when she realizes Caleb is dipping his head to hers.

Maddy's breath hitches as their lips meet. The kiss is brief, there are others standing nearby, after all, but the gesture makes Maddy's stomach swirl. So much emotion was just compressed into that one, tender touch. Caleb pulls away slowly, gives Maddy a small smile, then turns away and jogs toward the Master's lair. The delighted sensation in Maddy sours into fear.

She swears that kiss tasted like a goodbye.

Maddy watches as Caleb pauses outside of the Master's lair and speaks to a couple of vampires. After a few tense seconds, they let him through the door. Maddy lets out a breath and turns to the others.

"He's in," she says. "He also told me we should wait out here until he lets us in."

One of the Order members, a young woman close in age to Maddy crosses her arms, a knowing smile on her face. "You're not going to listen to him, are you?"

"Absolutely not." Maddy peers at the building, eyeing the pair of vampires in the distance. "We can't just sit here and do nothing. Marlowe sent us here for a reason. Caleb is focusing on taking down the Master, but once he does so, chaos will erupt. As far as we know, the Master has been waiting on Caleb to bring him the Chalice before he starts killing the humans that were abducted. We don't know what the vampires loyal to the Master will do if their leader is killed, but they could retaliate and start helping themselves to the captives."

A man with shockingly red hair nods. "You want us to go in and look for the prisoners." He looks at his companions. "She's got a good point. The vampires may be restraining themselves from harming the captives now, but once their Master is out of the way, there will be no one there holding the leash. We need to get the prisoners out before the Master is killed."

"So, what's your plan?" the young woman asked Maddy.

Maddy raises her eyebrows as the Order looks at her expectantly. Clearly, they are going to be following her direction. Though she feels as if she lacks the experience for a mission such as this, she takes up the mantle.

"Let's get around the back. Some of you wait outside the building and stand guard. If the vampires are alerted by our presence, you can take them out. Otherwise, leave them. We don't want to raise suspicion."

The young woman, the red-haired man, and another man who is lithe and fast, go with Maddy. They are swift and quiet as they make a wide arc around the house, then creep up toward the back. After a quick search, they find a small window. Maddy looks around, then kicks the glass, wincing at the sound as it breaks. Using the toe of her boot, she knocks the jagged edges away. Then, she crawls inside. The others quickly follow.

Inside, they hold still for what feels like hours. But there's nothing. No shouts. No boots clattering through the house. It seems luck is on their side. They're in.

"Caleb said the prisoners were being held in cells in the basement," Maddy whispers. "We need to find stairs."

The team works quickly. They roam down corridors and peek into rooms, alert for any movement or sound. Most of the vampires seem to be with the Master, no doubt alerted to Caleb's presence.

"Over here." The female hunter jerks her head to an open door leading to a set of descending stairs.

"Stakes out," Maddy says. She starts down the stairs, heart racing and sweat beading on her forehead. They're so close to finding the captives and she prays Cora is still okay.

They reach the bottom and find a door. Maddy frowns at the lock. "Damn." The prisoners could be just on the other side. "Any ideas?" she asks the others.

The young woman smiles and pulls a pair of slender metal pins out of her pocket. "I keep these with me for just an occasion." She gets to work picking the lock. Time ticks by and with each second, Maddy grows more antsy. Any second the Master could be killed and it will be a race to the buffet line.

Finally, there is a click and the lock opens.

"Great job." Maddy gives the young woman a smile. Then, she opens the door and her team rushes in. The heels of Maddy's boots scuff across the cold concrete of the basement as she slides to a stop, her blood freezing in her veins.

A dozen vampires glare back at her.

CHAPTER 38

CALEB

The walls of the Master's home seem to press in on Caleb as he walks across the floor. He took a quick detour, one he hoped no one saw, and is now making his way to the Master's meeting chamber. His thoughts are a frenzy of worry and determination. He walked into this building knowing there's a good chance he won't be walking out of it again. He'd said nothing to Maddy about his fear, and walking away from her after their tender kiss had punched a hole through his chest. This was necessary, though, and he tells himself Maddy will be much safer if the Master is no longer a threat in this world.

After making his way down a corridor lined with old portraits of people Caleb doesn't know, their still faces nearly seeming alive in the flickering lantern light, he arrives at a set of stairs which wind downward. At the bottom, he comes to a stop in front of a large door. A pair of guards stand sentinel outside and regard him without a hint of emotion.

"I'm here to see the Master." Caleb's uncertain if they are aware of the stipulation the Master had given him, but one raises an eyebrow in question. "He'll want to see me. Trust me." The Chalice is in his hand and the guard eyes it with curiosity.

Finally, the guard nods and lets Caleb pass. Inside is a large, circular room. The air is cool and the shadows fight against the lanterns and candles lining the cold stone walls. In the center of the room is an altar of sorts, and Caleb sees the curls of midnight smoke writhing atop it. Like a mass of inky worms, it thrashes and twists, seeming to devour and feed on itself all at once.

The obsidian.

Their suspicions were correct. The Master has the obsidian, which confirms he is in league with the mysterious organization beginning to influence those in the supernatural world. Had the Master known Felix had also been in league with them, or had he seen the opportunity to take out a supposed ally for the chance to bolster his position in the organization's eye?

The Master stands near the altar with several members of his inner circle. His eyes lock on Caleb as the door closes at his back.

"I have taken care of the Order." Caleb holds the Chalice up high, letting all those in the room see the object.

"You have done well, Caleb." The Master gives the barest incline of his head, the only sign he would ever show that someone in his following has impressed him. "It is time to prepare for the sacrifice." He holds his hand out toward Caleb, indicating the young vampire is allowed to approach.

Caleb draws closer to the altar, his grip firm on the Chalice. The Master doesn't reach for it. Instead, the vampire ruler's attention has gone to a slight, hooded figure parting from the shadows along the wall. The members of the inner circle part as she makes her way to the altar. She lowers her hood, revealing deep purple eyes and hair like spun stardust. A necklace with a pentagram locket rests just above her collarbone. Caleb recognizes it from the portrait of the missing boy, Alex.

"Zariah is a witch who works for me," the Master explains.

An eager light begins to glow in his gaze. "You may begin the spell."

The witch flicks a glance at Caleb for a brief moment, then starts murmuring an incantation.

A door on the far wall opens and the captives are led in. Caleb's muscles are taut, but he doesn't dare act just yet. The timing needs to be perfect. He spots Alex, his body frail-looking from being held in the dark, cold dungeon. Then there's Aubrey, shivering and hunched. And even Olivia, the girl abducted before her. His chest tightens when Cora is shoved through the doorway, her red hair limp and dull, dirt smeared up her arms. She spots him and her eyes go wide, and then betrayal crumbles over her. He wishes he could go to her and assure her everything will be okay. But he can't even risk giving her a reassuring glance. Instead, he looks on as if the sight of the prisoners isn't putting a bad taste in his mouth.

Another vampire yanks a prisoner into the room and Caleb stops breathing. He's stunned to see Morgan pulling a fighting Maddy. The other Order members who had accompanied them are there, as well. Maddy meets his gaze and his heart cracks at the fear he sees there. Caleb wants to yell at her for defying his orders and scoop her up in his arms all at once. Maddy's gaze sweeps to the Master, and Caleb notices a bruise forming on the side of her face. His lip twitches but he keeps the snarl trapped in his chest.

"A fine collection of sacrifices, isn't it?" the Master says. Around the room, the others murmur their agreement. "But I must say, the addition of the hunters, especially the young Madeleine, is quite a treat. I must thank you, Caleb, for leading them here."

Caleb slowly shakes his head. "I didn't—" Beside Maddy, Morgan's lips press into a hard line and he stares at Caleb with something akin to defiance. "I don't understand."

The Master's lip curls up in a sneer. "A vampire falling for a hunter is disgustingly disgraceful, but betrayal of your Master and your kind is beyond forgiveness."

A spike of fear jolts Caleb. "I have betrayed nothing."

"Do not patronize me, Caleb. I have known of your double dealings for quite some time." The Master looks at Morgan and gives him a thankful nod.

Burning hurt seeps into Caleb's marrow as he peers over at his friend. He knew Morgan was loyal, but he hadn't expected him to betray him. His nostrils flare as he pulls in a sharp breath, trying to ignore the pain of the knife Morgan has thrust into his back.

Caleb wants nothing more than to dash over to Morgan, slam his fist into his friend's face, and save the girl he is falling for, but it isn't time yet. His plan is crumbling before him, and he's trying desperately to keep a hold of the pieces.

The Master approaches Caleb and clicks his tongue. "You should be thankful for the gift you have been given. To be turned into a vampire means immortality, strength, and power." He curls his lip, revealing just a hint of fang. "You have cast away your human shell, and yet you cannot shed your Order skin. You are determined to save the lives of humans, which only proves you are weak beyond measure."

Around the room, the other vampires sneer and hiss, casting insults at Caleb. He glances at Morgan again, hoping this is a mistake, but his friend won't even look at him.

"It is time for the vampires to rise." The Master's voice echoes off the curved walls and domed ceiling. Behind him, Zariah continues chanting and swaying slightly, weaving her spell. "I will use the Chalice and channel its power to sacrifice our prisoners."

The darkness of the obsidian swirls, drinking in the hate and fear coating the room. The Master eyes it with a hungry glint in his eyes. He turns his back on Caleb and walks back to the altar. The cancerous ribbons of the obsidian curl around the Master like tempting wisps of serpents, whispering in his ear and guiding his hand.

"The obsidian is our god, now."

Madness. The Master speaks madness and none of his followers raise a single word to question him. Morgan, to his credit, looks a bit uneasy. He sweeps a quick glance at Caleb, but any doubt is quickly chased away as his face shutters again. Caleb stands rooted to the spot as the Master continues.

"We will gain enormous power the likes of which is unheard of. This power of the obsidian is not yet full, but when it happens, the powers will form something too great for anyone to defeat. The remaining threads of the Order and others who would stop us will find nothing but unforgiving resistance. And death."

Caleb takes a step forward and several of the nearest vampires snap their attention to him. "You can't do that," he spits. The gaze he sets on the Master drips in defiance. "This isn't right, and it isn't the way vampire kind will thrive. You and this organization you're wrapped up in are messing with nature's hierarchy. You're going to destroy everything if you continue down this path."

A deep and dark laugh rolls through the Master. "There will be a new hierarchy. Breaking the chains of this world's order is the only way for us to live. We will reign supreme."

"You will be stopped." Caleb sweeps a hand over the gathered vampires. "All of them will be stopped. You are no match for the Order or any of the others who will stand against you."

Anger ripples through the gathered crowd but the Master is unbothered. "There is no one who will be able to defy the powers of the obsidian." The darkness curls around his fingers, slick and oily-looking. "Even though this essence is a mere fraction of its original power, it will still be enough to bolster our cause. As for the humans..." The Master peers at the group of captives being held by his followers. "They will all be enslaved, used as nothing more than blood bags for vampire kind to feed on anytime and anywhere. No more will we hide in the darkness and fear retribution simply because we need to survive. It is time for us to rise from the shadows."

Caleb looks between Maddy, the Master, and the followers who look at the obsidian like it is some sort of messiah. Arguing will do no good, and he can't see how he can get across the room to Maddy without being stopped. His mind is in overdrive as he tries frantically to come up with a way out of this deadly mess. The vampires in the room cheer at the Master's words and the vampire leader turns to face Caleb once more.

"You see, Caleb? There is no stopping this. It is our right, and our destiny. I am only following the King's plans before he was killed by Kenna." The Master points at Caleb. "Even you had a part to play in this, though it isn't the one you thought. You came here to slay me, and yet, all you did was bring me the most favorable sacrifice I could ask for, didn't you?" His voice raises and he holds his arms up. "We will begin our exodus with the sacrifice of the hunter, Madeleine Grimes."

"No!" Caleb starts forward but is quickly blocked by a group of the Master's inner circle. The vampires grab him, grunting when he fights with everything he has. But there are too many of them, and within seconds, his arms are pinned and someone is holding him with a fist in his hair. They hold Caleb captive, forcing him to watch what is unfolding.

Maddy jerks against Morgan's hold as he drags her up to the altar. He forcefully lays her down, four vampires holding an arm and a leg each.

The Master reaches for her, a glinting blade in his other hand.

"No!" This time, the word is a scream. A denial that it has somehow all come to this.

Maddy can't be sacrificed.

She can't die.

He promised her she wouldn't be harmed.

Caleb struggles, eyes stinging at the tight hold of his hair, grunting at the pain as the vampires yanks his arms back, trying to immobilize him. He fights as his heart fractures. Maddy's eyes lock on Caleb's, her pale face drenched in panic.

His heart stops as the Master swipes the blade across Maddy's throat. Her face freezes in terror as her back arches in agony. Crimson pours onto the altar.

Caleb's screams fill the room.

CHAPTER 39

MADELEINE

Shock and searing pain war in Maddy's mind. She tries to suck in a breath and blood gurgles in her throat. Panic seizes her heart. She needs air, but she chokes on each breath. A metallic taste fills her mouth as her body goes limp. A scream tears through the room right before she folds into darkness.

Caleb...

She was supposed to help him. Save him.

The scent of rain confuses Maddy and she blinks, finding herself staring out at a scene of distant mountains, dark under a cloud-laden sky. Thunder rumbles in the distance and wind howls past the balcony she stands upon. She frowns. There's no pain. No death claiming her. Was everything a terrible dream?

"I have always found something both cleansing and fortifying about an unforgiving storm."

Maddy whirls toward the voice to find a man staring at her. He's dressed like an ancient royal, with tall leather boots, dark breeches and a black tunic. A red overcoat edged in fur is belted over his clothing and something that looks like a mix between a crown and a cap sits on his head. It's hemmed in rows of beads with a large black stone set in the front. An opaque mist swirls around his feet, covering the floor and creeping up the walls behind him so nothing can be seen except him and the balcony they stand on. Startled and confused, Maddy retreats a step, her back pressing into the stone railing.

"You have nothing to fear here, blood of my blood." The man has a strange accent, but the smile on his face is almost kind.

"Where am I?" Maddy asks.

The man tilts his head side to side, contemplating. "The best way I can describe it is limbo. You are neither alive, nor dead. You are not on earth, or yet in the afterlife."

Maddy lifts a hand to her throat, but feels nothing there. If she isn't dead, then why is she here? She eyes the man before her. He's tall, with handsome rugged features, pale skin, and eyes black as ink. "Who are you?"

"I am Count Dracula, and I would like to welcome you. You are my kith and kin, and the only descendant worthy of being called as such." He walks over to Maddy and stands beside her at the railing, peering out at the storm rolling over the horizon. "My real name is Vlad Draculea, and when I was a human, I found out I had strange powers. My mother told me they came from my warlock heritage." He angles his head, staring down at Maddy. "A heritage you share, Madeleine."

Maddy turns to face him. "So, you're saying I'm not only descended from the most powerful vampire that has ever lived, but also from some sort of magical entity, as well?"

The man frowns, his expression not exactly angered, but one may have when being stern with a child. "Being a warlock doesn't mean you're some sort of fanciful magical entity. There is so much more to it than that. Discipline, for one. I began to train with warlock powers when I was a child. It wasn't easy, and was far more dangerous than you can even imagine. However, while a warlock is susceptible to death like any other mortal, we also have the ability to come back to life."

Sounds convenient, Maddy thinks. Yet, also horrible. What if you didn't want to come back to life? "What does this have to do with me being here?"

The man, her ancestor, she supposes, lets his stern expression fade into a small smile. "I'm getting to that. One day, while I was still human, I learned of a small section of the Knights Templar who seemed to have found a part of a black stone which emitted some sort of darkness the likes of which I'd never seen before. I watched them for a time, and soon realized this particular faction of the Knights Templar venerated this stone as a god of sorts, as the darkness gave them immense power beyond imagining."

"The obsidian," Maddy whispers, a crack of thunder rumbling through the sky over the mountains.

Vlad nods. "Yes. It wasn't easy, but I foiled their plans when I saw the obsidian had started to infect the humans. I returned the stone to its original crypt, hoping nobody else would find it, and then cast a spell to protect the stone."

Maddy tries to remember the history she knew of Dracula, but nothing is adding up. "The stone didn't twist you into a vampire?"

"No. The Knights Templar found out what I had done with the obsidian, and in retaliation, they found a way to nullify my warlock abilities by tricking me into drinking vampire blood. The next time I died, I returned as a vampire instead. When they discovered their mistake, they sought to kill me, but they were unable to do so. My warlock abilities had turned me into a vastly more evolved creature than a typical vampire."

A cool breeze brushes against Maddy's cheeks as she

watches the dark gray clouds swirl in the distance. "I don't understand why you are telling me all of this. Why am I here? I should be dead."

"Would you rather be dead?" Vlad lifts a dark eyebrow.

Maddy thinks of Caleb, Cora, and the Order members trapped in the Master's lair. It's tearing her apart thinking they could be getting slaughtered at that moment and she isn't there to help them. She shakes her head. "No, I don't want to be dead."

"You possess powers, same as I. They passed to you when the King died. Due to a curse, his line could only bear one warlock every generation. Though warlocks are often thought of as immortal, there are ways to kill them." Vlad rested an arm on the railing of the balcony. "What I am saying is, you are free to make the choice. You can return to your time on earth, or you can pass on to the afterlife. If, however, you do choose to return, I want you to channel your warlock powers and finish off the Master. I do not wish for the obsidian to corrupt the world anymore."

Maddy looks from Vlad, to the storm, then back again. There is no question which choice she will make. Before she can open her mouth to give an answer, a lightning bolt flashes down from the sky and strikes her in a spear of fire.

A gasp fills Maddy's lungs as her eyes fly open. The first thing she sees is the Master. He stumbles back with wide eyes and a startled yell. Maddy hears her name on the lips of more than one person. It takes her mind a few seconds to catch up, and then realize both Caleb and Cora are calling her name. Maddy scrambles to her feet and finds Caleb. A smile begins to lift his lips. He says her name again, and the amount of relief in his voice is both beautiful and heartbreaking.

Shouts break through the room as the Order members

Maddy had left outside crash through the door. Chaos explodes, and where Maddy had found she was saved from death one moment, she suddenly finds it staring her down in the next. A stake is in her hand before she can think and she stabs at the Master. He's far too quick and flashes far from her reach in a split second. To her horror, Maddy realizes the Chalice in his hands. He must have taken it from Caleb after he slit her throat.

A snarl rips from the Master's lungs and he raises the Chalice. He locks his gaze on Caleb. "Stop!"

Maddy's heart drops to her stomach when Caleb stops in his tracks. He stands, frozen, eyes wide as he glares at the Master.

"Good." The Master's voice drips with wicked mirth. "You will all do as I say. Caleb, you will watch me kill your Madeleine again, and again, if necessary. You stay put."

A chuckle sounds from Caleb. "I think not, *Master*."

Confusion and indignation cross the Master's face. He holds the Chalice out. "You will obey me."

"I will do as I please," Caleb snarls. Then, he lifts his chin. "Before I came here, I sought out a certain witch who told me of a boy named Alex you most likely had kidnapped. After a bit of tracing and a phone call, I got into contact with Zariah."

The witch, who still stands by the altar, looks at the Master with a spark of mischief in her eye.

"You see," Caleb continues. "Zariah is Alex's older sister. She manipulated her way into working with you so she would have the chance to save her brother and the other captives. Once I found out, the pieces fell into place." He nods toward the witch.

Zariah lifts a hand toward the Chalice in the Master's fingers. Maddy's eyes grow round as the Chalice simply shatters into shards like glass. The jagged pieces scatter across the stone floor as the Master steps back. Then, Caleb raises his hand up high, and in his grasp is the true Chalice. He'd had the witch create a decoy! A subtle glow surrounds this Chalice, and when Caleb glares at all of the vampires and speaks, his voice rings with authority.

"You will all stand down and release the captives. You will do no harm to them or to yourself."

Maddy watches in awe as the vampires have no choice but to do as Caleb commands. His face is granite and his eyes steel as he turns to the Master. Caleb walks to Maddy and grabs the stake out of her hand. He throws it at the Master's feet.

"Take this stake and plunge it into your own heart."

The Master's lip curls up, revealing his long, sharp fangs, but he has no choice except to reach down and pick up the stake. "This isn't over," he snarls.

"I'm pretty sure it is," says Caleb, watching as the Master's hand extends, the tip of the stake aimed for his heart.

The Master's arm trembles as he fights the compulsion, fights the very same power he's had over countless vampires. His face twists with strain and he shakes his head, as if the denial can stop what's coming.

With a flash of vampire speed the stake drives into his chest. The Master throws his head back, but never sees the motion through. He explodes into a cloud of ash.

The shocked silence is fractured as the other vampires hiss and curse. But Caleb ignores them, slowly turning to face Maddy, a smile blooming across his handsome features and making her heart leap. Triumph glows on his face as his gaze drinks her in. "We did it, Maddy," he says. "We actually did it."

Relief washes through Maddy on a shaky breath as she starts toward him, but then, she pauses. Behind him, the coils of darkness erupt outward like some sick firework. The obsidian vibrates with fury, a silent roar seeming to shake the very air.

The swirls of midnight rise, curling and writhing in the air as if searching for an escape from the circular room.

In a blink, it streaks across the room, condensing into a single, deadly spear.

And drives straight into Caleb's chest.

CHAPTER 40

CALEB

Cold, inky blackness assaults Caleb, the pain taking his breath away. Not that he can breathe. His entire body is frozen in agony. Knives of ice flood his throat, dividing into his lungs, then fanning out, intent to reach every part of his body. It feels like he's being shredded from the inside out.

He locks his muscles, trying to stop the spread of the obsidian. This is never what he wanted. Being turned into a vampire against his will was devastating enough. Being a puppet of evil will destroy any shred of goodness he's desperately clung to.

The ice blooms through his chest like cancer and his sight dims. Caleb's vaguely conscious that his back is arched, his arms thrown out. Every tendon feels like a wire about to snap. Maddy's screaming his name, but she feels so far away.

The ice constricts in his chest, turning every cell into a shard of midnight. His hands and feet go numb. The darkness flies up his neck, ready to take the last part of him. His mind. His ability to choose. Caleb can feel the feverish excitement of the obsidian. Flashes of the blood and death it craves are all he sees.

No!

The vile blackness explodes in his head, swallowing him. Suddenly, the pain is gone. All he feels is...cold nothingness.

Yes, hisses the obsidian. *Kill them. Kill them all.*

Caleb turns to Maddy, breathing hard. He doesn't have long. "Get away from me."

She shakes her head. "We can fix this, Caleb. You just need to fight—"

"It's too late!" he roars, and he's not sure who's speaking, himself or the obsidian. He steps back, then back again, registering the eyes watching him with wariness. And fear.

The vampires are twitching, their fangs peeking from curled lips. The members of the Order all have their hands hovering over their weapons. The prisoners look terrified. Maddy's mom moves closer to her daughter, eyeing him with open distrust.

She always knew you were rotten to the core.

Caleb twitches, hating the insidious voice. "Let me pass or you'll all die."

The words are a warning from the obsidian.

And a desperate plea from himself. There's so much power thrumming through him, there's no way he'll be able to control it. A power that's baying for blood far more forcefully than any vampire lust ever has.

Maddy shakes her head again, this time more resolutely. "You can't run, Caleb." Cora rushes to Maddy's side, to support her or possibly to tell her to shut up. "We'll figure this out together."

"You can't save me," he growls, taking another step back.

Behind him, he hears movement, then Marlowe's low voice. "We won't kill him, but we need to incapacitate him."

Yes. Fight us. It will make your deaths all the more satisfying.

"You're good, I know it," says Maddy, taking a step closer. Cora sticks close to her side.

The obsidian roars with excitement. *So much blood. So much death.*

Caleb spins on his heel, using every shred of his control to move his body toward the door. Except the members of the Order rush in, blocking his way.

Trapping him.

"Let me out," he demands. They have no idea what he's capable of.

"We're not letting you go," Maddy says behind him, her voice charged with determination.

Caleb growls low in his throat, noticing the way one or two Order member's eyes widen. Before Maddy can speak again, before the Obsidian can pierce it's evil even further into him, Caleb spins back. He's grabbed Cora and yanked her to the center of the room before anyone's moved. The scent of her fear is overwhelming.

Maddy freezes as Cora whimpers, but her determination doesn't waver. "You can run, but I'll never stop searching for you. I'll follow you for as long as it takes to make this right."

Kill this one first, pants the Obsidian. *Give them a sample of what's coming*

If Caleb could feel his heart, it would be constricting right now. Each beat would be painful.

But he can't. He now carries the obsidian and it wants nothing more than to kill. Which leaves him no choice. Maddy, the Order, need to let him go.

Yes! Kill her!

"This is who I am now," says Caleb, holding Maddy's pleading gaze.

With a swift motion, he twists Cora's head to the side. Her gasp is cut short by a crackly pop. Her body slides down his and crumples onto the ground. Maddy cries out, taking a step forward, then stops.

"Don't follow me," he growls.

With a hard glare, he spins around again and walks away. The Order members shift away from the door, their uneasiness blending with disgust. Caleb walks straight past them and then up the stairs. All he has to do is hold on until he's far away enough.

Outside, the sun is shining but he can't feel it. The evil of the Obsidian is slithering through his veins, his mind, trying to burrow into his soul. And there's every chance it will win. He breaks into a run, surprised at the speed. He was always fast, but not this fast. What's more, he has little control over where he's going.

Not that Caleb fights it. Away from Maddy and everyone else is all he wants right now.

He stops when he reaches the outskirts of Creed. A few houses are to his right but little else. Caleb strides past, working up the strength of will to run some more. A movement from the corner of his eye has him glancing down. A small bed of daisies wilt as he watches, the petals twisting as if in pain as their center turns black. Within a blink, the whole plant withers and dies.

And so it begins, hisses the Obsidian.

Caleb's jaw clenches tight. He needs to get as far away as he can from anything and everything.

No. This is where we're supposed to be.

A car appears and slows as it approaches him. Caleb yanks his gaze away and tries to move, only to find he can't. He tries again, this time with more determination, but his feet are glued to the cracked pavement. A man climbs out of the car and walks toward him, the collar of his jacket turned up and his hat pulled low. Caleb stills. Fear that he's going to have to repeat what he did with Cora floods his body.

The man pulls down the brim of his black hat even further as he stops in front of Caleb. "Give it to me."

There's only one thing Caleb has, one thing the man could be talking about. The Chalice of Solomon.

He watches, his body once more outside of his control, as he pulls the Chalice from his jacket and passes it to the man.

"My organization is looking forward to working with you." The man walks on and Caleb's unable to look over his shoulder to try and get a good look. He has no idea who he just gave the Chalice to, or why. Or what it will mean.

He arches his back as the power explodes again, consuming him. The world dims as his sight both sharpens and fades. The obsidian has him in its hold.

It's time for blood.

It's time for death.

CHAPTER 41

MADELEINE

The moment Caleb is gone, Madeleine falls to her knees beside Cora. "No, no, no," she gasps through choked sobs. Cora can't be dead.

And yet she saw Caleb kill her.

Maddy's hand falls onto Cora's shoulder as she lies on her side, her red hair fanned across her face. Tears are hot on Maddy's cheeks, but the anger in her heart is blazing like an inferno. Caleb killed Cora without a flicker of emotion.

"Maddy," says a voice behind her. She turns to find the witch, Zariah, standing there. "It was the obsidian that made him do it."

She shakes her head, even as she's not sure what she's denying. She tells herself it doesn't matter. Cora's dead and it's all her fault.

"We have to find a way to stop the obsidian's influence," Zariah continues. "It's power will already leaching into the world, destroying it."

Maddy's about to tell her to go to hell so she can mourn her best friend in peace, when Cora's shoulder twitches. Maddy's hand tightens, knowing she must've nudged her friend in her desperate with she's still alive.

Except Cora's chest expands.

With a smooth motion, she sits up, drawing in a sharp lungful of air. Maddy falls back on her heels, shocked into silence in the same way the rest of the room is.

Cora glances around, blinking in confusion. She brushes her hair out of her face, eyes roaming the room as if she's trying to understand how she got here. Her hand is just dropping away when she clutches her throat. Her gaze flies to Maddy. "I'm hungry. Like, *really* hungry."

No. The denial only echoes through Maddy's mind. Her lungs are too frozen to work. What has Caleb done?

"She's a vampire," says Zariah. "Caleb must've turned her to save her life. The obsidian would've demanded her death."

Cora's brow crimps in confusion. She stands, glancing down at her body as if she's expecting to see something different. "But..."

Maddy slowly pushes to her feet, the basics of vampire lore whispering through her mind. If Cora feeds on blood, she will cement her transition to a vampire. If she doesn't, she'll starve to death.

Which leaves Maddy with an impossible choice to make. Watch her best friend become the same beings she hunts. Or make sure she dies...

And it's all Caleb's fault.

The fury turns to cold, hard shards in her chest. She'll never forgive him for this.

Ready for the next installment in the Keepers of the Chalice series? Check out VAMPIRE UNVEILED!

VAMPIRE UNVEILED

Vampires could be exterminated. But what if they're the solution?

Maddy's world has been turned upside down. She's a hunter, but the Order isn't what it seems. And the one guy she can't forget is a vampire, even when Caleb's making choices that go against everything she's been taught.

Caleb can't afford to have feelings for Maddy. Evil is rising and vampires have the power to stop it. Pushing her away seems like the only solution. It's safer for her...and his heart.

Especially now that a cure for vampirism is being engineered.

As the fight to gain power intensifies, they discover nothing is as it seems. Where do Caleb's loyalties lie? What does

Maddy's dark blood mean for them all? And can they claim victory when they have to do the impossible — trust each other?

GRAB YOUR COPY HERE
http://mybook.to/VampireUnveiled

HAVE YOU READ THE KEEPER CHRONICLES PREQUEL?

As an exclusive for my subscribers,
you can download it for free!!

When Sierra sneaks out, determined to escape her over-protective family, she stumbles across a young man covered in blood. His last words are a plea. *Find the Grail Keepers. Warn them.*

Ryder is the young cop who was last seen with the murdered victim. Sierra doesn't trust him, no matter how drawn she is to him. Except it turns out they're both looking for the same thing—the Holy Grail.

They're quickly drawn into a dangerous hunt involving cryptic clues, a mysterious stone, and a Grail that hasn't been seen for centuries. One that leads to more questions than answers. Can Sierra trust her impulsive emotions? Should she believe Ryder's words or the truth she sees in his eyes? And ulti-mately, should she follow her heart?

Especially when every decision will decide the fate of count-less lives.

CLICK HERE TO DOWNLOAD FOR FREE!
https://BookHip.com/TTBMTTV

THE KEEPERS-VERSE IS ALWAYS GROWING!

The Keeper Chronicles will continue to grow, with each new addition adding to its epicness. Each interlinked series will have you falling for unforgettable characters, being swept away by captivating romance and thrilling adventure, and re-visiting old friends (you'll discover all your favorites popping up when you least expect it!).

Check out what's coming your way!

Keepers of the Light
Angels and demons have battled for millennia. Their inevitable war has begun.
Check out Book 1, Hidden Angel, HERE.
http://mybook.to/HiddenAngel

Keepers of the Grail
Seven Gates of Hell. Seven deadly sins.
One impossible choice.
Check out Book 1, Gates of Demons, HERE.
http://mybook.to/GatesofDemons

Also by Tamar Sloan

PRIME PROPHECY SERIES

He failed to shift like every one of his ancestors.

Until he met her.

KEEPERS OF THE GRAIL

The legendary Holy Grail is real.

Yet everything known about it is a lie.

KEEPERS OF THE CHALICE

A vampire. A huntress.

A cure that will change everything.

KEEPERS OF THE LIGHT

Angels and demons have battled for millennia.

Their inevitable war has begun.

KEEPERS OF EXCALIBUR

A fated love. A cursed wolf.

A supernatural war only they can stop.

DESTINED DEMIGODS
Love that defies the gods.

Powers that define destiny.

ELEMENTAL GAMES
Elemental powers. Deadly Games.

No escape.

THE SOVEREIGN CODE
Humans saved bees from extinction...and created the deadliest threat we've seen yet.

THE THAW CHRONICLES
Only the chosen shall breed.

ZODIAC GUARDIANS
Twelve teens. One task.

Save the Universe.

ABOUT THE AUTHOR

Tamar hasn't decided whether she's primarily a psychologist who loves writing, or a writer with a lifelong drive to make a difference. She must have been someone pretty awesome in a previous life (past life regression indicates a Care Bear), because she gets to do both. She divides her time between helping families and writing emotion driven YA stories set in amazing imaginary worlds that surprise even her.

The driving force for all of Tamar's writing is sharing and connecting. In truth, connecting with others is why she writes. She loves to hear from readers. Find her on all the usual social media channels or her website, www.tamarsloan.com where can download one of her books for free.

(Seriously, I LOVE hearing from you guys!)